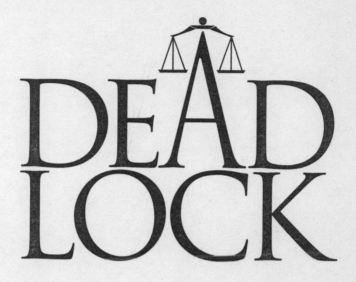

DEAD LOCK

JAMES SCOTT BELL

ZONDERVAN™

Deadlock
Copyright © 2002 by James Scott Bell

Requests for information should be addressed to:
Zondervan, *Grand Rapids, Michigan 49530*

Library of Congress Cataloging-in-Publication Data

Bell, James Scott.
     Deadlock / James Scott Bell.
        p. cm.
     ISBN 0-310-24388-2
     1. United States. Supreme Court—Fiction.   2. Near-death experiences—
Fiction. 3. Washington (D.C.)—Fiction. 4. Spiritual life—Fiction. 5. Women
judges—Fiction. 6. Liberalism—Fiction. 7. Agnostics—Fiction. I. Title.
     PS3552.E5158 D43 2002
     813'.54—dc21

                2002010450

Interior design by Beth Shagene

Printed in the United States of America

02 03 04 05 06 07 08 /❖ DC/ 10 9 8 7 6 5 4 3 2 1

*This book is for
Tracie Peterson*

PROLOGUE

The girl heard herself scream.

Oh, God, don't let them do it!

Her words were only in her mind. Her mouth was open, but only sputtering gasps came out, issuing an awful *ak ak ak* sound.

Her eyes felt puffy, raw. Where was she?

A bed. She was in a bed. Hers.

She put a hand on her stomach.

Don't let them!

Hand on stomach and head spinning. Warm sweat on her face. She had been sleeping.

And she knew she'd had the nightmare again, the same one, the one where they were dressed in black. Not white smocks. Black robes. They had her tied down on the cold, hard ground. Her wrists, in the dream, were fastened to stakes. She could not move. One of the robed ones laughed at her.

It always seemed like an image from a horror film, one of those devil movies where the devil actually comes to life.

Life. That was what she'd had inside her. A life, a baby. She knew that now. They hadn't told her. In the dream she had seen him, a son, a little boy. Her stomach was like a window, and she could see into it. A dome of glass, and under the dome her baby.

He had opened his eyes and looked at her.

Don't let them!

But in the dream the robed ones closed in, and one of them had a knife. He was going to do it—she had *said* he could, but now she didn't want him to, and she tried to move, but she was tied down.

That was always when she heard herself scream.

This was the fourth night in a row she'd had the dream. It had come and gone before, but now it came every night, and she knew it would never go away. She had tried to end the dreams before, with a razor blade. But Mama had found her and the doctors brought her back to life.

She did not deserve life. That was another thing she knew. That's what the dreams were telling her. At sixteen she had lived too long, long enough to let them kill her baby.

Barefoot, in underwear and a T-shirt, she slipped out of bed so her mama wouldn't hear, and then out the window into the warm southern night. The smell of old tires and rusted car parts hit her, and the buzz of cicadas was as loud as her beating heart. She headed for the highway, for pavement, so she could run flat out. She knew she'd have to make a decision soon. What could she do? Wait for a truck and throw herself in front of it?

Or maybe the bridge.

Yes, that was it. Just like in that song her mama used to sing to her, about that girl named Billie Jo who jumped off a bridge. There was one just a mile away, over the gorge. She'd thrown rocks off it once with Cody. He'd said he loved her then but it was a lie. He said get rid of the baby and he wouldn't tell. Then he told her to leave him alone forever.

Now she'd go over the gorge like a rock herself, and Cody would know about it. They'd all know about it. They'd all suffer like she had suffered.

For one second she thought about not doing it, because of Mama, even though Mama yelled a lot. She would be alone.

But in that second the hurt inside took over and she remembered the dreams and knew this was the only way.

Once she looked back and thought she saw something, a scary something. The people in black robes. Only this time there were hundreds of them and they were running behind her, almost pushing her. She thought she heard them whispering in unison, *do it, do it, do it.*

She *would* do it. She reached the bridge and saw it outlined against the moon. She could hear the rush of the river below, deep in the gorge, sloshing over sharp rocks. When she started over the bridge, the waters sounded like they were singing.

Singing . . .

No, it was voices singing. Real voices. Somewhere close. There was a campground on the other side of the bridge. That meant people.

She stopped for a moment. What were they singing? Something about . . . *Jesus*. A church camp maybe? A bunch of kids singing church songs. She'd done that once, a long time ago, before Mama stopped going to church. She had once sung songs about Jesus. No more. Jesus hated her.

She thought of God then, and wondered why God hadn't stopped them from doing it, hadn't stopped *her* from letting them. If God was real he would reach down right now and make it all better, bring her baby back.

God should have stopped it before it happened. He gave the laws, didn't he? She thought about the law that was supposed to protect her. Wasn't that why they'd made her sign the paper? She didn't understand it, but they said to sign it, so she did. They said it was the law, and the law was good and it would protect her.

It didn't.

And if the law didn't protect her, and God didn't, nothing else would either. She moved to the middle of the bridge.

There was a narrow strip of asphalt road across the bridge with small steel rails on either side. She'd be able to hop it, no trouble.

The singing got louder. They were praising Jesus. He hadn't reached down to help her either, any more than God had.

She hesitated. One second between life and death. It wouldn't be so bad. And then she wouldn't have the dreams anymore, and everybody'd be sorry, and they'd know they killed her and her baby, and they'd cry. All of them.

She thought she heard something. Someone coming. A voice said, "Hey . . ."

She jumped up on the rail.

PART ONE

We are very quiet on the Supreme Court,
but it is the quiet of a storm center.

JUSTICE OLIVER WENDELL HOLMES

CHAPTER ONE

1

Millicent Mannings Hollander could not stop looking at evil.

She sat, along with her eight colleagues, on the raised dais facing the marble frieze over the main entrance to the United States Supreme Court. The frieze depicted the forces of evil—deceit and corruption—overcome by good: security, charity, and peace. The scene was dominated by the triumphant figure of justice, an enduring testament to the greatest virtue of the law.

As a ten-year veteran of the Court, Millie Hollander had seen that artwork hundreds of times. Why should it jump out at her now? Was it simple judicial fatigue? Though in relatively good shape at fifty-two (she liked to shoot hoops in the Supreme Court gym), every term was a challenge.

Work on the Court was a day in, day out cavalcade of cases, court petitions, emergency appeals, oral arguments, conferences, analyses, and draft opinions. The same held true even for the three hundred other employees of the Court—everyone from the private police to the cafeteria cooks—who did not don the robes.

Though she loved everything about the Court, by mid-June Millie was ready for the recess, the summer break that lasted until Labor Day.

But mere weariness wasn't behind this perception—this *sensation*—of evil. She'd been tired before. No, there was a feeling of something deeper, something *out there*.

She blinked a couple of times and then thought it might just be the lawyer at the podium. Not that lawyers were evil (though some might be inclined to disagree with her there) but he was phrasing his argument in apocalyptic terms. "The matter is not simply what is right for this student," he had just said, "but for all the future students who must decide if life has any meaning at all."

Millie Hollander, in all her time as an associate justice of the Court, had rarely heard an advocate cast so wide a net. *Got to admire his ambition,* Millie thought, *if not his grasp of the Establishment Clause.*

"What business is it of the public schools to teach anything about the meaning of life?" Thomas Riley thundered at the lawyer.

Millie had to smile. How many times had she heard that voice, now eighty-four years young, plow right into the heart of an issue?

As the lawyer for the high school student stammered a reply, Millie once again found her gaze pulled, almost magnetically, to the frieze and the rendition of evil. There seemed to be something new about it, though that was absurd. Her legal mind clicked a notch and informed her that there couldn't be anything new about artwork that had been in place nearly seventy years.

"Public schools have some sort of mandate to prepare students for life, don't they?" Justice Byrne asked the lawyer. Raymond Byrne was the Court's most conservative member— the polar opposite of Tom Riley—and often asked soft follow-up questions after Riley had skewered some hapless lawyer.

Millie knew it was all part of the dance. The two most extreme justices were really trying to pull the middle three swing votes—herself, Valarde, and Parsons—to their side of the fence. Millie almost always came out on Riley's side. Thus her label as a moderate liberal in the popular press.

And on this issue, the role of religion in schools, Millie had long made her position clear—no role. Strict separation of church and state.

". . . so yes, Your Honor," the lawyer for the student said, "we must allow the free discussion of the most important issue in any student's life, as—"

"But, Counsel," Millie said, "isn't the Establishment Clause's very purpose to *prevent* any governmental stance on a *religious* issue?"

The lawyer cleared his throat. "I believe, Your Honor, that to allow discussion is not really a 'stance' on a religious issue, it is a—"

"But it's happening on school grounds, isn't it?"

"Yes, it—"

"And students are compelled to be there by law, aren't they?"

"That's true, Your Honor, but—"

"Then what you are arguing for is tantamount to legal coercion, is it not?"

"I don't believe it is," the lawyer said, his voice warbling a bit. Millie was about to tell him that the only thing that mattered was what the Constitution declared, but let it go. The man had suffered enough.

Ten minutes later, Chief Justice Pavel announced the adjournment of the Court for the last time this term. The nine justices rose to make their magisterial exit through the burgundy velvet curtains behind the bench.

Just before she did, Millie took one more look at the frieze. There was that sense again, of something from the evil side moving toward her. That was enough. She told herself to get a very serious grip.

Then she looked down from the frieze to the packed gallery, and immediately locked eyes with someone in the back row.

The eyes belonged to a United States senator, one the *New York Times* had recently named the most powerful politician of the last twenty-five years. And Senator Samuel T. Levering, D-Oklahoma, was giving Justice Millicent Mannings Hollander a very enthusiastic thumbs-up sign.

Not something she usually got from politicians. But she knew this was no ordinary time. In two hours she would be meeting with Levering, at his request. She also knew he was probably going to offer her the dream of a lifetime.

2

Charlene Moore closed her eyes and sang.

Oh, God, don't let me mess up, no no. Her voice was a whisper in the elevator. *Oh, God, don't let me sweat. Oh, God, this is my one good suit! Ain't got money for a new one, Lord. Oh no, oh no, oh no.*

At least the elevator air was cool. As the elevator charged toward the thirtieth floor, Charlene wondered what would happen if she just stayed in the car, rode it back to ground level, and ran from the building.

She sang again, which was how she prayed when she was nervous. *Lord, take my feet and make 'em walk on fire.*

A fire it would be, going up to Winsor & Grimes! Little Charlene Moore, born twenty-seven years ago in Mobile, Alabama, the great-granddaughter of a slave. A girl who wanted nothing more than to sing like Patti LaBelle. What was she doing here, a lone, unmarried lawyer with only one client and a very large tiger by the tail?

Because God had spoken to her?

The elevator bell rang, startling Charlene. She smoothed her skirt and checked the clasp on her briefcase. The doors opened. With one last prayer, Charlene stepped into the largest reception area she had ever seen. At just over five feet tall, she felt a little like Frodo Baggins looking up at Mount Doom.

Over a desk the size of an aircraft carrier were huge brass letters: *Winsor & Grimes*. Founded just before World War I, it had prospered even through the Great Depression. A Spanish American War veteran, Captain Beauregard Winsor, was the legendary founder. Malcolm Grimes was an equally storied personality who had joined the firm in 1920.

Though both names were now part of regional legal lore, neither had achieved the stature of the man Charlene was about to meet. Beau Winsor III, who many said had engineered the election of the current president of the United States, was the one who had summoned her here.

After a cursory check-in with the receptionist, Charlene was ushered into a conference room by a young woman who looked as if she could gnaw metal. Winsor & Grimes was known for toughness, even in its assistants.

Ten minutes later the door to the conference room opened. A lean square-chinned man in an impeccable navy blue suit, with a full head of graying hair and a blindingly white smile, extended his hand. "Beau Winsor," he said.

Charlene swallowed. "Charlene Moore."

"Welcome." He spun the chair next to her so he could sit down. Charlene was unnerved. She had anticipated he would sit across from her, like an adversary. "You get up here to Mobile much?" he said.

"No, actually," Charlene said, certain her throbbing pulse could be heard by everyone on the thirtieth floor.

"How I envy you," Winsor said.

"Excuse me?"

"Oh, that simple life down in Dudley. The way things move, easy and nice. Not like up here, where things are a bit more hurried, more harsh."

He drawled that last word in a rich, honeyed tone. And his was the smile of a killer. Hardly a word had been spoken and already Charlene felt like a plug of red meat dangling by a thread over a lion's cage.

Charlene cleared her throat. "I'm sure it could be a little dangerous to come to the city unless a person knew exactly what was going on."

"Words of wisdom, Ms. Moore. It'd be more than a little dangerous. A person could get hurt pretty bad. And I hate to see people get hurt."

He nodded at her, like an uncle. An uncle hiding a stiletto behind his back.

"You know," he continued, "federal court is like the city. When you filed your case it was in state court. Nice, easy-going judges and juries. When we moved it to federal court, well, it's a whole new world. You ever tried a case in federal court?"

Charlene had never even been inside a federal courthouse. "This will be my first," she said.

"Can't say as I'd recommend this case to be your debut."

She could feel him circling her, looking for cracks in her façade.

"My policy is to meet with opposing counsel face-to-face," Winsor said, "before a trial starts. Talk some turkey. Now it seems to me you've invested quite a bit of time and money in this whole thing."

How true that was. Her bank account was precariously low, her credit cards maxed out. "I believe in this case," she said.

"'Course you do, darlin'. Mark of a good lawyer. And when I see a good lawyer, I want to make sure he—or she—gets a fair hearing. So before we go taking up a lot of time and trouble in court, how about we settle this right here and now?"

"What," Charlene said slowly, "did you have in mind?"

"Well now, you're asking for a whale of a lot of money, Ms. Moore. We know that's how you play the game. I've got no grudge against a good game. Did you know my grandpappy played ball against Ty Cobb?"

The sudden turn threw her off balance. "Really?" she said, trying to sound interested.

"Sure enough. Baseball was a game for men back then. Tough men. And Cobb, well, he was one of the toughest. Used to slide into base with his spikes high, hoping to rip up the legs of anybody in his way. Well, my grandpappy stood in his way once. He played pro ball before settling on the law. And old Cobb, he came flying at him heading into third base, and what do you think my grandpappy did?"

Charlene could only shake her head.

"He took a step to the right, caught the ball, and slammed it into Cobb's face. Bloodied his nose. And Cobb never tried that again with Beauregard Winsor. So, darlin', instead of getting bloody over this, why don't you take four hundred thousand dollars home with you? Give two thirds to your client, who will be very happy. And you'll have more in your pocket than you've seen in your whole career."

A flame ignited inside Charlene. "I'm not in this to make money," she said. "This is about punishing an organization that scars young women."

Winsor hardly blinked. "Why don't you just think about it? Talk to your client. You see, if we go to trial, we'll have to come at you with spikes high, just like ol' Ty Cobb."

Charlene bristled. "Then maybe we'll have to bloody your nose."

Winsor smiled. "Brave words, darlin'. But you ought to know one more thing. We added Larry Graebner to the team, as of this morning."

If he had literally spiked her, the shock would not have been as great. Larry Graebner! The Yale law professor reputed to be the finest Constitutional lawyer in the country, a man on the short list of possible Supreme Court nominees, a scholar whose treatise on Constitutional law Charlene had used in law school ... he was now part of the largest, most frightening legal opponent Charlene had ever seen?

"So you be sure to think it over," Winsor said, "and get back to me now, ya hear?"

3

"You beat God back with a stick," Senator Sam Levering said to Millie. "That's no small feat."

They were seated in Levering's oak paneled office in the Senate building. The senator sipped a bourbon on the rocks. Millie drank a sparkling water. She did not drink much more than a little champagne on New Year's. She had made her career with a clear, sharp mind, and did not want that to change. Especially now.

"You're overestimating the role of one justice," Millie said. She was still trying to figure Levering out. She'd spoken to him maybe half a dozen times in the past, but only cursorily and in a semi-official manner. Now they were face-to-face, chatting amiably.

Levering smiled his charming Oklahoma grin, the one that had gotten him reelected four times. He was sixty years old with perfect chestnut hair. "You know better'n that, Madame Justice. Which is precisely why I invited you here."

With a short nod Levering took a sip of his drink. He wore a perfectly pressed white shirt and a maroon tie. There was a rumor he'd be in the next round of presidential candidates. Millie had no doubt he'd acquit himself like the winner he'd always been.

"They're gonna look back on this time in history, Madame Justice, and you know what they're gonna say about you? That you stood in the breech. That the country could have veered off in a terrible direction, but Justice Millicent Mannings Hollander was the woman fate had selected to keep her country from dying a horrible death. How's that sound?"

Millie cleared her throat. "A little like Justice Hollander, Warrior Princess."

With a laugh Levering said, "Maybe just like that. I mean, you handed that fancy lawyer his head today, didn't you?"

"A justice has to ask the hard questions," Millie said. "The lawyers know that going in."

Levering waved his glass dismissively. Ice clinked on the sides. "You know what I'm saying. We can be open here."

"I'm not sure I follow, Senator."

"I'm a plain talker, Madame Justice," Levering said. "The people in my state get up, go to work, raise kids, and what you and your colleagues do is going to affect them for a long, long time. Maybe forever. And you, Justice Hollander, are the five on the most important 5–4 majority in the history of this country."

Deep down, she knew what he said was true. But that was not how she liked to think of herself. She wanted to be just another justice sworn to uphold the Constitution to the best of her ability. That she happened to be the key swing vote on a highly polarized court was simply the way the gavel slammed.

Levering went on. "We'd have a law against partial-birth abortion if it wasn't for you. Can you imagine what that would have done? To women? To girls? We'd have Pat Robertson and James Dobson arresting doctors for murder. What a nightmare."

Millie stared at the lime slice floating in her glass. That had not been an easy decision, even if Levering liked the outcome.

"And this case about religion in the schools," Levering said. "Again with the Christian Right. You can't get rid of 'em. But you held them back, Madame Justice, and next term—"

"Senator," Millie interrupted, "I would prefer that we don't discuss anything about next term or about cases that might be considered. You know I can't do that."

"Well, *can't* is a pretty strong word. A little bit of chat wouldn't hurt, would it? Just between friends?"

"Senator," Millie said, gripping her glass thoughtfully in two hands, "when FDR tried to pack the Court, you will recall, he was at the height of his popularity. He had a huge majority in the Senate and a 4–1 majority in the House. But his plans failed. You know why?"

Levering waited for her to answer.

"Because the American people knew it *would* hurt. They knew it was wrong even for a great president to blatantly meddle with the Court. I believe in the judgment of the people, Senator. Not only that, I hold it in trust."

For a moment Levering looked at her, then finally nodded. "That's all I need to hear. How'd you like to be Chief Justice of the United States Supreme Court?"

There it was. She had been certain he was going to ask. It was still amazing to hear it. The first woman chief justice. Through all the political machinations of the last decade—the fractious Court appointments and hearings, the calculations and in-fighting, the public outcries and battling newspaper editorials—she had wondered if this moment would ever come. And now it was here.

Any justice with an ounce of ambition—and that was all of them—had thought about the CJ's chair. She thought about it because the Court was her whole life, and she wanted to serve it in the highest and best way possible. To be named as the first woman CJ would be something even her mother might finally applaud.

"I can make it happen," Levering said. "We all know Pavel wants to retire. That would mean the president would appoint the next chief, and the president and I are very good friends."

"What about Justice Riley?" Millie said.

"Too old, too controversial."

"He deserves it."

"We don't always get what we deserve in this life. Much as I admire Tom Riley, there is no finer mind on the Court than yours."

Millie looked again at her water glass. The little bubbles seemed to be exploding everywhere.

"Now don't be modest about it," the senator said. "It's true. You are a towering intellect, your opinions are models of style. Larry Graebner says he uses you as *the* model in his classes at Yale. The question is not, can you do it? The question is, do you want it?"

Millie paused, took a deep breath, and met the senator's eyes. "Senator Levering, I love two things in this world above all else. The law, and the United States Supreme Court. I would do my level best to lead it in the finest traditions of the greatest judicial body in the world."

Levering smiled and nodded slowly. "That's about the most eloquent acceptance speech I've ever heard." He put his glass down on his ornate mahogany desk. "You are the right woman at the right time, like I said. And that brings me to my next question. It's rather personal. Do you mind?"

It was clear he was going to ask anyway. "All right."

Levering leaned forward. "I wonder if you'd do me the honor of having dinner with me sometime."

Before Millie could respond, Levering added, "I know I dropped that kind of sudden, but I'm a sudden sort of fella."

4

Sarah Mae Sherman looked as skinny and scared as the first time Charlene Moore met her. She had big eyes, like the children in those black-and-white photographs taken during the Depression. Sarah Mae, if she had not been a real girl in terrible torment, would have been a perfect casting choice for a remake of *The Grapes of Wrath*.

She looked lost in the wooden chair in Charlene's office, even though her mother was with her. Aggie Sherman was a larger, plumper version of Sarah Mae. Unlike her daughter, who wore her hair in long strands, Aggie had hers cut short, a look that matched the severity of the expression she always wore.

It was even more severe now, after Charlene had advised them to turn down the settlement offer from Winsor & Grimes.

"That's almost half a million dollars," Aggie said, sitting on the edge of her chair. "That's more money than we'll ever see in our whole lives. You sayin' not to take it?"

Charlene folded her hands, trying to stay calm. "What I am saying is that we started this case because we wanted not only to compensate Sarah Mae, but also to punish the abortion clinic and doctor who did this to her. To send a message. The amount they are offering is just the insurance company's idea of nuisance value. They want to get rid of us. They do not want to try this case."

Aggie grunted dismissively. "When we went into this, we warn't in no federal court. You told me that's a lot harder."

"I can't deny it is very different from our state courts," Charlene said. "But the jury is still made up of people, just like you and me."

"We ain't their kind," Aggie said. "And they ain't our'n."

"When Sarah Mae first came to see me with Pastor Ray, we had a long talk about how she felt about filing a lawsuit. She said she wanted to do it so the whole country could hear what happened to her. So it wouldn't happen to other girls. You remember that, Sarah Mae?"

The girl nodded slowly.

"And do you still feel that way?" Charlene asked.

"You talk to me now," Aggie said. "Sarah Mae ain't old enough to make that decision."

Charlene noticed a slight twitching in Sarah Mae's cheeks when her mother said that.

"Of course, Mrs. Sherman." Charlene needed to respect this woman, a single mother struggling day to day. It was a precarious situation. Her daughter's suicide attempts had shaken Aggie to the point where her defensiveness was understandable.

Charlene continued. "Sarah has undergone such trauma that her story needs to be told. The abortion industry is engaged in a willful practice of deceiving women about the dangers and consequences of abortion. They are especially deceptive about the psychological dangers. They refuse to admit such dangers exist. And women continue to suffer depression, guilt, shame. Studies show that the guilt gets worse as time goes on."

At least Aggie Sherman appeared to be listening. When Charlene had first interviewed her, Mrs. Sherman seemed to be completely oblivious to the long-term effects of abortion. Most people were. The media never reported on the studies that indicated such effects.

"Post-abortion trauma is real, Mrs. Sherman, and it will continue unless people find out about it. I believe most Americans are fair-minded but aren't getting the whole story. If they hear Sarah Mae's story it will make a difference."

"Why can't we tell the papers or the TV or something?" Aggie said.

"Leverage," Charlene said. "As it stands now, your daughter's story might make the local news, but that's where it will stop. A lawsuit has a way of getting attention."

Aggie Sherman chewed on this for a moment, then her eyes narrowed. "That's what you're after, ain't it?"

The tone in her voice puzzled Charlene. "What do you mean, Mrs. Sherman?"

"Attention. This'll bring a lot of attention to you."

Charlene shook her head. "That is the furthest thing from my mind."

"Is it? You ain't the busiest lawyer in these parts. And you're a . . ." She stopped short.

Charlene didn't have to hear the word to know it was in Aggie's throat. A black lawyer, especially a female, was rare in the region. Charlene fought hard to keep her emotions in check. "I am a lawyer, Mrs. Sherman. When someone like your daughter is hurt, the law should provide justice and maybe prevent the same thing from happening again. That's all I am interested in."

"Well," Aggie said, "my daughter is what I'm interested in. And four hundred thousand sounds more than interesting to me. I want you to get us that money."

"Mrs. Sherman, please—"

"No. I don't want to have to go through a whole trial. Sarah Mae don't either."

Charlene's heart plummeted. She had invested not only time and money in this case, but her very soul. It was a case she passionately believed in. A battle she was sure God had entrusted to her. It couldn't be yanked away.

"You can't do this, Mrs. Sherman," Charlene said desperately.

"I can!" Aggie Sherman said. "You get us that money."

Charlene looked at Sarah Mae. The girl said nothing. Her mother grabbed her arm, pulled her off the chair, and out of the office.

5

The first time Millie Hollander saw the Supreme Court she was on her father's shoulders. He had a business trip to Washington, D.C., and insisted on taking her along. She was eight. They had turned the corner, Daddy giving her a ride that was bracing in the cool breeze, and suddenly there it was.

It literally took her breath away.

Great white steps led up to a main portico flanked on either side by two large marble figures. Seated majestically, the twin statues looked ready to hand down decisions of timeless wisdom. The portico itself was supported by sixteen massive Corinthian columns. It was like some palace of the gods.

And over everything, etched in stone for all the world to see, were the immortal words: *Equal Justice Under Law.*

The impression was overwhelming. Millie knew there had to be something of incredible importance housed here.

Perched on her father's shoulders, she felt ten feet tall. She also sensed immediately that whatever she was going to do in her life would, in some way she couldn't possibly know, have something to do with this building.

Millie recalled those feelings at the end of every term. Today was no exception. Official Court business was wrapping up. She gave her clerks her traditional sendoff—her famous cheesecake—along with a gold watch with the Supreme Court symbol on the face.

Other than her mother in California, Millie's clerks were her only family. Each year she grew close to each of them before they left to make their way in the world of law. Of course they sent cards, letters, e-mails; but they had, in a sense, left the nest. Though that was the way it should be, Millie always felt more than a pinch of sadness about it.

Now she was alone in her chambers, getting ready to leave for the summer recess. And she began the little ceremony she'd started ten years ago.

First, she paused to look at her judicial hero. From the start of her legal career she'd kept a portrait of Justice Oliver Wendell Holmes in her office. Beneath the famous face—the sweeping white mustache and Yankee patrician nose—were his words: "Every calling is great when greatly pursued."

Then she walked through the Great Hall, passing the marble busts of the former chief justices, and exited into the late D.C. afternoon.

Finally, descending the magnificent steps, she paused to look back at the Supreme Court building itself. It seemed as if she were on holy ground. She drew strength from the thought, knowing she had been given the greatest privilege in the law—to serve on the Supreme Court.

"Never gets old, does it?" Thomas J. Riley had come up to join her. He was dressed in his usual manner—a suit about ten years out of fashion—and carried his favorite walking stick.

"Did you follow me out?" Millie asked.

"We all know this is what you do. Sort of your ritual."

"You might call it that."

"You bet I do," Riley said. His eyes, sharp blue, were the most intelligent she had ever known. Behind them was a legal mind that had become legend. Millie could hardly believe that a little girl from rural California could call such a man her colleague—and friend.

"This is our temple," Riley said. "And ritual is an important part of our practice. When we don the robes, shake hands before taking the bench, listen to the oyez—it is all part and parcel of our religion."

Millie laughed. "We wouldn't want our friends at the ACLU hearing that word now, would we?"

The old justice smiled. "A purely secular religion, my dear, that flows from our allegiance to the Great Paper." That was Riley's name for the Constitution, which he always carried with him in small paperback form. He'd gone through roughly twenty copies in the ten years she had known him.

"I suppose that's true," Millie said.

"'Course it's true. Walk with me." He began his descent of the steps, his cane clicking briskly. The town was beginning to light up as evening slipped in. Riley headed toward Maryland Avenue. Millie had to move fast to keep up with him.

"Ed's making noise about retiring again," Riley said. Edward Ellis Pavel, the chief justice, was a spring chicken at seventy-five.

"Do you really think he will?" Millie asked.

"If it looks like President Francis will be reelected."

Millie nodded. "People seem to think it's a lock."

"That's the trouble. Everybody thinks about what everybody else thinks. Nobody thinks for himself. Millie, you're going to get the nod."

He stopped and turned to her. She felt his knowing gaze bore into her. "It just makes sense," Riley added. "Anybody approached you yet?"

"I had a meeting with Senator Levering a couple of days ago."

Riley's eyes narrowed. "Levering's a good man to have on your side. If he's for it, it's a done deal. I just want you to know I'll support you all the way."

"Thank you, Tom," Millie said, feeling the warmth she always did when speaking to the man who was like a second father to her. "I wish it was you."

"Ah." Riley waved his cane. "I'm too crotchety. Too old. Though I do plan to serve till I'm a hundred. Then I'll go out singing, if I remember any words."

He stopped at the corner and faced her. "Millie, I've been around a good long time. You get a feel for things. Back when I was a trial lawyer in Wyoming, during the Bronze Age, I learned to get a feel for what a jury was thinking. You know how I did it?"

"Tell me."

"By walking around. By getting out in the city and the country and reading newspapers and listening to folks. It's a wide world out there, and the good lawyers know how to get to it."

Millie wished she could have seen Riley in action back then, defending mostly poor people accused of crimes.

"Now I've got a feeling," Riley continued, "that we're in for some rough times in this country. Terrible times. And this time it's not because of terrorists or anthrax or anything you can touch. It's more insidious. And if you get tapped to be court justice, the barbarian hordes are going to come after you. They may say some nasty things."

"My only concern is for the Court. I don't care what they say about me."

"That's the ticket. We'll take 'em all on." He extended his hand, his grip firm with energy. "See you in a few months. *Vincit omnia veritas.*"

"Truth conquers all things," Millie said. It was Riley's favorite quotation, and Millie had often heard him say it from the bench, confusing lawyers with the Latin phrase.

Riley winked at her. "Don't ever stop believing that, Justice Hollander."

6

"What's your read?" President John W. Francis asked.

"She's a slam dunk, Mr. President," Senator Levering answered.

It was near midnight in the presidential study. The lights in the wood-paneled room were low. A bottle of A. H. Hirsch bourbon sat open on the table—a detail, Levering mused, that would have sent the religious right to the thesaurus to find new definitions for outrage. Especially since the topic of discussion was control of the Supreme Court.

Next to the bottle, a small replica of the Declaration of Independence in a paperweight cube hugged the edge of the table, as if it might fall off at the slightest bump. Every now and again Francis would reach out and tap the cube with his index finger.

"Think she'll get through the committee?" Francis asked.

"In a New York minute," Levering said. "Think they're gonna turn down the first woman CJ? We've got a majority, and everybody loves her. And having her as CJ will help you enormously."

Francis shot him a look. "You poll watching again, Sam?"

Levering smiled, enjoying the slight tinge of uncertainty in the president's voice. The balance of power in the conversation had shifted his way. His interior gauge for such transfers of power had served him almost infallibly for over thirty hard-fought political years.

Francis took a swig from his drink, another sign of nerves. Levering had seen the president lose control like this once before, when they had haggled over a pocket veto that Levering opposed. Levering had prevailed over the president's inner circle, just as he planned to now.

"And she'll be consistent for us?" Francis said.

"As she has been."

The president tapped the Declaration of Independence again. "Sam, I've decided to hang my legacy on the domestic partnership act."

Levering nodded. "Good choice. It will be the civil rights act of our time."

"If it's not declared unconstitutional."

"Relax. The way the Court's made up now, it'll pass."

"So we name Hollander chief justice. Who's on our short list to fill the other chair?"

"Some good names. We have a couple of stealth candidates who are probably unbeatable."

"Nobody's unbeatable," Francis said.

"John," said Levering in his best schoolteacher tone of voice, "let me remind you how it's done. Pavel retires, you move Hollander into the chair, and then you appoint a good liberal law professor. Like Larry Graebner."

"Graebner? He'd never get by. His paper trail is too long."

"Exactly. It's like the picador. Ever seen a bullfight?"

"Only in the movies."

"The picadors soften up the bull, using long spears to slice up the bull's neck muscles. Then the matador comes in and finishes him off. Graebner is our picador; we drop his name and the conservatives go crazy. We get a big fight, and Graebner steps aside. And then you appoint the right judge. We'll find him—or her. Someone in their forties. All the fight will be gone from the other side. They've fired their big guns. And then you know what you'll have?"

"What?"

"A solid 5–4 majority. For years."

The table lamp reflected in Francis's eyes, and Levering knew the president understood.

"It sounds perfect," Francis said. "Just one thing, though. Hollander."

"What about her?"

"I just have a feeling about her. Are you absolutely sure she's the one we want?"

"Sure as I can drink you under the table, Mr. President."

"What makes you so sure?"

Levering leaned over the table to address the leader of the free world face-to-face. "Because I know women," Levering said. "And I'm about to get to know Millicent Mannings Hollander in a very special way."

Francis's smile was of the locker room variety. "You old dog," the president said.

7

On Tuesday morning Millie spoke to a group of fourth graders at a public school in D.C. Sharing her love of law and learning with children was one of the things she enjoyed most. She hoped a seed would be planted in those who might otherwise have considered dropping out by the time high school rolled around. And maybe, just maybe, she'd be talking to a future Supreme Court justice.

Today's appearance was different. Millie's closest friend in town, Helen Forbes Kensington, had prevailed upon Millie to allow a camera to videotape the session for future public relations use. Helen, having reached a seventy-million-dollar divorce settlement from publishing tycoon Richard Kensington eight years ago, could support whichever causes she chose. Women's reproductive rights were at the top of her list. She served on the board of the National Parental Planning Group, and often appeared as a media spokesperson.

At lunch, over Pelegrino water with lime, Helen congratulated Millie on her answer to a delicate question from a little girl who asked why she could not pray in school. "You handled that brilliantly, kiddo," Helen said. She was Millie's age, but the best plastic surgeons in the country had made her look twenty years younger, especially in the soft lighting of the upscale restaurant Helen had chosen.

"I wasn't handling anything," Millie said. "I was merely trying to explain to them why separation of church and state is a good thing. That's hard for a fourth grader to understand."

"I don't think she wanted to understand. It was like she was planted just to make you look bad. Wouldn't put it past them."

Them. Millie knew exactly to whom Helen was referring. She often referred to conservative Christians as *them.*

"You're a little paranoid," Millie said.

"It's not paranoia if it's true." Helen reached for another jicama-date canapé from the appetizer plate. "There are fronts opening up all over the place now, and frankly I'm getting a little frustrated. I just heard this morning about an informed consent case down south."

Millie said nothing. In conversations with friends she had to walk a fine line between innocuous opinions and subtle politicking. Helen usually respected that line.

"It is an insult to women," Helen said. "These laws assume we don't know what's going on, we're stupid or incompetent to make decisions. When is this country going to grow up?"

"When you are elected president," Millie joked, trying to change the subject. Talking with a friend who was so issue driven had to be done delicately. Millie wanted no undue influence on matters destined for the Court.

Helen understood and smiled. "Okay. So why don't you tell me about this super secret meeting you had the other day."

"Not super secret."

"What's going on?"

"Nothing much. Just a meeting with Senator Sam Levering."

Helen let her jaw drop melodramatically. "You stinker! You didn't tell me!"

"It was an informal meeting," Millie said. "He just asked me if I wanted to be chief justice."

Helen let out a celebratory howl. "Now we're talking! Oh, honey, I knew this day would come."

"It hasn't come just yet," Millie cautioned. "But it may."

"And Sam Levering is on your side? You cannot miss, girlfriend. Do you want it?"

Millie took a sip of water. "Of course I want it."

"This is great. This is wonderful. We have to celebrate. How about you and I dress to the nines and hit Antonio's tonight?"

"Sorry," Millie said.

"You don't want to go out with your nearest and dearest friend?"

"I have other plans."

Helen put her elbows on the table. "What aren't you telling me?"

Millie couldn't keep it in any longer. "Sam Levering called me last night and asked me to dinner."

Again, Helen's mouth opened like an automatic door. "You. Are. Kidding. Me."

Millie smiled.

"Stop the presses! When was the last time you went on a date?"

Millie thought a moment. "Thirty-five years ago, I think."

"Sam Levering," Helen said, "is a notorious ladies man."

"I'm a big girl," Millie said.

"You're a lamb in sheep's clothing."

"Don't be silly," Millie said, but she felt a little heat rising on the back of her neck.

Helen looked at Millie. "The truth now," she said. "What on earth made you say yes?"

For a moment Millie hesitated. She was not one for massive self-reflection. She had settled interior matters long ago. But this was Helen, the closest friend she had.

"I really don't know for certain," Millie said. "Maybe it was insane. But the man is handing me the greatest prize a judge could ever have. How could I say no?"

Helen raised and lowered her eyebrows. "It might be kind of fun, if you know what I mean."

"Oh, stop it," Millie said. "You really are insufferable."

"But this is Senator Sam Levering, Millie dear."

"A nice dinner is enough for me."

Helen huffed as if she didn't quite buy it. "Just watch your backside, honey. And your front side, too."

8

Millie looked at herself in the mirror and said to the reflection, "You have got to be joking."

She was actually dressing up to go out on a date. Was the dress she held against her body too fancy or not fancy enough?

She had the right clothes for official dinners, and speeches, and appearances. But this was different, radically so.

Was the color right? Was the length out of fashion? If only Helen were here to help her, but that would have been a cure worse than the disease. Helen would have taken her on a dress-buying binge and quantum makeover for what was supposed to be a simple dinner for two.

Millie lowered the dress and considered her body. It wasn't so bad, was it? She was not thin nor heavy, though she would have preferred a little less in the thighs. Her lower body seemed to have developed a mind of its own lately, issuing dissenting opinions to her desire for firmness. The treadmill and basketball helped, along with a sensible diet. But she knew she would never be one of those middle-aged women who could wear bicycle pants to the market with impunity. Not that she would ever *do* it. But the option would have been nice.

She had never considered herself pretty; reporters were fond of describing her "dignified" face. What exactly did that mean? A face to be etched in the side of a mountain? Terrific. Right up there with Teddy, Tom, Abe, and George.

She wished now she had said no to Senator Levering. What on earth had she been thinking? Going out with a United States senator? One who had a reputation with the ladies? How could she have let herself get into this?

She remembered vividly the last time she went on one of these gruesome social rituals called a date. It was a memory etched in stone, like the words on the Supreme Court building. It was only her second time being asked out by a boy. She'd said no the first time. But this time it was Marty Winters, the second smartest kid at Santa Lucia High. She, of course, was the first, and that was one reason she didn't get asked out.

She had actually liked Marty, had been drawn to him, unlike any other boys she had met. Growing up brilliant made her extremely self-conscious and withdrawn in a way that worried her parents. She had never given boys a serious thought—who would ever find her appealing?—until Marty.

They went to the movies. *Romeo and Juliet* was the big sensation. Marty had placed his arm around her the moment the coming attractions started and did not remove it until Romeo and Juliet were quite dead. She knew Marty was in more than a bit of arm pain after the movie, but she didn't mention it.

He took her to a burger place afterward. They saw some kids from school, who made a few cracks about Marty and Millie sittin' in a tree. Marty made a joke that put them to shame, and she thought then that she was in love. He was almost handsome, in a scholarly sort of way. His acne was clearing up and she could see him inventing things someday.

She remembered the music that night. The radio in the restaurant played "Hey Jude" by the Beatles. And then Herb Alpert's "This Guy's in Love with You." She made a girlish wish that Herb Alpert was singing about Marty.

Marty did not drive her home. Instead, he took her up to The Rim. She didn't protest, though she was so nervous she almost threw up. The Rim was a mountain road that offered a great view of the valley. It was a make-out place, of course, where the kids always went. Where she never went.

She hoped Marty wouldn't do something wrong. She would allow him to kiss her, though she didn't know how to kiss. She had spent the afternoon kissing the side of her fist, trying to get the pressure to feel right.

And Marty did kiss her. A lot. Too much. She tried to turn her head away and he kept twisting it back with his hand. But that wasn't the bad part.

The bad part happened when she would not let him put his hands on her chest, when she said, "Let's stop, huh?" He reeled back like he'd been slapped.

And then Marty Winters told her that she was ugly and he was doing her a favor, and none of the boys liked her because she was so ugly and smart, and she'd never have a boyfriend and why didn't she just dry up and blow away?

Millicent Mannings Hollander, dressed up in her home in Fairfax County, remembered how she had almost burst out in tears. How unfamiliar feelings pushed up in her like flood waters behind a dam, and how her mind—the one thing she had always been able to rely upon—fought them back for her and forced her not to cry. Not in front of Marty then, and not alone in her room when he dropped her off.

And not in front of her mother when she had asked about the date. Millie simply turned her emotions inward, forming the start of a rock-hard interior.

That hardness had held her together through the death of her father, working to get through college, and finishing first in her law school class. It had given her a steadiness and strength that served her well as her career took her from teaching constitutional law at Boalt Hall, to the Ninth Circuit Court of Appeals, and finally to the Supreme Court.

During her career she'd had occasional offers to date but turned them all down. She had determined not to seek the intimate companionship of men. If she was to be married at all, it was to the law.

So why was she doing this now?

In truth, she had been feeling somewhat odd for a few months now. She could even pinpoint the start of it—the argument in the late-term abortion case. Because of her vote, the law outlawing the procedure had been declared unconstitutional. But the graphic nature of the operation had been emphasized by the attorney for the state. Ever since that afternoon she had felt moments of uncertainty. Not so much with her decision—based as it was on her reading of the law and precedent—but on the whole idea that such an issue should arise at all in a civilized society.

But the right of women to control their bodies was the primary value she upheld, and she would stick to that. She just wished she'd stop being bothered by a particular case.

That must be it, she suddenly decided. *The senator is a diversion I am hoping will put me back into equilibrium. That's unfair, to him and to me. This was a bad idea.*

She went to the phone to call Senator Levering. He'd left his direct mobile number. What would she tell him? Headache? He wouldn't believe her, but that was not important. She could not go through with this. It was, aside from everything else, silly. She was too old for dating. Besides, she had David McCullough's John Adams biography waiting for her, and that would be enough. Books had always been enough.

She picked up the phone and started to dial. Then she heard the doorbell.

9

Senator Levering said, "You seem a bit edgy, if you don't mind my saying so."

He sat facing Millie in the back of the limousine. She was on the side, near the wet bar, castigating herself for being so transparent. *This is just a dinner with a man, a senator, an ally,* she told herself. *Don't be such a baby.*

"I'm a little rusty at this," Millie said.

"It's like riding a mule," Levering said. "Nothing to it if you hang on. How about a drink?"

"Do you have 7-Up?"

"I was thinking Perrier-Jouët '95."

"Sounds French and imposing."

"It's only the finest champagne this side of the moon."

"Why not?" A bit of celebration was in order, wasn't it? A chief justice appointment didn't happen very often.

The senator fished the bottle of champagne from the ice bin. "What shall we talk about? The Takings Clause?"

She laughed a little, and it felt good. "If that's your passion," she joked.

Levering removed the cork and poured the champagne into two flutes. "I am a man of many passions," he said, handing her a glass. He clinked his against hers. "To our new chief justice."

"Perhaps," Millie said.

"So shall it be written," Levering said. "So shall it be done."

"That sounds familiar."

"Yul Brynner in *The Ten Commandments*."

"Ah yes. Pharaoh. Is that how you see yourself?"

Levering slid back to his seat which did, indeed, look like a throne. "I see myself as a man of the people, Millie. May I call you Millie?"

"Certainly."

"But some of us are called by fate to positions of great power. You. Me. Yul Brynner."

Millie smiled. "Didn't he drown in the Red Sea?"

"Not Yul," Levering said. "A survivor, like me. In this life we have friends and enemies, Millie. The trick is to know your enemies, treat 'em like friends, then stick 'em when they're not looking." He said the last with a wink, but Millie felt he was deadly serious.

"Where are we going tonight?" Millie asked.

"Thought we'd drive around a little," said Levering. "Take in the city lights. Talk. We'll end up somewhere."

He drank the rest of his champagne, then poured himself another glass. Millie had the distinct feeling Levering had had a few drinks before picking her up.

"Tell me about yourself," Millie said. If this was going to be a date, she was going to treat it like one.

"You've read the papers," Levering said.

She waved her hand dismissively. "Indulge me with a summary."

"The particulars are I'm divorced, have a . . ." He hesitated. "A son."

She perceived in him a desire to talk, and waited patiently. It was the first time she had seen any sort of vulnerability in his face.

"You've read about my son, I'm sure," Levering said. "He ran off some time ago, joined a religious thing. We—his mother and I—tried to get him out of it. He went back to it about five years ago, and I haven't spoken to him since. How's that for confession?"

"I'm sorry," Millie said, wishing she could say more. But she was not used to intimate talk with men. Or women, for that matter. Not even Helen.

"No need to be," Levering said. "You have a personal religion, Millie?"

The question caught her off guard. "I believe in the law," she finally replied.

"Well said. Hey, take a look at that." He pointed out the tinted window. Millie recognized the lights of the Jefferson Memorial. It was, for her, the prettiest of the major memorials in the city.

And then Levering was on the seat next to her. "A little more champagne?" he offered.

"No, thank you," Millie said.

"May I be so bold as to give some advice to a Supreme Court justice?"

"All right." She could smell his cologne now, mingling with the scent of perspiration.

Levering leaned toward her a little, unwavering in his gaze. "I think you need to live a little."

Millie swallowed. "Oh?"

Levering put his hand on hers. "We're cut from the same cloth, you know."

Millie tried to gently pull her hand away. Levering held on.

"From the people," Levering said. "We worked our way up the hard way. I know all about you, Madame Justice."

She wondered what he meant by that, and by the half smile on his face. For a moment she thought he would try to kiss her. But he leaned back, reached behind her to the bar, and poured more champagne for himself.

"You grew up poor, like I did," Levering said. "You pulled yourself up by your bootstraps and made it. Boalt Hall Law. Editor of the *Law Review*. Number one in your class. You were slated for greatness from the start. So was I."

The limo approached the Lincoln Memorial. Millie saw the flocks of tourists dotting the stairs, and Lincoln presiding over it all.

"And now," Levering said, "here we are."

He squeezed her hand again. Millie felt her face heating up. How silly this all was. That she should be acting like a little schoolgirl.

Levering leaned over and kissed her neck.

Alarms went off through her body. Part of her, the rational part, told her to take it easy. This was a harmless development; she could handle it. But the other part, made up of instinct and feelings she hardly knew, cried out at full volume.

She smelled alcohol on his breath as Levering reached his hand behind her neck and pulled her toward him. She pushed back.

"Stop it." Millie slid away from him. "Take me home, please."

He backed away. "Let's take a walk." He grabbed the limo phone and told the driver to pull over.

"Senator Levering, take me home." She said it firmly, but knew he had no intention of doing so. Now what?

The limo pulled into a crowded parking lot. The driver opened the door, offering his hand to Millie. She decided to get out. Maybe she could catch a taxi.

Levering stumbled out behind her. The air was crisp for early summer. A tour group ambled past them heading toward the Lincoln Memorial. Levering staggered a bit as he watched the raucous teens.

"They don't even know who we are," he said. "And couldn't care less."

Millie started to worry that someone would recognize the senator, a group leader perhaps, and before long she'd be staring at herself on the cover of the *National Exposure*. She shuddered.

Levering grabbed her hand. "Come on, let's walk."

She tried to extricate her hand from his, but he pulled her toward a grassy area. The thin sliver of moon seemed like a sardonic smile.

"Please let me go," she said. "I really want to go home."

He turned toward her. "You don't have to be afraid of me," he said. "I'm on your side. I'm your friend."

"Friendship is fine," Millie said. "I don't mind that."

"But I need more." In the gloom she could barely see his face, but it looked sorrowful. For one moment she thought of him not as a senator, but a boy. The look quickly faded as a smooth smile returned.

"Don't you want to give it a try?" Levering said.

"Give what a try?" she asked.

"This. Us. Just give it a try. You'll like it."

He moved quickly, grabbing her around the waist and pressing his face on hers.

She broke his hold and stumbled back. "Stop."

His arms shot out again and pulled her toward him. He kissed her mouth. She struggled in his embrace, but he was strong.

It was all so surreal. She was no longer a judge on the highest court in the land, but simply another woman being pawed by a drunk in the dark.

She slapped him.

It landed clumsily, not with the loud pop that a Bette Davis might have managed. And when he smiled at it, she turned and found herself running, stupidly, the heels of her shoes poking holes in the soft grass.

10

Charlene's prayer tonight was not a song. It was a crying out.

This is our case, Lord. You're not yanking it from me now, are you?

Four hundred thousand, of which Charlene would get over a third, was not pocket change. But this case was not about money. It couldn't be.

It was dark outside her apartment, almost moonless. She had an indescribable feeling of evil hovering not just here, but over the whole country. And she had to do something about it.

She fell to her knees with her hands on the old sofa she'd nabbed at a yard sale while still a law student. Back then she'd been full of confidence. Now, with only the sound of crickets drifting in through the screened window, she felt confused and alone.

When she had gone into law, she thought she could make a difference in the world. Use the law to make the country a better place to live.

She had drifted away from her Christian roots by the time she'd enrolled at LaBlanc. It was not a prestigious school, but it allowed her to complete her degree at night. The curriculum was no-nonsense bar exam preparation. During the day she worked two jobs—as a waitress at Shoney's and as a tutor for elementary students.

Stress was a constant companion. Charlene juggled tasks like a plate spinner, ever at risk for a crash. Then Ty Slayton came into her life.

He was a ruggedly handsome fireman. It was as if he had arrived at her own fire, the one raging in her life, and offered rescue. She fell for him like a collapsing roof.

When she got pregnant, the collapse was complete. Ty Slayton pressed her to get an abortion. That was his condition for continuing the relationship.

It was the turning point for Charlene. She knew she could not abort. She knew she carried life. And she knew God had created that life in her.

The very night Ty had given her his ultimatum, Charlene asked God to take her back. She felt no sense of his presence, but knew in her mind she had made a decision she would never back down on again.

When she miscarried two weeks later, she wondered if it was a punishment from God. Well then, so be it. She would make it up to him one day.

That day came when Charlene read in the paper about a local sixteen-year-old girl who had tried to commit suicide. Twice. The first time it was with a razor to her wrists. The second was an attempt to jump off a bridge into a rocky gorge. This girl, Sarah Mae Sherman, had been pulled back by a Christian minister right before she jumped. A miracle.

While reading the story, Charlene had an overwhelming sense of God's leading. She prayed for an hour. And two days later Pastor Ray Neven had shown up in her office with Sarah Mae Sherman.

Now she wondered if she were being punished again. Sarah Mae's case had been yanked from her. Why? What did God want from her?

He couldn't want her to give up. He needed her. He needed this case. She was going to get it back.

Charlene grabbed the phone and called Aggie Sherman.

"It's late," Mrs. Sherman said.

"We can get more money," Charlene said.

The silence on the other end of the line was heavy. Then Aggie Sherman said, "Well?"

"Never take the first offer. We keep going forward. Start the trial. There will be a bigger offer before the trial ends." This was not a certainty, only likely. But it would get the trial going. That was the main thing.

"How much?" Aggie said.

"More than they're offering now."

"I don't know."

"Aggie," Charlene said, "I've put my heart and soul into this case for you and Sarah Mae. I won't let you down."

Another long pause. "Get us the biggest settlement you can. Then take it."

Yes, Charlene Moore sang in her thoughts. *We're going all the way.*

11

Slowing down from a fast walk, Millie realized she had not been in this park for years. She'd done quite a bit of sightseeing when she'd first come to the Court. But very quickly her life had developed a routine that made simple excursions to monuments and tourist sites difficult.

She glanced back and did not see the senator. Had he been too drunk to follow?

Over the course of her judicial career, the one thing Millie Hollander had avoided was publicity. If a judge was making headlines, either through judicial opinion or personal transgression, she wasn't doing her job.

She was angry at herself for allowing this to happen. She should not have let her guard down, even for a moment. She was not cut out to be with men in any romantic situation, nor they with her. She'd made that decision years ago, after Marty Winters. She should have stuck with that decision.

As she reached the sidewalk on the edge of the park, looking for the roof light that would indicate a taxi, she noticed a figure slowly making his way toward her, from the right.

He was dressed thickly, as if in several layers of clothes. His hair and face were caked with dirt. Even in the dim light she could tell that this was one of the city's homeless.

She turned her back and started to walk slowly away from him. Her body buzzed with an adrenaline surge. Was this what it felt like to be mugged? She had been so long in an ivory tower, and suddenly she felt ashamed. Her judicial decisions affected people like this, all people, really. But how much did she know about what went on in their daily lives?

She glanced back and saw that the man, in a slow but steady shuffle, was following her.

Millie's nerves crackled. She looked desperately to the street and saw a taxi coming her way. She put her arm up, more frantically than she wanted to, and waved stupidly at it. It passed by. She saw people sitting in the back. A man and a woman. They appeared to be laughing.

She turned. The homeless man was only a few feet away now. For one moment she could not move.

"You still have time," the man said.

He took another step toward her, and she could barely make out his eyes. They were wild yet full of some crazy earnestness. Pleading almost.

"You still have time!" he shouted, jerking forward.

Fear engulfing her, Millie stumbled backward. Her shoe caught the edge of the curb. Her body lurched into the street.

She heard the squeal of tires, and suddenly light seemed all around her, coming from every angle, blinding her. And then every part of her body felt as if it had exploded as she was hit by a force that lifted her up for a sprawling moment. Then she felt herself falling, and the ground, unforgiving, slamming her head. And then the light turned to darkness.

CHAPTER TWO

1

No one would have faulted her for staying seated at her age, but Ethel Hollander had to kneel. Tonight she knew she had to pray on her knees.

She and fifteen prayer warriors were at the church for the weekly prayer meeting. It started late, usually around nine o'clock, so Allard Jones could make it. He worked in Bakersfield, an hour north of Santa Lucia, and never wanted to be left out. Allard, like Ethel, had helped build Santa Lucia Community Church.

The building was built by a congregation of twenty back in 1964. It was simple and boxy outside. But inside there was a history as full of warmth and life as anything the Lord had created.

Ethel Hollander had over fifty years invested in this church congregation. She'd seen the good times and the bad. The old building went down in the earthquake of '57. They built it right back up. And when they broke ground for the new building in '64, they'd given the shovel to Ethel Hollander.

If someone had asked her what held the church together, Ethel wouldn't have hesitated to say prayer.

She knew Pastor Holden agreed. He was such a man of prayer. He hadn't been here long but he was already, in her mind, the best preacher they'd ever had. And he had a line on prayer, like his soul was attuned to things in a special way.

It had to be, in part, because of what he'd gone through. Ethel knew only part of the story. He'd come to the valley to be restored. He was just over fifty, but he'd had enough tragedy for two lifetimes.

That was why he prayed.

And tonight, Ethel needed those prayers. All day she had felt that something was wrong with Millie.

Ethel prayed for her daughter daily. Somehow she had ended up on the United States Supreme Court, and Ethel was certain God had intended that for some great good. Ethel held on to that belief, even though the last ten years seemed to move Millie further away from Christ. She knew that only God's miraculous hand could change her daughter's heart.

So each day without fail, Ethel uttered the same prayer, that her daughter would find her way back to the God she had grown up with.

Yet tonight she felt Millie was in trouble. What sort of trouble she could not name. But when she had that feeling she always prayed.

The prayer meeting lasted till almost midnight.

2

Millie heard someone whisper her name.

She was in total darkness. Her first thought was that she had gone blind. But somehow she knew it was not blindness, just lack of light. She reached out, looking for a wall or a switch. She felt nothing but air.

For some reason she felt she had to scream. She tried, but no sound came out. What was this? Paralysis seized her. Had she lost sight *and* voice?

And then she heard her name again.

The voice that whispered sounded neither like a man nor a woman. It was seductive, in a way that was both irresistible and deadly.

Was she dead?

No, couldn't be, for she was walking. Not walking, really, but being moved. Upright, as if on some belt made of air. Weightless.

And powerless. Powerless to stop her thrust forward into deeper darkness. Powerless to resist the force—it was a force, she knew that now—drawing her.

Then she felt a slimy thing around her ankles.

She could not scream or recoil, only feel a slithering like a wet snake. No, a pair of wet snakes. Then another pair and another, on both her ankles and her legs.

She opened her mouth, but all was silent.

Then she realized that they were not snakes, but fingers. Fingers on horrible hands that writhed upward from some abyss, grasping at her, trying to pull her down.

This was no nightmare. This was a reality beyond dreams, beyond comprehension, yet fully existent, woven from the cords of every terror she had felt in her life.

Her name was called out again, this time louder, and then the word *surrender.*

Surrender . . .

Yes, a surrender that would end this. And yet she knew if she did surrender now, she would be forever lost.

Her will told her to resist, but she had lost all ability to resist. She could not move. She could not control her limbs. She could not scream. She felt a drawing downward, downward.

And then in some far place in her mind—if she still had a mind—in a voice that sounded distantly like her own, she willed herself to say, *Oh, God, help me.*

3

"I messed up," Sam Levering said. "Oh, boy, did I."

"Just tell me," Anne Deveraux said.

Levering popped another aspirin into his mouth. Anne was everything to him—legal counsel, advisor, and spokesperson. She was also the sharpest politico on Capitol Hill. He depended on her for his every move, from schedules to meals to troubleshooting statements drafted on the fly.

This time she'd have to come up with a strategy, and it would have to be a masterpiece. He would need to break it to her a step at a time.

"I had a date last night," Levering said.

"Not exactly news," Anne said. She was the only one he would allow to talk to him that way. Part of it was pure sexual power. With her flowing raven hair, her form-fitting red suit, and her impeccable makeup, Anne Deveraux could, as the saying went, make a bishop kick out a stained-glass window. The one and only time Levering had made a move on her, however, she had frozen him out with an icy glare. Anne made it clear to him that she was all business.

"This wasn't an ordinary date," Levering said, clearing his throat. "It was with Millicent Mannings Hollander."

Anne threw her head back, the way she did when signaling overdrive in disaster-handling mode. "Tell me that's not true."

"Unfortunately, it is."

Anne began to pace in front of the oil painting near Levering's office door, the one of Gordon McRae as Curly in *Oklahoma!* It had been the gift of a wealthy donor.

"So you are telling me you were with Justice Hollander last night, and that she is about to die this morning? Have you seen the *Post* Web site yet?"

"No."

"Well, it's all over the place. And the big question is what was she doing alone, in an evening gown, in the middle of a Washington, D.C., park? And you're saying there are only two people with the answer?"

"Three."

Anne thought a moment. "You had the limo?"

"Sylvan won't talk."

"What about her friends? Did she tell anybody she was going out with you?"

"I don't know."

"Well, we better find out. Anybody see you pick her up?"

Levering shrugged.

Anne stopped for a moment and fished a cigarette from her pocket. She put it in her mouth and "smoked" it, though it remained unlit. Levering had seen her do this many times before. It was the ritual of a supreme spin doctor.

"All right," Anne said. "Detail me."

"I was going to take her to dinner," Levering said, longing for a drink but deciding he better not until this meeting was over. "Then I thought we'd ride around a little. Have a couple of drinks."

"Does she drink?"

"Not much."

"Did she have anything to drink?"

"Some champagne. Why?"

"That may come in handy. Keep going."

Levering rubbed his temples. With his eyes closed he continued. "So I'd already had a snort before picking her up. Believe it or not, I was a little nervous."

"Why shouldn't I believe it?" Anne said. There was a challenging tone in her voice that Levering ignored.

"So I drank a little more with her, we talked. She was uptight. And, I don't know, I got forward with her, I guess."

Anne dragged deeply on the unlit cigarette, then put her hand on her hip. "Keep going."

"Do I have to?"

"You want me to help you?"

"Fine. I kissed her on the neck."

Anne Deveraux threw her head back again, looked at the ceiling, and did a complete turn in the middle of the office. When she finished, she said, "You're telling me you tried to score with a justice of the United States Supreme Court? On the first date? Before you even got out of the car?"

Smiling sheepishly, Levering said, "That's about it."

"What were you thinking?" Anne said.

"You know me."

"I can understand it with the others. Interns, yes. Socialite widows, fine. But Millicent Mannings Hollander?"

"I don't know why I wanted her." He paused, pondering his reasons. He had not grown up with very much attention from girls. He had always felt shy and self-conscious—all the way through college. Even when he got married he considered it a lucky blunder. But when he won his first public office in the state legislature, he found that power held a certain attracting force. Women began to gravitate toward him. He was always careful about it. He'd never had a scandal during his married years. Even after the divorce he kept things as discrete as possible. He'd had his pick of women. So why Millie?

"Let me answer for you," Anne said. "She's Jaws."

Levering tilted his head at her.

"You know," Anne said. "Jaws. The shark. The big one. She was the big one. You wanted to land her."

Levering, with reluctance, nodded. "Maybe."

"Millicent Mannings Hollander is the most famous virgin in the country. Everybody knows she never got married and doesn't date. But you thought you'd be Mr. Excitement for the great score, didn't you?"

"Fine. Guilty."

"Good. Confession's good for the soul."

"I don't believe in souls."

"Then it's good for your digestion, okay? Now let me do what I do."

Levering sighed, glad to be back on familiar ground. Admissions always made him nervous. "What's the first step?"

"I'll go down and figure out what her status is. I've got to see if I can get to her before she talks to anybody."

"Can you swing that?"

Anne took a drag on her unlit cigarette and smiled. "Who's your Huckleberry?"

4

Millie opened her mouth and finally a sound came out.

"Help. Oh, please help." She heard her voice as if it came from outside of herself, a frightened whisper.

Light invaded darkness. She opened her eyes. A foglike veil shrouded the room.

She felt as if she were being pulled through that veil, pulled like dead weight toward consciousness. Her body fought against it, shrieking to go back to sleep.

Her eyelids were like bags full of rocks. But she knew with a certainty bordering on hysteria that she could not go back to sleep. If she did, they would have her. The ones she had felt in the darkness.

Circles of fear rippled outward from her stomach. She had to fight to stay awake.

"Help . . ."

Something at the back of her head. A throbbing, painful thing, reaching around to her temples like burning tongs.

Did they have her in a torture chamber?

Sight of curtains, smell of linen and disinfectant. Sounds of voices outside the room, beeping noises, the soft whirring of machines.

She was not dead. She was in a hospital room.

The realization came to her, and with it a wave of such sweet relief that she almost wept.

Come back, she told herself as her eyelids pressed downward. *Don't sleep!*

A nurse—Millie assumed it was a nurse, hoped it was—floated in through the mists.

". . . feeling?" the nurse said.

Millie heard herself groan.

"How are you feeling?" the nurse repeated.

"Help."

"Are you in pain?"

Was she in pain? No, it was beyond pain, as if she were awakening into a thick, burning substance. She felt things attached to her body.

"Help," Millie said.

"I'll get the doctor."

Millie wanted to shout *Don't leave me*, as if this nurse represented the last lifeline. But the nurse was gone.

She was alone. Would she die? The word *again* popped into her mind. Why should she think that? Her mind slogged forward, barely, frustrating her. She knew who she was, that her mind was a sharp one, well oiled, trained. Or had she suffered some sort of damage?

What was happening?

She did not have any idea of time. The next span could have been minutes or hours. But she fought to stay awake. Sharp pains helped her. She became aware of a monitor next to the bed, issuing peak and valley lines. Her heartbeat. She still had a beating heart.

She heard a voice. A familiar one. "How does Justice feel?"

Myron Cross. Her doctor. He always called her Justice. Not Madame Justice. Just Justice, as if she herself were the principle of law itself.

Dr. Cross was one of the best. He had been the doctor to many Supreme Court justices over the years, even getting a spread once in *Time* magazine about his practice to the powerful.

But he was a gentle and humble man who loved his work. Millie had never felt a moment's anxiety around him, until now. Dr. Cross must have seen a tortured look on her. He said, "Are you in much pain?"

She was, but the physical pain was not what concerned her. "What happened?" she asked. Her voice was thick and slow.

"You are lucky," Dr. Cross said. "You survived a bad accident."

"I thought I . . . was dead."

"Truth told, we almost lost you. You were in surgery four hours. Dr. Dickinson performed brilliantly. I was there."

"How did I . . . ?"

"You don't remember?"

Millie was barely able to shake her head.

"A car hit you," Dr. Cross said. "Don't try to talk about it now. Let me just tell you you're going to be all right, but you'll need a lot of recovery time. You have three broken ribs, a collapsed lung, bruises like you wouldn't believe, and a blow to the head. You were unconscious for twelve hours. It could have been so much worse."

But it was. What she had felt in that darkness had been worse than anything she had ever experienced. Yet how could she explain it to Dr. Cross? She had enough sense, even in her foggy condition, to know that what had happened was psychological, not physical. He would have no remedy for that.

"Did I . . ."

"Go ahead, Millie."

"Was I ever . . . gone?"

He straightened up. "You mean close to death? The answer is yes."

"No. Actually . . . ."

"There was a moment when you flatlined. But it was only a moment."

"When?"

"Do you really want to go into this?"

"Please."

"Your accident caused what we call simple pneumothorax. It happened when one of your broken ribs punctured your lung. You were unconscious and not breathing."

A trembling disquiet swept over Millie's body.

"So the paramedics brought you in with a bag-valve mask to keep you breathing. What that did, though, was fill you up with air, not in the lung but in the pleural space. That collapsed your lung completely and put pressure on your heart. And that is probably . . ."

"Yes?"

Dr. Cross glanced at the chart in his hands. "At 1:35 A.M. we had a flatline that lasted about one minute."

Millie said nothing.

"But you're here now," Dr. Cross said. "That's the important thing."

Pain exploded behind her eyes.

"You have some heavy bruising to the legs," the doctor added. "It's going to be painful to walk."

"Will I be able to play the violin?"

"You think I'm going to fall for that old joke? No, you won't be able to play the violin unless you could before. Yes, you will be able to walk and do everything else you used to do. Over time."

"Thanks," Millie said, feeling a tiny spot of relief.

"Don't talk," Dr. Cross said. "I should tell you the place is crawling with reporters, police, and all sorts of people who want to see you. I'm keeping them as far away as possible. But they'll want a report, and I'm happy to say I can tell them your prospects for a full recovery are excellent. Is there anyone you'd like to see?"

Her mother. That was who sprang to mind. She would be worried when she heard the news. "I want to call my mother," Millie said.

"I'll arrange it," Dr. Cross said. "Anything else?"

"Who hit me?"

"Oh, a man named Rosato or Rosetta, something like that. He is extremely remorseful, I understand. The police are questioning him."

"Tell them . . ."

"Yes?"

"It wasn't his fault."

Dr. Cross nodded. "I'll take care of it. You rest."

She could do nothing else. Her body felt like it had been put through a harvester and dumped in a bale on a road. But her body was not what concerned her.

It was that vision. She wondered, for a few moments, if the blow to her head meant she was going to lose her mind.

5

Down the hall from Millie Hollander's room, Anne Deveraux stuck a finger in a cop's face. "Did you not hear me?" she said.

The cop nodded. "And I'm telling you—"

She flashed her credential again. "United States Senate, okay?"

"Nobody sees her," the cop said. "Not the president, not the Dalai Lama, unless the doctor says so."

She looked around at the milling masses, recognizing some members of the press waiting for the impending press conference called by Dr. Myron Cross. That would be a whitewash, of course, telling her nothing she needed to hear.

But she'd hang around anyway. Maybe there would be an opening somewhere. What would they do if she walked right in?

She'd say she was paying her respects from a senator. A man concerned about her health, as he would any prominent member of the Court or Congress. A man who had admired her judicial integrity for years.

She would not reveal the real reason she was there, of course. She would not mention the word *Jaws.*

She felt a touch on her arm. She whirled around hard. Anne did not like to be touched.

She faced a short man with sweat beads on his forehead.

"You're Anne Deveraux, aren't you?" he asked.

"Who wants to know?"

"You work for Senator Levering, right?"

She was getting rapidly ticked at this guy. He was—what was the word?—ratlike. He had a longish, pointed nose and eyes that seemed to be scouting for food.

"What business is that of yours?" Anne asked.

He smiled, showing two prominent front teeth. Rodent choppers. "I know everything that goes on in this town, every poop that's a scoop. Dan Ricks." He extended his hand.

Anne ignored it. "I'm busy now, Mr. Ricks. If you'd like an appointment—"

"Get off it," he said. "I write for *The National Exposure.*"

"Tabloid guy?"

"Reporter," he said defensively.

"Oh, yeah."

"Don't get huffy. You remember when the *New York Times* sat on that Congressman Conley story?"

Lawrence Conley had been forced to resign over an allegation that he'd had sex with a sixteen-year-old girl. "What about it?" Anne asked.

"I broke that."

That's right, Anne recalled. It was originally an *Exposure* story. And suddenly Anne felt like Bogart in *Casablanca,* when he realized the ratlike Peter Lorre had murdered two Nazis by himself. *I am a little more impressed with you.*

"You have an angle on this?" Anne asked.

"You're an angle," Ricks said.

"Me?"

"What's the senator sending you over here for?"

"Who says he sent me?"

"Why are you here?"

"Why is that your business?"

"Everything's my business in this town."

"Everything?"

"What isn't, I *make* my business."

Anne nodded. The *Exposure* was not to be trifled with. It could indeed break things that would follow you around like a bad smell.

"I like you, Ricks," Anne lied. "I'll level with you. Senator Levering is concerned about Justice Hollander's health. It's no secret she might be chief justice someday."

Ricks nodded. Anne did not like the way he was studying her.

"She's also a woman," Ricks said.

"Gee, Ricks, you are a good reporter."

Ricks didn't flinch. "What do you know about the accident?"

"I don't know anything about anything," Anne said. "I'm here on an official call, and that's it. No more, no less."

"Uh-huh. The senator has quite a reputation."

"You're scampering up the wrong monument."

"Tell me where I should scamper."

"Why should I do that?"

"It pays to be nice to the *Exposure*."

Anne fingered a cigarette in her pocket. "That almost sounds like a threat, Mr. Ricks."

"From the press?" he said with over-the-top outrage. "We only want the truth, Ms. Deveraux. Remember our motto— 'All the news that fits, we print.'" He took out a card and snapped it between his thumb and forefinger, like a magician producing the ace of spades.

"Call me if you hear anything," he said. "Maybe we can help each other out sometime."

And with a political instinct born of countless spin sessions, Anne Deveraux took the card.

6

"Is that you, Mom?" Millie whispered hoarsely into the phone.

"Oh Millie, your voice," Ethel Hollander said. Her mother's voice sounded reedy, as it always did when she worried about something.

"I'm going to be fine, Mom. They tell me."

"When I heard it on TV, I about jumped through the phone line. I couldn't get through. I called and called . . ."

"They're being careful with me."

"It's on all the programs. They show that picture of you from five years ago."

"What are they saying on the programs?"

"That they don't know why you were out there."

"Where?"

"Alone. At night. What happened?"

Millie put her hand on her pounding head and closed her eyes. It was coming back now. She wished it wouldn't. Would she have to tell the story? To the police? They would want to know who she had been with, how the whole thing happened. More publicity.

"Millie?"

"I'm here, Mom."

"Can you talk?"

"It's kind of hard now, Mom. But I'll be all right."

"I want to come to you."

"Mom, don't—"

"I have to see you, Millie. I have to. I feel I do. I can have Royal get me a ticket and take me to the airport. I—"

"Mom, it's going to be a madhouse here." Millie pressed a finger to her right temple. She didn't want her mother here with all this going on. In fact, Millie herself did not want to be here. She could already feel the clamoring of media.

"Then you come out here," Ethel said. "Stay awhile."

"I really can't—"

"It's been too long and I . . ." Ethel stopped, and Millie could only wonder what her mother was feeling. In some ways Ethel Hollander, shaped as a child during the Depression, would always be tough as nails and not easily impressed. Indeed, Millie could not remember a time when her mother had said she was proud of her. As a little girl, that had hurt sometimes. But that was Ethel Hollander.

"Mom," Millie said, "I have to do what Dr. Cross says. I'll call you every day if you want."

"I do."

"I'll call you again tomorrow, huh?" Millie said.

"Yes," Ethel said. "Don't forget. And, Millie?"

"Yes?"

"God is with you."

"Bye, Mom."

Millie hung up the phone. She looked at the ceiling and thought about what her mother had said. Prayer, that was the fabric of her mother's life. It was a fabric Millie had long since abandoned.

When had she rejected her childhood faith? she wondered now, lying in the bed. It had been a slow transition, but Millie did remember waking up one morning in her dormitory at Berkeley and thinking explicitly, *I don't believe that anymore. I do not believe in God. How will I ever tell Mom?*

She hadn't, for many years. When her mother would call to check up on her, she'd always manage to ask her daughter about her church attendance. Millie could anticipate the question coming, and formed several clever ways to steer the conversation elsewhere.

Finally, after she had been a judge for a year, she could not hide the fact from her mother any longer. It was the most difficult conversation of Millie's life. Sitting in the living room of her childhood home, where she had once sung Sunday school songs her mother had taught her, she told her mother she had developed another sort of faith—in humanity, in principles of justice.

When the tears came into her mother's eyes it was like a death had occurred. And in a way, it had.

"I will never stop praying for your soul," her mother had said, almost with defiance. The thought of her mother continuing to pray for her was sometimes like a curse. Millie overcame it by learning to live in forward motion, not dwelling on her mother's spiritual concerns.

So why was she thinking about them now? And then the most disturbing thing happened. The word *hell* popped into her mind.

Her whole body clenched. Pain shot through her limbs like liquid fire.

Hell? Where had that come from? Why should she have thought it? Because of that vision when she'd almost died?

She would go mad if she didn't get that vision out of her system. She had always been able to think her way out of any dilemma. Her psychiatrist had been her reasoning, rational mind. She could always rely on it.

And she would now. What she needed was to get back into her own world as soon as possible.

7

By Wednesday, Millie finally felt like she could see visitors. Helen had called every day—faithful Helen—and there were requests from all sorts of people for a personal one-on-one. Reporters, mostly. All the network anchors had requested interviews. NBC had even sent along a huge gift basket filled with flowers, Godiva chocolates, and an assortment of gourmet almonds.

She turned them all down. She was not going to let an accident become an open door to the press. But she called Helen and asked her to come.

Helen Forbes Kensington came in looking like she was the star of her own movie.

"You look fantastic," Helen said, grabbing Millie's hand. "For someone who almost bought the farm."

Helen's tone and temperament were cheering. "Maybe a farm wouldn't be such a bad idea," Millie said.

"The reports I keep hearing say you'll be good as new. Are they right?"

"So Dr. Cross says."

"We need you, girl."

"We?"

"All of us. The United States of America. We need you to write those opinions."

Millie was about to say something in assent but she stopped. Something shifted in her mind. It was subtle and almost unidentifiable.

"Are you okay, girl?" Helen was leaning over.

"What? Sorry," Millie said. "I guess I had a moment."

"You looked like it. Pain?"

"No, no. I'm all right."

"You sure?"

Millie looked at her friend. Should she tell her about the vision? In all the years they'd known each other, Helen had looked upon Millie as a sort of Rock of Gibraltar. In fact she had once called her that, and for several months thereafter even nicknamed her "Rocky." And Millie had liked it. She liked it a lot. If that was to be her main reputation in the Court—to be a rock-solid justice who did not break under pressure—she would be pleased.

Now a fissure, however slight, seemed to be developing. How serious a break it would turn out to be, Millie did not know. But she did not want it to alarm anyone, especially her close allies. No, she would deal with it first, figure it out, like she always did. Think it through and get rid of it. Then she would be able to talk about it.

"I'm sure," Millie said.

"Good," Helen said. "Because I've got to tell you something. Big."

Millie tensed. Her ribs fought her. "Ow."

"Sorry," Helen said. "Relax. It's about your boyfriend, Senator Levering."

"Helen, please."

"I know. That gadfly of his, Anne something-or-other, tracked me down."

"Tracked you?"

"Asked me all sorts of roundabout questions. What I figured out is she wanted to know if I knew about you and the senator. I played dumb. I told her I didn't know anything about anything. I don't know if she believed me or not. Frankly, I don't care. But I'm certainly not going to spill any beans."

"I've issued an official statement that I was with a friend, and my private life is to remain private."

"Yeah. But these things can take on lives of their own. Like those awful *Survivor* shows. Well, you're a survivor, and you're going to stay that way. But I got from this Anne babe that the press might get all over this story if we don't watch it. I think it might be a good idea for you to get out of town awhile."

"What?"

"Lay low. You need to get confirmed as CJ—and you need to recuperate." A little light flickered in Helen's eyes. "Hey, why don't you go out to California?"

"Back home?"

"Your mom's still got a house, right?"

Millie nodded. "I don't know, Helen. Santa Lucia? It's the other side of the world."

"But that's the point, kiddo. It's *quiet*. And you'll have the whole summer."

Maybe Helen was right. Millie could get away from this unwanted attention and see her mother at the same time. She'd have to endure some religious talk, but that was a small price.

And there was something else about it. The desert community that she'd grown up in had a certain simplicity. Maybe that's what she needed to forget all that had happened the last couple of weeks. Maybe it would help that troubling vision to fade.

"I'll think about it," Millie said. "But remember, it's California we're talking about."

"What do you mean?"

Millie smiled. "A lot of weird stuff happens in California."

CHAPTER THREE

| 1

Charlene Moore took a sip of her mother's coffee on the front porch, and breathed in the morning. She'd spent the night with her family, a once-in-a-while thing. They lived an hour away from Dudley, and it was good now and then to have a home-cooked meal and see the folks. And Granddad. She loved the man who had taught her to love God when she was a little girl.

Once she had come to him after a Sunday school lesson about God and the Red Sea. Charlene told him she'd thought about it and she didn't think it could happen. Granddad had laughed his deep, jowly laugh and said, "Sometimes, Charlene, God kicks thinkin' in the pants."

As Charlene sat on the porch swing, where she'd spent many an hour as a girl, she glanced at the local paper. The front page was running yet another story on the accident that almost killed Millicent Mannings Hollander. It had been two weeks, and she was going to be released from the hospital.

Charlene read the story with keen interest. Hollander was something of a secret foe in her life. In law school, Charlene had written a law review article that took apart one of Hollander's most controversial opinions, one strongly upholding the *Roe v. Wade* decision. That had been a 5–4 disaster in the long fight against abortion.

Charlene took a long sip of coffee, wondering what the death of a sitting Supreme Court justice would do to the country. There would be a firestorm of political debate, of course. President Francis would move to put up a liberal, and thus preserve the liberal court majority. If one of the conservatives died, then another liberal would make the Court 6–3 in that direction.

Such were the calculations going on constantly, Charlene knew. And then a thought struck her. Millicent Hollander had been on the very edge of dying. Would that change how she now viewed life?

One could always hope. And pray. Things were supposed to happen when you prayed, weren't they?

The screen door opened and Granddad came out with his own mug of coffee.

"Hi," Charlene said. "Want to sit?"

"I do," Granddad Clarence Moore said. He was a veteran of the Korean War and a retired mechanic. He still smelled of grease because he was always tinkering with the lawn mower.

"How's my baby today?" he asked, sitting next to her. The rusty chain creaked a little.

"Ready to get back to work," she said. "I'll be leaving soon."

"Your big case?"

Charlene nodded. She had told the whole family about it last night at dinner. Everyone had agreed it was going to make her famous. Except Granddad. He hadn't said much at all.

"You worried about me?" Charlene said.

"Yes I am," Clarence Moore said. "Now that you mention it."

She put her hand on his arm. "Don't. I am all over this one. I feel good about it. I can win it."

"That's not what I'm worried about, baby."

"Then what are you worried about?"

He pushed with his feet so they rocked a little. "I'm worried about your insides. You sure you're not running ahead of God on this one?"

Charlene felt a little irked. She was not five years old. "Come on, Granddad, I'm a lawyer. This is what I've prepared for, to get a case like this and use it to—"

"Use it?"

"Why not?"

"Are you using it to prove something about Charlene Moore?"

"No," she said, wondering how much she meant it. "This is a once-in-a-lifetime case. It's mine and I have to take it all the way."

"You don't own it," Clarence Moore said. "We don't own anything, do we? You just keep praying about it, baby. And I mean the kind of prayer that lays you flat. Not the gimme-gimme kind. Promise your old grandpappy?"

"Of course," Charlene said, wanting to leave right away. "Don't you worry about a thing."

2

Sam Levering had a TV room at home. Four monitors, each beaming in a different channel. With the touch of a couple of buttons on the remote, he could increase or decrease the volume of any set, so he could concentrate on the story that seemed most relevant.

Right now it was on Fox News. He hated Fox. It regularly held him up to scorn, but it was also the leading cable news outlet so he would just have to deal with it.

Tonight it was all about the story that still occupied Washington, if not the entire country: Who was Millicent Mannings Hollander with the night she got hit?

The Fox reporter in the field, standing outside Walter Reed Hospital, was saying, "All we know is that police have questioned Justice Hollander, and she has stated that she had been with a friend. That's the word she used, *friend*. She was dropped off near the Lincoln Memorial, though she didn't say why, but was going to try to catch a taxi to take her home. Here is where the story gets a little confusing. There is some speculation that the friend was . . ."

Levering gripped his glass of bourbon like a lifeline.

". . . one of the other justices of the Court. Justice Hollander does not have the reputation of socializing much in Washington circles . . ."

Levering breathed a little easier. A *friend*. She was not going to say anything. Good for her. Now he would not have to use the little contingency plan Anne Deveraux and he had hatched. He could save it. Keep it in his back pocket, as it were, and with it control the next chief justice of the Supreme Court. Man, he was good. With Anne Deveraux, he was unstoppable.

His phone rang. The direct line.

"You been watching?" President Francis asked.

"It's under control," Levering said.

"I just want to know if this is going to become a problem for us."

"Don't worry. A few days and it'll be on A–20 of the *Post*, and then gone."

"What about Hollander?"

"What about her?"

"She still the one?"

"Oh, yes. This will garner her all sorts of sympathy. You'll be a hero."

"I still get this feeling."

"Trust me."

"I have to, I guess."

And that was just the way Sam Levering had planned it all along.

3

From her wheelchair, Millie tried to smile gamely for the cameras. The press coverage was inevitable, and it was best to just get it out of the way now.

Flashes burst around her and voices threw questions like baseballs.

Dr. Cross, pushing the wheelchair, ran interference. "Allow Justice Hollander to make a statement please. Please! And then she will answer only a few questions. I will update you on her condition momentarily."

The reporters waited, cameras whirring and microphones thrusting.

Millie was not an accomplished public speaker. When she made speeches she read them, preferring to prepare her statements in logical order beforehand. If she spoke off the cuff, she might say something that could be misconstrued. And the one thing she wanted to avoid as a Supreme Court justice was misunderstanding.

"Thank you," she said, "for your concern. And I thank the American people for their well wishes." She had received flowers and cards and stuffed animals, along with telegrams and even a bathrobe with capitol domes on it. So much for the separation of powers.

"I am continuing to recuperate under the care of Dr. Cross. Aside from a bad headache, I am doing quite well. I hope to take a little time to rest back home in California. I will be ready to resume my seat on the Court when the new term begins in October."

She paused, and immediately a reporter shouted, "Can you tell us why you were walking at night alone?"

There were a few groans at the question, but mostly, Millie noted, keen interest from the newspeople.

"I had been with an acquaintance, and that is all. I appreciate that you will respect the privacy of all concerned here."

"Are the police respecting that privacy?" another reporter asked.

"This is not a police matter. As I told them, I was in the process of getting a taxi to go home. I lost my balance and fell into the street."

"What do you think of Edward Ellis Pavel's retirement?"

While she had been recovering in the hospital, Pavel had announced his retirement.

"Chief Justice Pavel has served honorably for over twenty years. He will be missed."

"Are you going to be the next chief justice?"

"I leave that to the people who make those decisions. Now if you'll—"

A smallish man, who looked—Millie couldn't help the analogy—like a rodent, shot out of the gathering as if emerging from a hole. "Madame Justice, how has your brush with death changed your life?"

Millie only vaguely heard the voices of disdain this question provoked. She felt the man's feral eyes boring into her, as if by will he could drag out her deep secrets. And she did have a secret, one she was not prepared to be examined on.

The truth was her life *was* different, but she had no idea how. There had not been time to assess it. But the disquiet she had felt ever since coming back to consciousness was not gone. She had always kept her emotions under strict control. But now—well, she might actually need to see a therapist. And that was something no one must ever find out about.

Thankfully, Dr. Cross stepped in front of the wheelchair. "That is all for today. Thank you very much."

With a great sigh, Millie put on a smile and waved for the cameras once more. The reporters began shuffling to give way. But the little man stayed close, staring at her, until security finally nudged him out.

She got a very strange feeling in her stomach. "I need to go home," she told Dr. Cross, "as soon as possible."

"I'll have a car brought around."

"No," she said. "I mean to California. Would it be all right if I flew out tomorrow or the next day?"

Dr. Cross folded his arms. "I want to check up on you. I can't very well do that if you're three thousand miles away."

"I promise to be good."

He smiled. "I have an associate out that way, in Bakersfield. Would you mind if I had him on call for you?"

"Not at all," Millie said. "God forbid I should need a doctor. What could possibly happen?"

Dr. Cross patted her shoulder. "You just never know."

4

Sam Levering woke up with a fuzzy feeling on his tongue. As he got older, the drinking seemed to do that. When he was a young buck, he could put away twice the amount and wake up fit and ready to run.

Those days were gone. A lot of things were gone for Sam Levering. His wife had divorced him fifteen years ago. That had actually been a career boost. Marla could not handle her liquor and was developing into a liability.

Sure, a divorced politician was suspect in those days, but Levering managed to charm the people again. He won the governorship and left early to run for the Senate.

He and Marla had shared custody of their son, Tad. That was another thing Sam had lost.

Each morning when he awoke, Levering felt a small hole inside him. It could not be filled. It was shaped like his son, the one he had once envisioned taking the governor's mansion and then joining him in the Senate. And then the presidency. A dynasty.

But Tad had turned away from everything, every value, Sam Levering ever had.

It started with teenage antics. Levering thought that was normal and would play itself out. Tad liked cars, liked girls, and liked them both fast. A chip off the old block. Levering had even felt a little pride when Tad stole a cheerleader from the football team captain and spent a weekend with her in a Tulsa motel.

Then in his late teens, Tad had become progressively odd and distant. All because of a preacher.

Levering had grown up in the Bible belt but renounced the faith of his youth when he was in the Army. He did attend church services when the political weather vane pointed in that direction. But on fishing or camping trips with Tad, Levering taught him the value of self-reliance and skepticism of all things religious.

"Use the religious folks to get yourself elected," he counseled his son. "But don't fall into it yourself. The American religion is finishing first."

Tad, he thought, soaked up every word.

But then that preacher got hold of his son, and Tad got "saved." How Levering despised that word. As much as he despised the preacher, a man named Doty.

When Tad announced that he was a Christian, Levering almost went nuts. There had been huge arguments. Levering called Tad names he had never used before, even for political opponents. Tad took off.

That was eight years ago. Levering did manage to locate his son once through a private investigator. But Tad's only response was to send his father a Bible with a note pleading for him to "turn to Christ."

Levering sauntered to the bathroom and splashed cold water on his face, trying to put the past out of his mind. He heard his cell phone bleeping on the bed and went to answer it.

"Who's your Huckleberry?" Anne Deveraux asked.

"Why do you keep saying that?" Levering asked.

"Heard it in a movie once. Now tell me who your Huckleberry is."

"You, Anne."

"Why?"

"Because you're the best."

"And do you know why?"

"Is this a personal call? Because I've got a ton—"

"I'll tell you why. Because I see things before they happen. I anticipate trouble."

"Yes, you do, Anne." It was true. She was the best in the business at not only getting out of a crisis, but steering clear of those that did not yet exist.

"Well," Anne asked, "when can I see you?"

Levering went through his mental checklist. "I have several short meetings today."

"Work me in."

"When?"

"Now."

"Why?"

"Let's just say I see something coming."

"What's it about?"

"Madame Justice Millicent Mannings Hollander."

Levering met Anne near Independence Avenue. The day was overcast but hot, making him sweat almost immediately. He felt like he was in detox.

She was waiting for him on a bench that offered a view of the Supreme Court building. She was eating a Power Bar and sipping a Starbucks.

"Breakfast?" Levering said, sitting next to her.

"And lunch and dinner," she said. "This will take me to eleven o'clock tonight."

The senator shook his head. "Aren't you afraid of burnout, Anne?"

"No. Spontaneous combustion. If I'm not moving forward, I'm afraid I'll explode."

"What about your personal life?"

She looked at him. At least he assumed she was looking at him through her dark glasses. "Why the sudden interest in my personal life?"

Levering shrugged. "I was just thinking. You haven't got a family. Maybe you should think about it."

"Don't go family values on me, Senator. I could not handle that paradigm shift."

"Hey, you're free to live your life."

"Thanks for the vote of confidence. But it's your life we should be talking about."

"Go."

Anne finished her Power Bar, tossing the wrapper into a trash can. Then she took a sip of coffee to wash it down. "Hollander," she said. "Caution."

"Why?"

"How much is Francis behind her for chief?"

"All the way. I made sure of that."

"Tell him not to say anything yet."

Levering used one of Anne's favorite lines. "Detail me," he said.

"The last thing you need is an unstable chief of the Supreme Court."

"You talking because of the accident?"

"Of course."

"But Millie Hollander has always been steady as a rock."

"Accidents do things to people."

"Yeah, but she's been given a clean bill of health."

"Physically, yes."

Levering said, "Just tell me what you're driving at."

"They allowed her to go home yesterday. You may have seen the news."

"I did."

"Well, it may interest you to know that Madame Justice did not go straight to her home."

Levering was duly impressed. "Are you telling me you tailed a justice of the highest court in the land?"

Anne fetched a cigarette from her purse. "Just doing my job. There's a Barnes & Noble in a mall just over the Virginia line. Hollander's car pulled up in front and the driver got out. He went into the bookstore and came out a few minutes later."

"Big deal," Levering said. "Maybe he wanted a magazine."

Anne looked at him with mock disdain. "Would I be telling you this if I didn't know what he came out with?"

"You know?"

"Of course I know."

"Mind telling me how?"

"Let's just say you can do a lot with a computer and a little money given to the right people."

That was a political truth Levering had long been aware of. "So?"

"Ever hear of Elisabeth Kübler-Ross?"

"She a judge?"

"No, an author. She wrote about death."

"Sounds like the life of the party."

Anne ignored him. "Her most famous book is *On Death and Dying*. That's one of the books the driver bought. The other was one called *On Life After Death*."

Levering thought about this for a moment. "What do you make of it?"

"Red flag, Senator," Anne said. "You've got a middle-aged woman who is almost killed by a car. She just happens to be a Supreme Court justice, but let that pass. She is suddenly very aware of her mortality. She wants to read books about death. On life *after* death. Now what would you say was going on?"

"Maybe she bought them for a friend?"

Anne blew an angry breath into the Washington, D.C., air. "Don't avoid the obvious. She got shaken up. Not just physically, but mentally. When somebody starts thinking about death, things happen. Who knows what?"

Levering shook his head. "I can't see it making a big difference."

"Oh, you can't. Well, do you believe in life after death?"

That one hit him like a question from O'Reilly. "No," he said, wondering at that moment if he really believed it himself.

"Right. Now who does believe we pass into some heavenly reward? Or get reprocessed as something else? Answer: religious folks. What would happen if Justice Hollander got a sudden dose of religion?"

A bus rumbled by, belching exhaust. Levering watched it for a moment, sensing things getting cloudy. "I'm not worried," he said.

"That makes one of us."

"Besides, we have our little backup plan if we ever need it."

Anne shook her head. "Only as a last resort."

"So what do we do?"

"Whatever I say," she said. "Agreed?"

Levering felt oddly secure. "Darlin', you da man."

CHAPTER FOUR

1

Walking gingerly up the ramp at LAX, Millie felt remarkably good. She did have a cane, one of those aluminum jobs that were standard hospital issue, but didn't need to use it. Residual pain, for the moment, was muted. Dr. Cross would be pleased.

She hoped Mom was feeling well. Millie knew her accident, and the aftermath, had been hard on Ethel Hollander. The last time they had talked on the phone, her mother's voice sounded a little slower than normal. As Millie hobbled through the gate, she was anxious to see her mother's face.

What she saw, however, was a chaos of reporters. Only this time Dr. Cross was not there to intervene. She had been offered a secret service escort, but declined. She had never been one for governmental intrusion—into the lives of citizens or on behalf of justices. When she was off the bench she wanted to be an ordinary citizen herself. And she couldn't imagine a secret service agent hovering around her in Santa Lucia. It would simply draw more attention.

Security was everywhere. Men in blue coats and Los Angeles police officers kept order. Lights glared and microphones bobbed at her face. A few questions were shouted simultaneously. Millie put up her hands.

"Thank you for your concern," she said. "I am feeling pretty well. Much better than I was a week ago, I can assure you. I've come out here for some rest and will be thankful if I can avoid answering questions at this time." She looked around the crowd for her mother. No sign.

"Have you had any word on becoming chief justice?" a female reporter shouted.

"No word. Thank you." She made an attempt to move forward but the reporters, like a giant amoeba, moved with her.

"Madame Justice, do you feel you can handle the job?" a male reporter asked.

"My only job now is to rest," Millie said, wondering if her face was giving her away. "I just need to . . ." And then she saw her mother waving behind the reporters.

"If you'll excuse me," she said, trying to move on through. An airport guard told the reporters to clear a path.

"Can you tell us anything else about the accident?" a voice shouted. Another asked, "Was it really an accident?"

The question jarred her, even as she reached her mother. Millie hugged her as cameras whirred and clicked. Her mother felt a little thinner than Millie remembered, but with the same tough hide.

The slick reporter shoved his microphone toward Ethel Hollander. "Is it good to see your daughter?"

Ethel scowled at him. "That's about the dumbest question I ever heard from a grown man."

Slick stood up as if slapped. Millie could not help enjoying his look. "Case closed," she said.

Ethel had a car, a giant Cadillac—circa 1970 and covered with desert dust—waiting in the short-term parking. Behind the wheel sat a stout, friendly looking man. Ethel introduced him as Royal King.

"That's my real name, too," he said.

But he drove like a joker. The trip was an adventure in near misses that finally got them to the 405 freeway, heading north. Millie, reclining in the passenger seat, at least felt relieved to finally be heading for some peace.

"How are things in town?" Millie asked her mother.

"Same as always," Ethel said. "Only more so."

"Ah," Millie said, enjoying one of her mother's famous non-sequiturs. She usually made sense once you unpacked the verbiage.

Royal King said, "We got some reporters in town."

"Oh, no," Millie said.

"Yep. You can tell 'cause they have them fifty-dollar haircuts."

"I'm sorry, Mom. I didn't want to bring trouble to town."

"Oh, fudge bumps," Ethel said. "We can handle 'em."

"That's right," Royal said. "Like a brush fire."

"Royal's the fire chief," Ethel said. "He moved up from Santa Clarita a couple of years ago. He drives me to church on Sundays and Wednesday nights."

It had been a long time since Millie had thought about her mother's church. Ethel had attended it faithfully for fifty years now. There was something magnificent in that, even if Millie did not share the beliefs she had been taught there many years ago.

"How is the church doing, Mom?"

"She just keeps rolling along, like that song about the river and the old man who lives in it."

"Old Man River?" Millie said.

"No, but there's a song like it with the same title," Ethel said.

Millie smiled.

"I think you're going to like our pastor," Ethel added.

So it begins, Millie thought.

"He's a real good preacher," Royal volunteered. "I like his style."

"Oh?" Millie said casually, being polite about the conversation. In her mind she pictured an older man, perhaps a few years short of retirement, who was making one last stop at the church before his dotage. He'd be full of the old bromides and warnings of hellfire, damnation, and the wages of sins such as dancing and drink. She hoped, if she did meet him, that it would be a short meeting.

"He's not the kind of preacher you might think," Ethel said. "He's had a lot of tragedy in his life."

"A ton," Royal said.

"And he received mercy," Ethel said, "so he gives it out. He ministers to runaway teenagers down in Lancaster. For nothing."

"Because of what happened with his own daughter," Royal added.

Millie felt a vague interest in knowing the story, but said nothing.

"And can he pray!" Ethel said. "You should have heard him the night of your accident."

"What?"

"Yep. That very night, at prayer meeting, I asked for prayer for you. I felt troubled about you for some reason. It was heavy upon me."

"I remember," Royal said. "She was almost crying."

This was odd. "What kind of trouble did you think I was in?"

"I didn't know, exactly. But I remember the time. I surely do. I felt the Lord leading and looked at the big clock. It was 10:35."

Millie said, "You were up late."

"We pray long sometimes," Royal said. "Pastor really believes in prayer."

Sure he does, Millie thought. *He's supposed to. So are church people.* When she was a little girl, she had, too. But now ...

Millie's mind suddenly snapped to attention. "What time did you say, Mom?"

"What time what?"

"When you looked at the clock."

"I said 10:35. Yes, sir."

"Are you absolutely sure?"

"'Course I am. I can still see. Why are you asking?"

Millie did not say, but began to feel cold all over. If it was 10:35 on the west coast, it was 1:35 on the east.

The very time Dr. Cross said she'd flatlined.

The very time she'd had her vision.

"You all right, dear?" Ethel asked.

"Sorry, Mom. I just got a headache."

"Don't let's talk anymore. Royal, you drive nice and smooth now. Let my daughter rest."

Oh, yes. Sweet rest. She needed that.

But she knew she could not rest. Not now.

2

It felt like a time warp when Millie saw the old house. Her mother still lived here, would never think of leaving. Wouldn't even consider changing the basic look of the place. Adobe style on the outside with a flagstone walkway. Cactus plants in the garden under the front window. The lone oak tree that stood like a sentry guarding the ghosts of the past. She'd read books under it as a little girl. Desert shade for an inquiring mind.

The house, built by her father and a group of locals when Millie was ten (she helped dig out the tiny portion of sandy dirt that became the back steps), looked just as it did in the sixties. The capricious weather of California's high desert (though the townspeople hated *high desert* as a designation; not good for tourism) seemed to have paid it respect and treated it gently over the years. There was a solidity about it that provided comfort.

Royal scurried around to the passenger side of the car and opened the door for Millie. She swung her legs out carefully, remembering what Dr. Cross said about her ribs—no sudden movements or turns.

A rivulet of warm desert air caressed her face, bringing with it the scent of sage and wildflowers. It was soothing and familiar. There was nothing quite like the breezes here, and she'd

loved them growing up. The air was simple, unpretentious. Above all, clean. Not filled with the waste of busses and cars and industry. The act of breathing here was unpressured.

Yes, coming home was the right thing to do. Healing could happen here. Quiet rest. She wouldn't have to think about anything. The desert did not make demands on you. It did not ask you questions. This was just the place to regain equilibrium, forget thoughts of death and dark visions. Become normal again.

Royal popped the trunk and started getting Millie's bags. A noise made Millie look up, toward the roof. The sun was behind the house and she had to squint. But there was definitely something moving on top of the house.

Her first thought was that a TV reporter had managed to precede them. He was lying in wait until the car came, ready to get his exclusive. She almost ducked her head. Then she noticed the ladder against the house. Whoever was up there must be a worker of some sort.

"Hey there, Ethel," the worker said, leaning over the edge of the roof.

"Come down offa there," Ethel said. "Meet my daughter."

Terrific. All Millie wanted to do was go inside, into her old room where her mother still kept a bed, and sleep. She was not in any mood to talk to strangers.

But this was her mother's house. She would follow the rules. A quick greeting, then inside.

The worker came into focus now. Millie first noticed his denim work shirt splotchy with sweat. He had a leather tool belt around his waist and wore blue jeans.

As he descended the ladder she noticed that his tanned arms, glistening with perspiration, were strong. This was a man who did not shy away from hard work.

When he turned from the ladder Millie was greeted by a friendly pair of eyes with a set of hard wrinkles at each corner. His hair was dark with a hint of gray at the temples. He looked about her age.

His face was not that of a construction worker, but of an academic. Strange, but he looked like a young Thomas Riley, her colleague on the Court. And everyone said when Tom Riley was a young lawyer in Wyoming, he was the spittin' image of Gary Cooper—solid, rugged, quintessentially American.

"Howdy," he said, taking out a red bandanna and wiping his hands. He extended it. "I'm Jack Holden."

Millie caught sight of her mother grinning off to the side. She shook his hand. "Millie Hollander."

"Welcome home."

She forced a smile and a nod, but felt the slightest bit put off by the sentiment. Who was he to welcome her to her own childhood residence?

"That's Pastor Jack," Ethel said.

Oh no, Mother, Millie thought, *you didn't. You didn't set me up to meet this man, did you?*

"So nice to meet you," Millie said without enthusiasm. Then she noticed what looked like a string of faded, colored beads around his neck. It reminded her of the hippies in the sixties.

"Heard a lot about you," Holden said. "Personally I'd like to say it's a privilege to meet you. I visited the Supreme Court once."

"How nice."

"Didn't hear an argument, though. Wondered what I'd do if I ever had to make one."

Millie wanted to get inside the house.

"Will you stay for dinner?" Ethel said.

No! Millie's mind screamed. She was about to say something about being tired when Holden spoke.

"Now, Ethel, your daughter's come a long way, and I'm sure she's tired. Probably doesn't feel much like socializing."

"Maybe after church on Sunday," Edith said.

"I'd love to," Holden said.

A firecracker of pain went off at the base of Millie's neck. "Mr. Holden," she snapped. "I am here just to get some rest.

Excuse me." She turned and walked into her childhood home.

Royal brought in her two suitcases, with Ethel close behind.

"Millie," Ethel said, in a way that made Millie feel like she was ten years old.

"Not now, Mom, please."

"He's my pastor."

"I know, it's just—"

"You could try to be pleasant."

"Mother, I'm sorry. I just want to go lie down."

"Then you do that," Ethel said. "Just remember, a tree doesn't fall too far from the fruit."

Millie had no idea what that meant. But she was no longer in any mood for talk. Her head was starting to pound like a gavel on a judge's bench.

3

She dreamed of dark clouds.

In the dream, Millie sat in her judicial robes, in her chair on the Court. The courtroom was empty. And the walls had been taken away.

Black storm clouds rolled in, like an advancing army. She tried to get out of her chair but found she could not move. It was going to start raining soon. She had to find shelter.

The rain came. Lightning flashed. Peals of thunder exploded around her. She could not get away. There was no shelter. And then she saw something on the horizon. Help. Someone coming to help her.

But as the figure got closer she realized he was in black, and sticking out of his robed sleeves were long, slithery fingers, like snakes . . .

She woke up breathing hard, her ribs protesting. Muted sunlight filtered in through the window, indicating late afternoon. She lay there several minutes until her breathing was back to normal, then carefully got out of bed.

Ethel was preparing a meal in the kitchen. When Millie entered Ethel barely looked up from the peas she was liberating into a Tupperware bowl.

"Have a little sleep?" Ethel asked.

"A little," Millie said. She was not going to mention the dream. "Can I help you with those?"

"Grab yourself a handful, why don't you?"

From the big bowl of rich, green pea pods Millie scooped up a healthy portion and set them in front of her. When she was a girl she'd always liked cooking with her mother. The love of cooking was the one thing they shared in common.

"How are you feeling?" Ethel asked.

"A lot of sore spots still. When I first get up it hurts most."

"I mean inside."

Millie pushed out three raw peas into the Tupperware bowl. "Inside?"

"That's what I said. I want to know what's going on in that head of yours."

"I'm fine, Mom."

"You goin' back inside your turtle shell, huh?"

Millie looked away. "I haven't heard that in a long time."

"You been in fancy Washington, D.C., is why," Ethel said. "You remember the first time?"

Millie did, very much so. But her mother had on her storytelling look, and Millie let her go.

"You were nine years old." Ethel said. "You came in from school with red eyes, like you'd been crying, and you ran in past me. I was cleaning or something. But I went right after you. And when I got to you, you wouldn't tell me what happened. You remember that?"

Millie nodded.

"I kept asking and asking," Ethel said, "but that old stubborn streak in you was a mile wide, even then. And you said you were going into your turtle shell. You took to your room with a book, like usual, and wouldn't talk about it."

A stab hit Millie between the ribs. She well remembered that day. Three fourth grade girls had approached her at recess.

Your mom's a goody-two-shoes, they said.

Millie tried to get away, but the girls grabbed her arms.

Nobody likes you or your mom, you Bible thumpers. That's what you are. Why don't you dry up and blow away?

"I told your father about it," Ethel said, snapping Millie back to the present, "and he laughed and said 'She's your girl.' And whenever you used to crawl away with a book, not talking about things, I'd say to myself, 'She's going back in her turtle shell.' "

"Mom—" Millie stopped herself. If only her mother had ever told her she approved of Millie, even though she had rejected her childhood faith, maybe they could talk more openly now.

"Why don't you take a walk?" Ethel said.

"Walk?"

"Like you used to. Can you? I mean, with your ribs."

"Oh, yes. Dr. Cross told me to walk."

"Down to the square. You used to like to do that. Go on. I'll have dinner for you when you get home."

4

As Millie strolled, dusk dropped its red and orange cloak over the valley. She followed a dirt path lined with rabbit bush and scrub oak that wound its way from the back of Ethel's home into town. Millie could see across the valley to the Santa Lucia range, where the legendary mountain, the Sleeping Giant, lay. The outline of the mountains, from around Henderson up toward the 232 highway, gave the impression of a man sleeping on his back if you looked at it just right. It was the only tourist attraction in the town of Santa Lucia.

Climbing a small rise, Millie came to the outskirts of town. Santa Lucia looked the same to Millie. It was as if a dome had been placed over it, preventing any aging. There were paint jobs, of course, and some sprucing up. City Hall had a new flagpole, with a grand, golden eagle on the top.

If there was any difference it was that fewer people seemed to be out at this time of day. She could remember balmy summer evenings when the streets were teeming with families. That was in the early sixties. When cable TV got to the valley, people stayed indoors more. They could watch the tube, and also avoid the bad things they thought might float down from San Francisco or up from Los Angeles.

Millie found a bench facing the town's only fountain—a double decker erected by the Rotary in '59 and dedicated to the fallen heroes of World War II. She settled into the bench and opened the book she'd brought with her, *On Death and Dying*. There was barely enough light to read.

"Howdy."

Millie looked up. Jack Holden stood there, dressed in casual blue jeans and a T-shirt—as if he were a rancher or a farmhand. He still had that odd bead necklace on. She hoped he would not ask to join her.

"May I join you?" he said.

She nodded reluctantly.

Holden sat down. "Saw you over here and thought I'd apologize for earlier. I think I sort of hit the wrong note."

"Thank you. I apologize, too. I was a little tired from my trip." *You can go now.*

"See, I've got this little problem. People sometimes think I'm a little, what's the word I'm looking for . . ."

Obnoxious?

"Persistent," Holden said. "I get a little carried away sometimes, especially when I talk about the church. But it saved my life, you see, so I guess that's why."

Millie gave him a quick nod but said nothing. She did not want to invite further conversation.

"So," Holden said. "What are you reading?"

Millie placed her hand over the cover of her paperback. "Oh, just a little book."

"Like to read myself," Holden said. "Wish I had more time for it."

Shifting uncomfortably—her blouse was sticking to her back—Millie cleared her throat in a way she hoped would finally end the conversation.

"May I ask you a question that's a little personal?" Holden said.

No. "Personal?"

"I don't mean to be ... persistent. You can tell me to go jump in the lake if you want to."

"What's the question?"

"We've been praying for you, after your accident and all. I was just wondering how you're feeling. Not just physically, but every way."

She didn't know which she liked less. The fact that he was looking at her so seriously, or the fact that she almost wanted to answer him.

"Reverend Holden?"

"Yes?"

"Perhaps that jump in the lake?"

Holden put his head back and laughed. "I will respect your privacy," he said. "But I wonder if I might try this again. Would you do me the honor of attending my church on Sunday?"

Millie had to at least admire his persistence. "Thank you, that's very nice, but I'm just not a churchgoer."

"Well, we don't discriminate at our church. Non-church-goers are welcome."

She shook her head slightly. "Again, thanks for the invitation."

Holden didn't leave. "It really would be an honor to have a Supreme Court justice visit us. Though in the interest of full disclosure, I must tell you that I don't agree with your judicial opinions most of the time."

She was aghast. Not so much that he would disagree with her, but that he had read enough of her opinions to reach such a judgment. "You've actually read my opinions?"

"All of them," he said.

"But why?"

"Why not? I'm a citizen. And your mother is, after all, a member of my flock." He stood up and nodded. "Well, hope to see you on Sunday. Thanks for the chat." And with that he turned and walked away.

Stunned, she watched him go, noticing for the first time that he had a slight limp. Now *she* was curious. He had, in the last few minutes, transformed from a stereotype to a man of much more complexity.

A clergyman who read her opinions? Now she wanted to know just why he disagreed with her. She wanted to ask *him* questions, like she would have done to a lawyer arguing before her. For a moment she considered calling him back.

"Don't," she said out loud. Then she forced herself back into her book. But, unable to concentrate, she finally gave up and walked back to her mother's house.

CHAPTER FIVE

1

The trick to fighting depression, Sam Levering thought, was to keep busy. You could busy yourself with staff work, public ceremonies, drink, female companionship—any one of a number of items from a United States senator's playbook. And he had tried them all.

That was true now, as he pounded his way out of the chamber of the Judiciary Committee. He had been unable to concentrate on the hearing, even though it was an easy one. President Francis had sent Preston Atkins, a judge from the Second Circuit, as his nominee to fill the vacancy created by Ed Pavel's retirement.

The media were full of speculation about who would assume the CJ's chair, especially after the accident involving Millicent Mannings Hollander. Most assumed Hollander was going to get the nod.

But Atkins brought his own set of credentials. Described by Francis as "middle of the road," Atkins was really a staunch social liberal. The conservatives were making a lot of noise, but Atkins was handling the questioning with poise and equanimity. He was going to sail through, despite a few bumpy waves.

Yet Levering couldn't keep his mind focused. He'd been distracted by a simple phrase one of the opponents had said in the middle of an argument. "We cannot leave our children with that legacy."

Children.

Thoughts of his son raced into Levering's mind, stronger than they had in a long time. Levering had fought against all thoughts and feelings about his son. But sometimes nothing seemed to help.

So, though it was only eleven in the morning, Sam Levering was on his way back to his office for a drink. He turned toward the east corridor when he heard his name called. It was Anne Deveraux.

"Don't you ever rest?" he said.

"What's rest?"

"I'm about to have lunch." *Bourbon,* he thought.

"Want to hear the latest on Hollander?"

"Yes."

Anne looked around. No one was within earshot. "She was talking to, get this, a minister."

"Minister?"

"Yeah. Heads up a little church. Now isn't that curious?"

Levering ran his tongue over his dry lips. He hated the word *minister.* It had been a minister who ruined his son's life. What was Hollander doing consorting with one of that ilk?

"Bottom line, what do you think it means?"

"Maybe nothing," Anne said. "Maybe something. It appeared to be a somewhat casual conversation, according to my source. But it went on for a bit."

It better not be more than casual, Levering thought. *Not for his pick for chief justice.* "Don't you think you're being a bit paranoid? I mean, isn't her mother a churchgoer or something like that?"

"Something like that," Anne said.

"So what's your gut instinct?"

Anne looked at him over her sunglasses. "I think Madame Justice is not herself these days."

2

Charlene Moore felt her legs trembling. But she had to stand for her opening statement.

The courtroom was huge, especially compared to the state court satellites she was used to. Judge Howard Lewis seemed to be a hundred feet in the air atop his bench, looking down like an Olympian god. And the majestic eagle rendered on the shield that adorned the wall seemed ready to drop the olive branches in its talons and swoop down, mercilessly, on Charlene.

And every member of the jury seemed better dressed than Charlene.

But they were people. She reminded herself of the advice she'd given Sarah Mae's mother. She was going to tell them the story as if she were talking to people in her living room.

"Good morning, ladies and gentlemen," Charlene said. Most of the jurors nodded at her.

"As you know, my name is Charlene Moore, and I represent Sarah Mae Sherman."

Charlene turned to her client. "Sarah Mae, would you please stand?"

The girl, looking terrified, got to her feet. Her plain summer dress—pastel blue—was hanging on her like a tablecloth draped over a chair. She tried to look at the jurors, but her eyes kept glancing down toward the floor.

"Thank you, Sarah Mae," Charlene said. Sarah Mae returned to her seat.

"Sarah Mae Sherman did not grow up in a nice part of town. Her mother, Aggie, has been raising Sarah Mae alone since her husband left the family ten years ago. Life has not been easy for them. Like many girls her age, Sarah Mae dreamed of one day moving to the big city, making her way in the world."

Charlene saw in her mind's eye the flash of a picture—herself, a little girl dreaming of a singing career.

"One day she met a boy and fell in love. He was older than she was, and he paid attention to her. Bought her things. Took her to the movies. Told her she was pretty. But when Sarah Mae told him she was pregnant, he told her she was a loser and she'd better get rid of it—that's what he called the baby, *it*—and forget about ever seeing him again."

Charlene paused, taking time to look at each of the jurors' faces.

"Sarah Mae was scared, like any girl would be. She didn't know where to go, who to turn to. She feared telling her own mama. But she did see a sign stapled to a telephone pole. 'In trouble?' the sign asked. 'Find help you can trust.' And it gave the name and phone number of a clinic run by the National Parental Planning Group right there in Dudley.

"Ladies and gentlemen, you will hear exactly how this clinic abused my client's trust. You will hear how the law was willfully broken by the doctor, Michael Sager, who is sitting at the defense table."

Charlene paused and turned toward the defense table, where Winsor sat next to Dr. Sager. Sager was in his late forties and dressed in an expensive gray suit. Apparently he didn't feel he needed to hide the fact that he was a success.

"You will hear how the requirement that the patient be fully informed of the nature and risks of a medical procedure was ignored. You will hear what happened as a result.

"Five months after the abortion she knew little about, Sarah Mae Sherman learned exactly what she had been carrying inside her womb. She learned what her baby looked like, what its heartbeat sounded like, exactly what she had given up at the hands of those understanding people at the NPPG.

"And you will hear about the torment that Sarah Mae suffered as a result. About the nightmares that would not stop, about the night she couldn't take it anymore, got a razor blade, and slit her wrists."

Charlene had to pause a moment. She was feeling electric currents snapping through her.

"And then you will hear how the nightmares kept coming until Sarah Mae ran out to a bridge to throw herself off. But she was rescued just in time, by a minister. Why, you might wonder. You might also come to believe it is so she could be here to tell you the whole sordid story."

Beau Winsor stood up. "Objection. Counsel is pushing the limits of acceptability here."

"Sustained," Judge Lewis said.

Charlene waited until Winsor sat down. He took his time doing it.

"When you have heard all of the testimony," she said to the jury, "I will be asking you to deliver a verdict that will punish this clinic and the doctor involved so that other girls like Sarah Mae will not suffer at their hands, or the hands of those like them."

She turned and walked back to counsel table. She noticed that Sarah Mae had tiny tears in the rims of her eyes.

Now it was Winsor's turn. He was dressed to absolute perfection. His deep blue suit had fine, muted pinstripes. The effect was not "rich lawyer" but "dignified professional."

Charlene felt an ice ball in her stomach. She thought, suddenly, that she was not in this man's league. He had not lost a jury trial in twenty-five years.

"Good morning, ladies and gentlemen," Winsor said. His honeyed drawl was not overbearing. It seemed to reach out and embrace everyone in court.

"My name's Beau Winsor, and I'm a lawyer. We've got to get that out of the way at the start. Folks don't much like lawyers these days, and I understand that. There's a lot of mischief lawyers do. I've done a lot of it myself. We all know about the lawsuit craze and all that. Abuse of the courts."

Charlene wanted to stand up and object. This was not an opening statement. It was a subtle attempt to tar her as a lawyer bringing a baseless lawsuit. But then she thought, no, he was baiting her on purpose. If he could get her popping up to interrupt him before he even got started, the jury might think she was trying to obscure something.

"But not all lawyers are like that. I have every confidence that you will listen to the evidence as it is presented, and not to the fancy words of the lawyers. Make up your minds based on facts and law. Nothing else. You swore that when you took your seats, and I believe you'll keep that oath."

He turned and looked at Dr. Sager. "I want you to get to know this man who has been accused so terribly by opposing counsel. You will get to know him over the course of this trial. And it will be a far different picture from what you just heard.

"You will hear about a man who has ignored threats to his very life in order to bring healing and hope to scores of young women in terrible trouble. You will hear about his work in inner cities, his volunteer efforts, his absolutely pristine reputation."

He turned back to the jury. "But most important, you will hear how Dr. Sager obeyed the law. And that is really all you will need to hear. Because if Dr. Sager obeyed the law, as the evidence will show, then there is no case. There is no case against the doctor, or the clinic, or anyone else. If you don't agree with the law, you can change it. You can make it tougher or you can get rid of it altogether. But you don't do that here, in a courtroom. You do that at the ballot box.

"The evidence will show that the law was followed by the clinic, by Dr. Sager. And we trust your judgment, ladies and gentlemen. Because being on the side of truth is the best defense we have."

As Beau Winsor resumed his chair, Charlene's mind sang. *Here we go, Lord. Here we go, go, go.*

Judge Lewis said, "Call your first witness, Ms. Moore."

3

Charlene's first witness was Pastor Ray Neven. He was forty-two and looked like a big kid. Longish brown hair curling at the shoulders, bright blue eyes, and a ready smile. No wonder kids like Sarah Mae warmed up to him. He seemed a little uncomfortable in his suit and tie, like a Tom Sawyer who wanted nothing more than to throw off such restraints and head back to the swimming hole.

Charlene asked after Neven was sworn. "You are the pastor of a church in Dudley, is that correct?"

"Yes, I am," Neven said. "We're an independent Bible church."

"How long have you been the pastor there?"

"I started the church back in 1995."

"And how many are in your congregation?"

"We're running about a hundred-fifty now."

Charlene stepped out from behind the podium. "Do you have a youth program at the church?"

"We have a good group of kids," Neven said proudly. "A lot of teenagers right now."

"Is Sarah Mae one of them?"

Ray Neven looked past Charlene to Sarah Mae Sherman and smiled. "Yes, she is."

"Will you tell us how you first met Sarah Mae?"

Charlene wanted to leave the question open ended, so Neven could tell the story himself. Neven told how he had been camping with a group of teens from the church, had felt something was wrong, like one of the group might have wandered off. He wandered over to the bridge and saw a girl about to jump and grabbed her just in time.

Charlene was sure the story had some impact with the jury. But it was only a foundation for the next part of Neven's testimony.

"As you began to talk to Sarah Mae," Charlene said, "what was your impression of her mental condition?"

"Your Honor," Beau Winsor said. "May I take the witness on *voir dire?*"

Charlene should have expected this. The rules of evidence allowed the opposing attorney to question a witness in the middle of testimony if that witness was going to be offering opinions that might require special expertise.

"I'll allow it," the judge said.

Charlene resumed her chair while Winsor arose from his.

"Good morning, Pastor Neven," Winsor said.

"Good morning," Neven replied amiably.

"It is *pastor*, and not *reverend*, isn't that correct?" Winsor said.

Ray Neven blinked a couple of times. "I don't quite understand the question."

"What I mean is, you don't have a degree from any theological seminary, do you?"

"No, I do not, I—"

"In fact," Winsor looked at his notes, as if to emphasize the next question, "you didn't attend college, either, did you?"

"No, sir. I went to work right after—"

"How about you try to answer just the questions I ask?" Winsor said with a rebuke so mild he sounded like a favorite uncle.

"I'm sorry," Neven said.

"That's quite all right, sir. You understand I have to ask these questions because my colleague wants you to give some rather specialized information?"

"I'm just here to tell the truth," Neven said.

"Of course you are. But Ms. Moore wants you to talk about things that require a certain degree of training. You've never taken a course in psychology, have you?"

"I find the Bible to be a very good course in human psychology."

"That's not what I asked, Pastor Neven, with all due respect. Have you ever taken a course from any recognized institution of higher learning, in the area of psychology?"

"No, sir."

"Theology?"

"No."

"You're a layman then?"

"I am a minister," Neven said.

"What denomination has ordained you?"

"I am nondenominational."

"Not ordained?"

"I believe I have been called by God to preach the gospel."

"And you have a right to. What you don't have the right to do is offer expert testimony on psychological matters."

"May we approach the bench?" Charlene said quickly.

Judge Lewis called the lawyers up.

"Mr. Winsor's last comment was inappropriate," Charlene said. "And he knows it."

"I apologize," Winsor said. "If Your Honor wants to admonish the jury to disregard my comment, that's fine with me."

Slick. Oh, how slick. If the judge did that it would only reemphasize what he said.

"That won't be necessary," Charlene said. "But this is a key witness for me."

"Mr. Winsor's point is well taken, however," Judge Lewis said. "He's not qualified to offer opinions on your client's mental state."

"What about spiritual opinions?"

"No," Winsor said. "This man does not have a degree or even an ordination from a recognized denomination."

"I agree," said the judge.

"But he's been a minister for twenty years," Charlene said. "Rule 702 allows someone with practical experience to qualify as an expert."

"But he must still meet a threshold level," Winsor said. "In *U.S. v. King,* for example, the court excluded testimony by a witness who had taken a correspondence course in handwriting analysis. The Fifth Circuit upheld the exclusion. Ms. Moore's witness has never taken any sort of course, correspondence or otherwise."

"He is a lay preacher," Charlene said. "That is a recognized office in the American church."

"But not in a court of law, Ms. Moore," said the judge. "I'm going to exclude any further testimony by this witness on these matters. Do you have another witness ready to go this morning?"

4

She did. And this witness was a real expert. Through Dr. Gardner Hutchinson Charlene hoped to establish the duties of a doctor both ethically and according to the informed consent law. Then she would move on to the events of June 7. With the testimony of Dr. Hutchinson, the jury would have a full understanding of what should have happened in the doctor's office— but didn't.

After qualifying her witness as an expert, Charlene got right to the main points.

"As a medical doctor," she said, "what is your primary ethical charge?"

"It is to the patient," the doctor said. He was in his late fifties and a bit paunchy, but in a friendly uncle sort of way. "The well-being of the patient always comes first."

"Do no harm?"

"Exactly."

"When a patient comes to see you for the first time, what is the first thing you do?"

"I find out about the patient's history. He fills out a medical form with his medical history. We go over that before we even touch on the particular problem he came to see me about."

"Why is that so important, Doctor?"

Hutchinson smiled as if the answer were self-evident. "Because one can do considerable harm if he doesn't know enough about the patient he's dealing with."

"That's common sense, is it not?"

"Objection," Beau Winsor drawled. "Counsel is making a closing argument now."

"Sustained," said Judge Lewis.

"I'll withdraw the question," Charlene said. "Now, Doctor, please tell the jury how the notion of informed consent is consistent with the ethical duty you have just described."

Hutchinson turned in the witness chair so he could face the jurors. "No one should be advised to undergo any medical procedure unless he or she is fully informed about the nature of that procedure and the medical risks associated with it. The doctor's responsibility in each instance is to make sure that the patient is so informed. That does not mean partially, or even mostly. It means fully. And that is what informed consent is all about."

"Thank you," Charlene said. "Now, we have in this state an actual statute mandating informed consent in any abortion procedure, is that correct?"

"That is correct."

Charlene walked to her counsel table. "With the court's permission, I would like to display an exhibit for the witness and jury with the exact language of the statute."

"Without objection?" Judge Lewis said.

"Without objection," said Winsor.

"Proceed, Ms. Moore."

Charlene took the poster board she had made at Sammy's Graphics—$34.95 total price—and placed it on an easel for the jury and Dr. Hutchinson. Winsor stood so he could read it as well.

> An abortion shall not be performed without the voluntary and informed consent of the woman upon whom the abortion is to be performed.
>
> Except in the case of an emergency, consent to an abortion is voluntary only if the requirements of this section are met.
>
> The referring physician, the physician who will perform the abortion, or an agent of either physician shall provide all of the following information to the woman by telephone, by audiotape, or in person, at least twenty-four hours before the abortion:

a. Information that medical assistance benefits may be available to the woman for prenatal care, childbirth, and neonatal care.
b. Information that the putative father is liable to assist in the support of the child.
c. Information that medical assistance benefits may be available to the woman for an abortion under certain circumstances.
d. The particular medical risks associated with the particular abortion procedure to be employed including, if medically accurate, the risks of infection, hemorrhage, breast cancer, danger to subsequent pregnancies, and infertility.
e. The probable gestational age of the unborn child at the time the abortion is to be performed.
f. The medical risks associated with carrying her child to term.

"I would like to call your attention to subsection d," Charlene said. "Would you please explain to the jury your understanding of the term *medical risks*?"

"Yes. Any risk to the well-being of the patient, including the obvious things that are listed there, such as breast cancer, which some studies show has a connection with abortion procedures. But it would also include information on Post-Abortion Syndrome."

Charlene expected Winsor to object. When he did not, a thin flame of nervousness shot through her. She pressed on. "What is Post-Abortion Syndrome, Doctor?"

"It is a variant of Post-Traumatic Stress Disorder."

"And how long has Post-Traumatic Stress Disorder been recognized in the psychiatric field?"

"Since 1981."

"Is PTSD or PAS a form of depression?"

"Absolutely."

"Are there physical manifestations?"

"Oh, yes. The body can literally shut down."

"Mental signs?"

"Yes."

"Would suicidal tendencies be one of those?"

"That would certainly be a strong indicator of PAS, yes."

"What should a doctor do to help prevent the risks associated with Post-Abortion Syndrome?"

"At the very least he should screen all patients for any prior history of depression."

"If he does not, then there would be strong medical risk, isn't that right?"

"That is correct."

"Thank you, Doctor. No further questions."

Beau Winsor stepped to the podium but not behind it. He held no notes. Charlene could only marvel at that. No doubt the jury would marvel, too.

"Dr. Hutchinson," Winsor said. "Would you take a good look at subsection d again for us?"

The witness, somewhat sheepishly, reread the exhibit. "All right," he said.

"Now where do you see the term *Post-Abortion Syndrome*?"

"Of course it is not there, but—"

"You have answered the question, sir."

Charlene stood. "Objection, Your Honor. Counsel did not let the witness finish his answer."

Judge Lewis said, "Overruled. It was a simple yes or no question. You'll have your chance on redirect."

Stung, Charlene sat back down. Sarah Mae seemed upset. Charlene patted her arm.

Winsor said, "Also in subsection d, Doctor, where do you see the word *psychiatric*?"

Hutchinson stared at the lawyer. "It is not there."

"And Post-Traumatic Stress Disorder?"

"Not there."

"And who drafted this informed consent statute, Dr. Hutchinson?"

"I presume the legislature."

"And they didn't include any of those terms, did they?"

"No, sir."

Winsor paused to look at the jurors. They seemed trans-fixed by him. Charlene fought to keep her heart steady.

"Doctor, this supposed syndrome after abortion, is it rec-ognized in any of the standard texts as such?"

"Well, there have been some articles in—"

"Doctor, please. My question is about the standard refer-ence texts in the field. Will we find this syndrome listed in any one of these?"

"I do not believe so."

"Fine. Just so we're clear on that. One last thing, Dr. Hutchinson. Are you being paid for your testimony here today?"

With a slightly victorious smile, Dr. Hutchinson said, "No, sir."

"Isn't that a bit unusual, Doctor? Don't expert witnesses get compensated for their time so they can come to court?"

"I think that's the usual practice, yes."

"And you chose not to be paid, correct?"

"Yes, sir."

"Is it because you are an anti-abortion activist?"

"Objection," Charlene heard herself say, and immediately knew it was a mistake. It would seem she was hiding the truth about her witness from the jury. Once again, Winsor had played her like a violin.

"Overruled," said Lewis.

"Do you need the question repeated?" Winsor said.

"No, sir," said Hutchinson. "I have been associated, proudly, with the pro-life cause."

"In fact, you were listed on the letterhead of the American Rescue Foundation, were you not?"

Hutchinson looked like he'd been hit with a bucket of cold water. Charlene could almost feel the jurors changing their opinion of him on the spot.

"I was for a time, yes," Hutchinson said.

"Was that the same time that family planning center in Minnesota was bombed?"

"Objection," Charlene said.

"Sustained," Lewis said.

Winsor looked unconcerned. Of course it didn't matter what the answer was, or that the judge had sustained the objection. The question had been asked, and it was in the minds of the jurors. Charlene considered asking the judge to admonish the jurors not to take any of that into consideration, but knew that would only play into Winsor's hands again. Telling a jury to disregard something was almost a guarantee they'd consider it.

Suddenly, Winsor's tone turned cold and sharp. "So you would have us all believe that your unpaid testimony here is not biased in any way, is that right, Doctor?"

"Objection." Charlene had no other choice. The question was clearly argumentative.

"Sustained," said the judge.

She'd won the point, but the big picture was cloudy. When Winsor said, "No further questions," it seemed to Charlene that the jury was suddenly in his corner.

CHAPTER SIX

1

The Santa Lucia Community Church had a homey feel to it, built as much by memories as materials. The people knew her as Ethel Hollander's little girl, the one who became one of the most powerful women in the country. She saw a few old faces who knew her way back when. The newer people sort of stared at her, like she was a rare fish in an aquarium.

Why had she consented to come? To keep her mother from harping about it, sure. Maybe this one time would be enough to appease Ethel's crusade for her daughter's soul.

But she also had more than a little curiosity about the pastor. What he might say. How he presented himself in the pulpit. Maybe she wanted, in her own mind, to check this man's intellectual bona fides. He had said he disagreed with her judicial opinions. Was there any real firepower in his thoughts?

Ethel, as if sensing her daughter's discomfort, settled with her in the back row. That was fine with Millie. Easy exit.

A few people came by to say hello to Ethel and perhaps gawk at Millie. She smiled politely and tried to seem human. She felt anything but.

A short, intense-looking man in a suit that didn't quite fit slipped into the chair in front of them.

"Morning," he said.

Ethel said, "Good morning to you, too. Happy to have you visit."

"Thank you," the man said. Millie had the feeling she'd seen him before. But where? Something told her he wasn't a local.

"And hello to you, Madame Justice," the man said, reaching his hand to Millie. "My name is Dan Ricks."

Millie shook his hand. It was sweaty.

"Sure would like to have a chance to talk with you afterward," Ricks said.

"My daughter has come here to rest," Ethel said. "I'm sure you understand."

He was a reporter. Millie was sure of it. And then she remembered him. It was at the hospital, the day she was released. He had poked his face out of the crowd of reporters and shouted a question at her.

"Well," Ricks said, "your daughter is a famous person. No getting around that now, is there?" He snorted a laugh. "I have an obligation to my readers, Madame Justice. I'm a gentleman of the press."

"I appreciate that, Mr. Ricks," Millie said. "But as I have consistently told reporters, I do not want to give any interviews at this time. If you'll give me your card, I'll make sure you get a copy of any official statements."

The man made no move for a card. "I'm into exclusivity, Madame Justice. That's my stock in trade."

"What paper do you write for?"

The man smiled, his teeth looking like they could gnaw wood. "*The National Exposure.*"

"Oh, my," Ethel said.

"News you can use and won't make you snooze," Ricks said. "You read our stuff?"

"I see it in the store," Ethel said. "You should be ashamed of yourself."

He laughed. "Now if I was ashamed of myself, I wouldn't be a good newspaperman, would I? After all, I'm protected by the First Amendment, isn't that right, Justice Hollander?"

For a moment he just stared at her, then he winked. "Be seeing you," he said. He slipped out of the row and walked toward the exit.

"What a disagreeable little man," Ethel said.

Before Millie could answer, a young man at the front holding a guitar said, "Good morning, everyone. Please stand as we praise the Lord."

After what seemed like an eternity of singing and announcements, Jack Holden took the pulpit for his sermon.

Millie studied him. He was dressed in a suit and tie and held a Bible. It looked as natural in his hand as a hammer in the hand of a carpenter. Millie wondered if he was still wearing those beads under his shirt.

"I have a cheery topic this morning," Holden said. "I'd like to talk to you about death."

The word hit Millie like a slap. In fact, a slap to the face might have been less intrusive. And then she had a terrible thought. He was preaching to *her*. He must have seen the book she'd been reading.

"You know what Woody Allen once said about death?" Holden continued. "He said he didn't fear it. He just didn't want to be there when it happened."

A smattering of laughter rose from the congregation. Millie thought about walking out, but her mother would be mortified. No, she had to stay, like a prisoner forced to listen to the warden's inspirational speech.

"Well, we're all going to be there when it happens. And we have to think about that. It's crucial that we think about it. Because as morbid as it sounds, our life is really about how we prepare for death."

Holden, Millie noticed, was speaking without notes. He made eye contact with his audience. She couldn't help thinking that as a lawyer he would make a great impression on the justices of the Court.

"But in today's world, we seem to spend most of our time trying *not* to think about death. In a famous book from the 1970s called *The Denial of Death,* the author said we are so afraid of death that this denial was the central fact of our lives. Furthermore, he said, since we have no way of knowing our purpose on earth, we just have to act as though we have one.

"That's the problem, isn't it? People do not know where to look for the answer. So they don't think about death. They play games, watch television shows, drink themselves into oblivion, take drugs, seek extreme experiences. Anything to keep from thinking about the reality of this thing called death."

Holden opened his Bible and started turning pages.

"But the Bible tells us that we need to think about death, because it is going to happen to us. The psalmist says each man's life is but a breath. And listen to what James says in chapter four: 'Why, you do not even know what will happen tomorrow. What is your life? You are a mist that appears for a little while and then vanishes.'

"Now James may not have been the life of the party," Holden said, "but he is telling it like it is. So, too, does the writer of Hebrews. 'A man is destined to die once,' it says in chapter nine, 'and after that to face judgment.'

"What happens after death is, you'll pardon the expression, of grave import to us now. One either believes there is life after death, or one does not. Those in the middle, whom we call agnostics, don't feel there is enough information to make up their minds. The tombstone of an agnostic reads, 'All dressed up and nowhere to go.'"

Again, the congregation laughed. Millie didn't find the comment funny.

"The truth is, however, we all go. *Where* is up to us. I love the book of Ecclesiastes. It's a book I wish everyone would read.

If you want to think about death, think about what Solomon had to say. When he considered death in this world, without regard to the next, he found that all was vanity, a chasing after the wind. That word *vanity*, in the original language, means 'vapor' or 'breath.' And all of our striving on this earth, if there is no immortality, is vanity. A chasing after the wind.

"In our day, we think we have become sophisticated about death. A school of psychology became popularized in the works of a Swiss-born psychiatrist named Elisabeth Kübler-Ross. Some of you may have heard of her book, *On Death and Dying.*"

Millie bristled and felt her hands clenching. He *was* preaching at her! And in the most personal of terms. If she had been stripped naked she couldn't have felt more exposed.

"Kübler-Ross and others believe that a dying patient goes through a series of stages, beginning with denial. After that comes anger and then a bargaining with the prospect of death. When that doesn't work, depression follows and then, if the right conditions exist, acceptance. But I do not believe the human soul can ever accept death unless it is convinced that death can be overcome."

Millie was going to leave. Right then. Slip out and deal with her mother later. But Holden brought her up short.

"You have all heard accounts of the so-called near-death experience. They've had TV shows about it. People report that they have died, and seen a great light, sometimes at the end of a tunnel, sometimes all around them. And it has been pure ecstasy. So it has been reported.

"But you may not have read much about the other side of the coin. For those who have almost died and reported something like a vision of hell."

How did he know about her vision? Millie was almost trembling with anger and shock.

"We are not being wise if we do not look at death square in the face, like the Bible does. Jesus talked about death in terms of eternity. And make no mistake. When he talked about men dying without God it was a horror of immense proportions. I sort of wish that stuff wasn't there, but I can't close my ears to what Jesus says.

"But in the New Testament, the Greek word for *dead* is used mostly in connection with another word—*resurrection*. Yes, the Bible compels us to think about death, but it shows us that for those who are in Christ death is not a period. It is a comma.

"One of my favorite passages of Scripture is in Romans, chapter eight. 'In all these things we are more than conquerors through him who loved us. For I am convinced that neither death nor life, neither angels nor demons, neither the present nor the future, nor any powers, neither height nor depth, nor anything else in all creation, will be able to separate us from the love of God that is in Christ Jesus our Lord.'

"Or as it says in the old hymn:

> 'Crown Him the Lord of life,
> Who triumphed o'er the grave,
> And rose victorious in the strife
> For those he came to save;
> His glories now we sing
> Who died, and rose on high,
> Who died eternal life to bring,
> And lives that death may die.'"

Jack Holden bowed his head then and began to pray. All around her, Millie saw heads bowing.

She did not bow.

She glared.

2

Charlene Moore had nowhere to run.

If she tried, she would have to mow down at least a dozen departing churchgoers—a teeming mass of upper-class evangelicals. This was not like her home church back in Dudley.

This was a city church, the one closest to her hotel. It must have seated three thousand people.

The service had been a good one. The music was upbeat, a balm for her soul. It had been a tough week in court. The trial was taking more out of her than she had thought it would. Singing helped, and Charlene belted out the tunes as if Patti LaBelle were right there by her side.

And the sermon was first rate. The youngish minister had preached on the comfort of the Holy Spirit. She needed that, too. But afterward, as people streamed from the church, she saw Beau Winsor making his way toward her. And all of the good feelings drained from her.

He made eye contact with her and smiled. She could not avoid him.

"Miss Moore," he said, extending his hand. He wore an ostentatious three-piece suit, with a gold watch fob dangling from the middle of his torso. In front of a jury he would never have worn such a thing. It screamed rich lawyer. Winsor had made a career out of painting himself as just the opposite.

"What a surprise," Charlene said.

"For me, too. Imagine bumping into you at my home church."

"Yes, imagine."

"You must be staying nearby."

"At the Madison."

"Fine old hotel. Been here since the Civil War, did you know that?"

"So it says on their brochure."

"I'm glad I ran into you. What would you say to a cup of coffee?"

"Thank you, but—"

"Come on along, there's a nice café just around the corner."

"I really should—"

"We need to talk."

The café he walked her to was called the Somber Reptile. It was one of those upscale places that were popping up in old downtown areas. It had a yellow and black awning with tables outside near the sidewalk. Each table had a yellow and white umbrella with a pattern of little black alligators.

Winsor sat them at one of the outdoor tables and ordered two coffees. His hair, as usual, was perfect. Charlene suddenly felt like a pair of old shoes with a new tuxedo.

"I want to say right off the bat what a great job I think you're doing for your client," Winsor said. "Yes, indeed. A fine, admirable job for your first big trial."

"Thank you," Charlene said, feeling set up.

"I remember when I was about your age," Winsor said. "And had my first big trial. A terrible accident involving a power saw. Man got his hand sawed off clean. Young man, too. Had his whole life ahead of him."

That was curious. "You were a plaintiff's lawyer?"

Winsor smiled, showing his perfect teeth. "No, I represented the insurance company. The injured man claimed the saw was defective in design. Had a pretty good lawyer, too. But when it was all over, the jury came back unanimously against him." He leaned forward. "See, not every injury gets compensation. The jury found that the man was responsible to read the directions and use the saw the right way. He didn't."

Charlene looked at him. "Are you suggesting, Mr. Winsor, that my client is in the same position? That she is somehow responsible for what happened to her?"

"Just an illustration, that's all. But today's juries do believe people have to be responsible for their actions. There's a real distrust of plaintiff actions like this one. And my intuition is this jury of ours has that feeling. Don't you feel it too?"

In truth, she did. She felt the jury, especially after seeing Winsor at work, slipping slowly away.

"But I'm not one to harp on the negative," Winsor said. "I'm gonna offer you eight hundred thousand dollars to settle this thing right here and now. Eight hundred thousand, Miss Moore. Now that's not bad for a case that might be worth zero after the verdict. Ah, here's the coffee."

Charlene hardly noticed the waiter placing the steaming cup in front of her.

"Let me grease the tracks a little for you," Winsor said. "I know how much you have put into this case. I know what it costs to conduct discovery, to put you and your client up in a hotel, to take time away from other cases you could be handling. I know what that's like."

She wondered if he did, really. Had he ever been on the side of the little guy? Or had his entire career been funded by checks signed by insurance companies?

"So settlement would not only clear up those expenses," Winsor continued, "but also let you go home with a nice chunk of change. Now how about it?"

Something in the way he said "chunk of change" set her off. She could hear part of her mind telling her not to say anything. But another part, a deeper part, could not turn back.

"May I ask you a personal question, Mr. Winsor?"

"Feel free," he said.

"How can you defend what these clinics are doing? How can you, as a Christian, defend a system that encourages the taking of human life?"

The words came out in a rush, and Charlene saw an immediate reaction in Winsor. For a long, uncomfortable moment he just stared into Charlene's eyes. Finally he said, "Are you questioning my faith?"

With her heart flitting like a bird in a cage, Charlene said, "I am asking you, a lawyer, to defend a position that goes against God's will."

Winsor sipped his coffee, thinking. "Do you presume to know God's will?"

"I think in the case of abortion it's pretty clear."

"It must be nice to see the world in black and white," Beau Winsor said. "Those of us who live in the gray areas actually envy you sometimes."

She saw in his eyes then a quick flash of vulnerability. It was brief, passing, but real. She had never seen anything at all like it in him before. And, she was sure, he would not allow her to see it again.

Winsor took a leather wallet from his suit coat, removed a crisp ten-dollar bill, and placed it on the table. Then he stood up.

"My offer is good until four o'clock this afternoon," he said. "I advise you to take it. If you don't, I will hold nothing back. I will see to it that you never see a dime. You know where to reach me."

He turned and walked away.

3

"Won't you sit down?" Jack Holden asked.

"No, thank you," Millie replied. "I will not be long." They were in his office less than an hour after the service had ended. Millie had walked around town, sore in more ways than one, waiting for the congregation to disperse.

"That's too bad," Holden said. He seemed oblivious to her feelings. "I was hoping to have a chance to talk with you a bit. How about something to drink? Coffee? Dr. Pepper? I have a fine Dr. Pepper, 2002. A very good year."

Millie chafed at the attempted humor. "This is not a social visit."

Jack Holden's face stayed friendly, but concerned. "I'm starting to get that feeling."

"I'll just ask you straight, then. What did you mean by your sermon?"

"Didn't you like it?"

"I did not. And I did not appreciate being put on the spot like that in front of my mother." A thought struck her. "Did she put you up to it?"

"Justice Hollander, would you mind telling me what you found objectionable?"

"You can't guess?"

"Was it scripturally unsound?"

"It had nothing to do with Scripture."

"Then it would be unsound!"

"I don't find that funny. You stood in the pulpit and directed a sermon at me. You took advantage of my situation, my accident, and delivered what was tantamount to a lecture for one. Well, I found it highly offensive and unethical."

The pastor swallowed. He looked like he'd been hit with a hockey stick. Good. He needed to be.

"You took something highly private," Millie continued, "and made a whole sermon about it. You even mentioned a book I was reading. If you wanted to shine a spotlight on me in front of this whole town you did a pretty good job of it. Is that your idea of Christianity? To embarrass people, stick needles in them?"

"This was not—"

"That is all I have to say. I will assure you, for the sake of my mother, that I won't talk about what I've said here with anyone. I will show you a courtesy you did not show me."

She turned toward the door.

"Justice Hollander."

"There is nothing more to discuss." She put her hand on the doorknob.

"Sixth Amendment," Holden said.

Millie whirled around. "Excuse me?"

"Does not the accused have the right to a trial?"

"I am not amused." Though she was surprised that he would be quoting the Constitution at her.

Holden stood and walked to the front of his desk. "I am not trying to be amusing, Justice Hollander. I would only like the chance to say something in my own defense."

"I am really not interested in discussing this further."

"You at least owe me that."

She was about to say she did not owe him anything. But now she was curious. What could he possibly say that would justify his offense?

"I'd just like to show you something," Holden said. He went to a filing cabinet by his bookshelf, pulled out the top drawer. Millie saw a line of manila folders.

"These are my sermon files," Holden said. "I plan my sermons months in advance. I know what subjects I'll be preaching on. About six weeks before a sermon, I start my research, jot notes, find material, and throw that into the folder. Four weeks out I start writing the rough draft."

He pulled out a folder and slid the drawer closed.

"This is my folder for today's sermon," he said, approaching her. "On the tab I have today's date." He took out some papers. "And this is my rough draft. I'd like you to take a look at it, if you would."

Reluctantly, Millie took the draft from Holden.

"You'll notice the date at the top of the draft," he said. "I wrote this three and a half weeks ago."

Millie started to read. Her head began to tingle and she felt her cheeks storing embarrassed heat. As she scanned the rest of the page, and the page after it, she saw, almost verbatim, the sermon he had delivered this morning.

"You see," Holden said, "six weeks ago I knew my subject was going to be death. But I had no idea you would be here today, just as I had no idea you would be in an accident."

Millie heard herself stammer. "But my book. You mentioned my book."

"Book?"

"The one I was reading in the square. *On Death and Dying.*"

"You were? Oh, yeah, you had a book. Was that what it was?" Holden walked to the bookshelf and pulled down a dog-eared paperback. "Here's my copy."

For a moment Millie stood there, feeling exposed and without control. For ten years on the Supreme Court, she had been able to control virtually everything, because of her dogged preparation. She never made an argument unless all the facts were clear to her.

The facts had not been clear this time. She had made a huge assumption. Had there been a convenient prairie dog hole outside she would have gladly held court there.

"I must apologize," she said.

Holden said, "No need. If I had a dime for every time I was misunderstood, this building would be made of crystal."

In spite of herself, Millie smiled. "I'll just run along."

"Wait."

Millie looked at him, wondering what he could possibly want.

"You feel up to shooting some hoop?"

4

Anne Deveraux flipped open her phone. "This better be good."

"It is."

"Ricks?"

"It ain't Yasser Arafat."

"Detail me." Anne shot a cigarette into her mouth. She was sitting on the balcony of her apartment, ripping through the *New York Times* and *Washington Post* via laptop. She wore loose jeans and a gray T-shirt, what she called her Sunday best.

"Our girl went to church with Mom this morning," Ricks said.

"Big deal."

"That's not all."

"Give it to me."

"She went back later to meet the guy."

"The minister?"

"Same one she was talking to before. She went back to the church and met the guy at the front door. Then they go inside."

"Where is she now?"

"That's where I left them."

Anne looked down at the street. From her fifth-floor perch the people looked like dolls. She felt like moving them around.

"All right," she said. "Stay on it. Just don't stick out like a sore thumb."

Click.

Anne leaned back in the canvas chair and ran her mind around Dan Ricks. There was nothing to worry about. She knew she could trust him, because he feared her. She knew he feared her because she never entered any relationship without the power to inspire fear.

Except one.

That relationship was not with one of the so-called power guys in D.C. They were really cupcakes when it came right down to it. They would go all soft and crumbly in the face of a woman like Anne. The sex would be great the first night, but after that feelings of inadequacy would creep in under the macho shell, and soon the guy would be goo. One time she'd picked up a lobbyist for a tobacco company, and right as he was fumbling with her buttons she started singing Pat Benatar's song "Hit Me with Your Best Shot." That was cruel, she knew, but also telling. The guy was out her door within five minutes.

The older power brokers held no allure for her. Guys like Levering. She respected them, of course, but was not interested in trophy status.

She was twenty-eight and beginning to think the single, professional life would be her lot. Not a bad thing. She didn't want kids. She didn't even know if she wanted a long-term relationship.

When she met Ambrosi Gallo, though, things changed.

Anne checked her watch, and noted she had three hours to get over to Dulles to catch her flight to New York. She wished it was sooner. She wished she was on the plane right now, the sooner to be in Ambrosi's arms.

Anne actually lit her cigarette now, and then felt something weird, something in her gut.

She'd always had great instincts. Had to. To survive. When her parents died helicoptering over the Grand Canyon, her stepdad at the stick—that might have messed up any other sixteen-year-old. But Anne had already overcome her stepfather's abuse, and she chose to get even stronger. Eventually got into Harvard. Made her way into the citadels of power. Her instincts were impeccable.

She took another deep, wonderful drag on her cigarette, and checked out the street again. Same activity. Same going and coming. Same—

Then she saw him. On the corner just below her balcony. The way he was dressed cried out homeless person. But even from five floors up she could read him. He had a scraggly beard, a dark face. His eyes were wide. And he was looking directly at her.

She went cold. Had to be a coincidence. He had to be looking at something else. From down there, he couldn't zero in on her. She paused a moment, waiting for him to turn away. He didn't.

So she did. She looked at her laptop again. Took another puff on her cigarette. Told herself to relax.

But she couldn't relax. She felt the guy's eyes on her. Angrily, she looked back down at the corner. She was going to give the guy a glare that would melt rock.

But the man was gone.

5

"I can't believe I'm doing this," Millie said. The sun was hot on the half-court asphalt behind the church. Her ribs and legs were still tender, but here she was. About to shoot a basketball with a Christian minister. If Helen could see her now . . .

"You sure you want to try this?" Jack Holden said.

"Yes," Millie said. "But no quick moves."

"I won't even play defense on you." He was in his shirt-sleeves, the little bead necklace exposed. "A Supreme Court justice lofting them in Santa Lucia? This is historic."

"How did you know I played?"

"I read a story about you once. Said you liked to play ball after court. I think that is so cool."

Holden flipped the ball to Millie. The ball felt good in her hands. It had a thin veneer of dirt on it, giving her a good grip. She approached the free-throw line, set herself, and shot. The ball hit the back of the rim and bounced out. But no pain in her ribs.

"Good thing we've got all day," Jack Holden said.

Cheeky fellow, she thought. "I *do* have other things to attend to, Mr. Holden."

Holden recovered the ball and passed it to Millie. "More important than b-ball?"

"Amazing, but true," she said, even as she spun the ball in her hands, readying herself to shoot.

"Tell you how we can make it more interesting," Holden said. "How about we play a game of Horse? I win, you decide to let the Bible back in public schools."

It was a joke, obviously, but still cut a little close. "You want to tear down the wall of separation right here?"

"I'll give you two out of three, how's that?"

Millie held the ball. "You are not what I expected," she said.

"Is that a compliment?"

A warm breeze from the desert caressed Millie's face. "I don't know yet."

"Shoot," he said.

She did. And missed.

Holden ran for the ball, limping slightly, and returned it to her. "Before you make up your mind, I actually have a confession to make."

Millie waited for him to explain. She was growing more curious about this man by the second.

"I did in fact give my sermon a little extra today when I saw you."

"Extra?" Millie said.

"Extra oomph," Holden said. "You know, energy. Like when an actor is out there doing Hamlet and discovers Spielberg is in the audience."

"It was for my benefit, this oomph?"

"Yep. Before I tell you why, though, I need to tell you the second part of my confession."

"There's more?"

"Yeah, the worst part, too. I'm a lawyer."

Millie tried to keep her face from showing stark surprise. "Well, I won't hold that against you." This was getting really interesting. "Where did you go to law school?"

Holden bounced the ball a couple of times. "Yale."

Another stunner. "Who was your Constitutional law professor?" Millie asked.

"Larry Graebner."

"Graebner! You're kidding."

"Life's funny, ain't it?"

More than funny. Incredible. "How on earth did you go from Yale to this?" She hadn't meant it to sound condescending, though it did.

Holden, if he was at all offended, didn't show it. Instead, a faraway look came to his eyes, with a tinge of sadness. "It's kind of a long story."

She found, suddenly, that she wanted to know what it was. "Go ahead," she said.

"Not now. We're about to play Horse."

"Please," she said. "I really want to hear it."

Holden took a deep breath and said, "Okay, but only in the interest of full disclosure. I guess if I'm going to change the course of legal history through basketball, it's only fair you know where I'm coming from. Let's grab some shade."

They walked to a bench under the church eaves. Holden spun the ball in his hands as he talked.

"After Yale I landed with a big-time civil litigation firm in New York. I was, as the saying goes, on top of the world. I had a wife and daughter, an apartment on East 86th. Season tickets for the Knicks. Bought all my suits at Bergdorf's. And, idiot that I was, I had an affair. With a temp in the office. A nineteen-year-old actress. My wife found out about it and, bam, left me, took my daughter. I tried to find them, but Yolanda, that was my wife's name, was good at what she did, which was to avoid me."

He reached into his shirt and held the bead necklace in his hand. "My daughter was six when she made me this. It's the only thing of hers I have left."

Millie almost reached out to touch it. The whole story felt ineffably sad.

"Anyway, I dealt with it by using drugs. Cocaine, mostly. It was the eighties, after all. The city was covered in snow. It didn't take long for the firm to boot me out. You know those stories they tell junior high school kids to keep them off drugs? All true. At least it was in my case. The low point came when a drug dealer shot me, tore a big hole in my leg. I almost bled to death."

A shadow passed over Holden's eyes, covering everything for a moment.

"Long and short of it, I got out of the hospital and had serious thoughts about ridding the world of one more loser. Me. Still couldn't find my daughter. So I had nothing left. I found myself holing up in a thirty-dollar-a-week hotel in Newark called the Nazareth. I kid you not. The Nazareth Hotel. And one night that first week, when I was thinking about the best way to kill myself, some of the guys in the lobby were watching Billy Graham on TV. I sat down to listen. And I got hit with a laser beam, right here."

Holden pointed to his chest.

"I mean, it was like somebody opened me up and poured hot liquid into me. I know this is a cliché, but he sounded like he was speaking right to me. Like he knew exactly what I needed, down to the letter."

He paused a moment, seeming to gather fragments of memory. "Next thing I know I'm crying, I mean bawling like a baby. The other guys, old geezers mostly, are asking me if I'm having a heart attack. Funny thing is, that's exactly what it was. An attack on my heart. And when Billy Graham gave that invitation, I got down on my knees on the cheap linoleum of the Nazareth Hotel and prayed for forgiveness of my sins."

Millie remembered hearing testimonies as a little girl. For some reason, they never really reached her. They were usually laden with emotion and Millie always filtered them through a sieve of cold objectivity. She could not recall ever being moved.

Now, for some strange and uncomfortable reason, she found she was moved by Holden. He was not embellishing or ranting or spouting preacher-talk. He told his story from a deep place inside him and, through some miracle of human connection, it touched her.

"Skip ahead a few years," Holden said. "I went into the ministry. Started pastoring a church upstate in Syracuse. Did that for a time, and felt called to rescue work."

The term sent a chill through Millie. *Rescue*, the anti-abortion term for doing things like shutting down family-planning clinics. She'd written an opinion once denying protesters the right to cross a certain buffer zone near such clinics.

"I ended up in prison," Holden said. "Now *that* was funny."

"Funny?" Millie said.

"Big-time Yale lawyer in the joint for pro-life civil disobedience. Larry Graebner must have had a conniption fit." Holden sighed quietly. "I finally got out and my lawyer had some news for me. He'd located my ex-wife and daughter. Only my daughter was dead."

Millie's chest tightened.

"Drug overdose," Holden said. "Fourteen years old." Holden looked down at his hands. "So I sued God."

His tone was even, unemotional, as if he were reciting the facts of some mundane petty theft case. Then he looked up at her. "I wanted to sue God, tell him what I really thought about him. Disprove him. To myself. I was going to walk away from the ministry."

"What happened?"

"I wrote up an indictment," Holden said. "I ended up with a huge legal brief against him. It started to work on me a little bit funny. I found myself arguing God's side, too. Back and forth. I felt like I was in a body-switching move. But I ended up with my faith back. It hasn't always been easy since then, but I find that brief is sometimes a lifeline for me. And it's taken on something of a life of its own."

"How so?"

"I distribute it in the prisons," Holden said. "I do some chaplain work at the Correctional Institute in Tehachapi, or down at Wayside. I'm told this brief gets spread around on the inside. And mailed out to other prisons across the country."

"The prisoners really read it?"

"Sure. Most of the prisoners are jailhouse lawyers to one degree or another. This is something I hope will interest them, get them thinking. And maybe . . ."

"Yes?"

"If I reach one person, maybe in a way it's like reaching my daughter. Or a way to atone for not reaching her. Does that sound crazy?"

"Not at all."

"Hey," he said jauntily. "Want to read it?"

That was a bolt from the hot blue sky. "I don't know," she said. "It's probably very personal."

"Yeah, that's exactly what it is. But I'd still like you to take a look."

To her surprise, she wanted to—part of her, at least. And she wanted to tell him about her vision, because he'd talked about something like it in church. For one small moment she wanted to trust this man, and reveal part of herself to him.

But another part of her didn't want anything to do with him or his so-called brief.

"Thank you anyway," she said diplomatically. "I really should be getting back to—"

"Tell you what," Holden said. "I make a fifteen-foot hook shot from the line, you read it. Deal?"

She looked at him, half admiring his persistence.

"I'll sweeten the offer," Holden said. "I'll make it a left-handed hook."

"Fine," she said, throwing up her hands. "Left-handed hook from the line."

He smiled and dribbled out to the free-throw line. He bounced the ball a couple of times, took a step with his right foot, and delivered a left-handed hook shot that arced beautifully into the afternoon air and down through the net.

Millie stood up and put her hands on her hips. "You are left-handed! What happened to all that full-disclosure stuff?"

"This is street ball we play here, Your Honor," Holden said. "Now I'll just get you a copy of the brief."

CHAPTER SEVEN

1

On Monday morning the wind came down from the north. Dark clouds conferred in the sky, portending rain. It was the sort of day in the desert Millie had always loved.

Millie took a lounge chair to the backyard with a big cup of coffee and one of her mother's homemade cinnamon rolls. She told her mother she wished to be left alone, no phone calls. She was going to go into court against Jack Holden. She was surprised at her enthusiasm and genuine interest in finding out what went on in that pastor's mind. But she had always loved the battleground of ideas, and here it was in her lap.

She settled comfortably in the chair and began to read the thick document. Under the section titled "Statement of Facts" the brief stated:

> I have been in jail. I have nearly died. I have lost the people
> I loved more than anything in the world. I wonder sometimes
> why I didn't take my own life. I think I now know why. God
> isn't finished with me yet.

The Statement of Facts went on to narrate Holden's story as he had told her, only in more detail. Millie was caught up in it immediately. She could tell Jack Holden must have been a very good trial lawyer. He had her attention from the start.

Section Two was titled "Issues." The wording was more casual than a true Supreme Court brief, but Holden was writing this for a lay audience, specifically those behind bars.

> I wanted to say that God does not exist, and that I know that to be true. I said that many times to myself, but began to wonder about the statement. I wanted to be an atheist. What proof did I have?
>
> I found that the one thing I could not say with absolute certainty was that God does not exist. One cannot prove the non-existence of anything. We would have to have absolute knowledge of everything to know for certain that God does not exist. And then we would be gods ourselves.
>
> I found that it is valid to be an agnostic, and to say, "I do not yet have enough evidence to convince me that God exists." This is why I decided to look at whatever evidence there was, and see where it led.
>
> After studying the evidence, I now believe the evidence is strong, not only for a god, but for the Christian God.

Millie sat up in the chair, ignoring the prickles of heat in her ribcage. She read the paragraphs again. She had to admit that his writing was not flabby noodles. She read on.

> I propose to do the following in the remainder of this brief. First, I will prove that it is more reasonable than not to believe in God. And then I will prove that it is more reasonable than not to believe that Jesus Christ is his only begotten Son, and that whoever trusts in him will have everlasting life.

"Mom!" Millie shouted.

Ethel came to the back door. "What's all the hubbub?"

"Can you bring me a legal pad, please? There's one in my briefcase. And a pen."

"Are you working out there?" Ethel said with rebuke.

"Please."

Her mother brought out the pad and pen. "What's that on your lap?" Ethel said.

"We'll talk later, Mother. I just need some time alone."

"What's with all those wrinkles in your forehead?"

"Mom!"

"All right, all right." Ethel started back toward the house, muttering.

Millie set the legal pad on her lap and got ready to take notes. Jack Holden wanted a real fight here, did he? All right. She was going to give him one. On the pad she jotted a note: *God may be, or may not be, but if you are proposing that he is, the burden is with you.*

She flipped to section three, which was titled, simply, "Beauty." That sent a small spike of anticipation through her. She had just been thinking about the beauty of her surroundings. She read quickly.

> Beauty exists. Everyone knows it, for everyone finds something beautiful. There is an amazing agreement on what is beautiful, all across cultural lines. Beethoven and Bach. Sunsets and flowers. Mountains and the Grand Canyon. You can't escape beauty.
>
> But where does beauty come from? You can't put it into a mathematical equation. You can't mix it in a bowl. It is a sense. It is something we feel as a consequence of being human.

Millie paused and looked out at the valley again. The colors, if it were possible, seemed even more vibrant. She felt the wonder of it, and then a small jolt of annoyance. Holden's writing was a bit too sure of itself, a bit thin on the evidence. Or was it? She jotted a note on the pad. *The sense of beauty may simply be a chemical component of our bodies, like the sense of smell.*

Holden was claiming that this feeling was from God, not from chemicals. *Not enough information,* she wrote. *We're going to need more from you, Pastor Holden.*

The next heading was "Morality."

> What has been said of beauty may also be said of morality. We all behave as if there is a standard, a real right and

wrong. Somebody who cuts me off in traffic either believes he has that "right," or wants to "get away with it." In either case, he believes in a moral standard.

This is true of all morality, in all cultures. As historian Will Durant writes in *The Lessons of History*, one who studies history will see "the universality of moral codes."

As with the sense of beauty, the sense of morality must come from outside nature, and it must be given by a Being who gives us morality, a set of laws designed for our own benefit, intentionally. A moral lawgiver, in fact.

Millie shook her head. At least he got to the heart of matters quickly. Verbose counsel never impressed the justices. Holden was clipped and assured.

But his assurance was still bothersome. Okay, she told herself, be objective about it. When she considered a case, Millie always spent at least a little time in the shoes of each party to better understand the opposing viewpoints.

So she asked herself, *What if I really did change my mind about God?* And her initial reaction was a kind of muted fright.

She breathed deeply. What would a belief in God actually do to her after so many years? Would it affect her judicial philosophy? Now wouldn't *that* be opening a can of political worms.

A loud crash interrupted her thoughts—the unmistakable percussion of metallic kitchenware falling on the hard tile of the kitchen floor.

"Mom?" Millie called out. She waited. No answer came. She called out again, louder this time.

No answer.

2

"Sarah Mae," Charlene said gently, "how old are you?"

This was it. Sarah Mae's testimony from the witness stand would be the deciding factor in the case. Winsor had undermined her expert witness. Now the story had to be told by the one who lived it.

There was no turning back. Charlene had used all of her persuasive powers to get Aggie to go along with continuing the trial. It was greed that did it. Aggie's. Eight hundred thousand could become at least a million, Charlene had said. They increased the first offer. They would easily go into seven figures next. You can trust me, Aggie.

But greed was not why Charlene was continuing the trial. The case was God's will, Granddad notwithstanding. Charlene was taking this trial to the limit, and there was no way she could lose. No way. Sarah Mae's testimony was too compelling. God's will was too clear. Charlene Moore was God's woman.

And the next few minutes were the key to the whole thing.

Big doe eyes looked back at Charlene. "Eighteen," Sarah Mae said.

"And where do you live?"

"Dudley."

"With your mother?"

"Yeah."

"And brothers and sisters?"

Sarah Mae nodded. Judge Lewis said, "You need to answer out loud, so the reporter can hear you. Do you understand?"

Again Sarah Mae nodded. Then quickly added, "Yeah."

Charlene paused to let Sarah Mae recover a bit. "Sarah Mae, tell us about that day two years ago when you found out you were pregnant."

The girl swallowed and took a deep breath. "I started to feeling sickly. But there wasn't nothing wrong with me. Least I didn't think there was. But I got sickly and threw up. I didn't want to tell Mama because I knew why I was doing that, throwing up. So I went to that place that I saw on the telephone pole."

"Was that the National Parental Planning Clinic?"

"Objection," Winsor said. "Leading."

"Sustained."

Charlene said, "What was the name of the place you saw on the telephone pole?"

"National . . . what you just said."

"Do you remember it in your own mind?"

"Yes, ma'am."

"It was in Dudley?"

"Yes, ma'am."

"You went there because you thought you might be pregnant?"

"Yes, ma'am."

"Sarah Mae, without mentioning names, tell the jury why you thought you were pregnant."

Sarah Mae Sherman looked at her hands. Her fingers were locked together. "I saw this boy for a spell. I thought we was in love. Turns out I was. He weren't."

Charlene paused. She caught a quick glance of Aggie Sherman, seated in the front row. She was also looking at her hands.

"Now, when you went into the clinic, what was the first thing that happened?"

Sarah Mae's chest went up and down as she breathed. "They was all friendly at first. They had a lady behind a desk and she sat me down."

"Do you remember this lady's name?"

"No, ma'am."

"Continue then. What happened next?"

"I told her what I thought. She said I could have a test to see. I asked her if I had to tell my mama, and she said no, I didn't have to tell my mama nothin', and there's no law said I had to."

Charlene paused. "And did you have a test?"

"Yes."

"What kind was it?"

Sarah Mae looked embarrassed. "Of my urine."

"What was the result?"

"I was pregnant."

Charlene paused a moment, letting the story take on a natural flow. "When it came time to talk to the lady about what to do, Sarah Mae, can you tell us what she said?"

Beau Winsor said, "Objection. Hearsay."

"State of mind, Your Honor," Charlene said.

"Overruled. The witness may answer."

Sarah Mae looked from the judge to Charlene. "She asked if I was wantin' to have an abortion."

"That was the first thing she said?"

"Uh-huh."

"What did you say?"

"Said I didn't want no abortion. Said I wanted to keep my baby."

"And what was her response?"

"She said it weren't no baby yet."

Again Charlene paused. This was crucial. "What did you say?"

"I said weren't it gonna be a baby?"

"And the response?"

"She said did I know what I was getting myself into, having a baby when I was sixteen? And then I was thinkin' that maybe she was right and all. I was gettin' scared. She told me everything would be all right if I got it."

"The abortion?"

"Yeah."

"Did this lady ask you any questions about your past medical history?"

"No, ma'am."

"Your background?"

"No, ma'am."

"Anything about your past at all?"

"No."

"Did you think about talking to your mama about all this?"

Sarah Mae looked to the first row, her eyes starting to tear up. "No, ma'am."

"Can you tell us why?"

"'Cause . . ."

"It's all right, Sarah Mae. Take your time."

"I was afraid she'd get mad." Tears started from the corners of Sarah Mae's eyes. Her voice warbled. "I was afraid she'd think I was a bad girl." Sarah Mae put her face in her hands and sobbed.

"Miss Moore," Judge Lewis said. "Do you want to take a short recess?"

Charlene did not want to if she could avoid it. Sarah Mae's emotion was important for the jury to see.

"Sarah Mae," Charlene said softly. "Do you need to stop?"

The girl sniffed and wiped her eyes with the back of her right hand. "No, ma'am."

The judge told the clerk to put a box of tissues on the witness rail. Sarah Mae took one and daubed at her eyes.

"All right," Charlene said. "Tell us what happened next."

"Dr. Sager gave another test, where they look at what's inside."

"Did he call this a sonogram?"

"Uh-huh."

"And that's where the doctor puts a device right on your stomach, so he can see a picture of the baby inside you?"

"Object to use of the word *baby*," Winsor said.

"Sustained."

"Sarah Mae," Charlene said, "did the doctor allow you to look at a monitor so you could see what the sonogram showed?"

"No, ma'am."

"Did he offer to let you see?"

Sarah Mae wiped a tear from her right eye. "No, ma'am."

"Did he allow you to hear the ultrasound of the baby's— excuse me—the sound of the heartbeat?"

"No. He didn't turn on no sound."

"And when this was finished, what did he tell you?"

Sarah Mae breathed in deeply. "He said I could have the abortion right then 'cause they had a slot."

"A slot," Charlene said slowly, just so the jury could hear it again. Implicit in the word was the abortion industry's dirty little secret, that it was more a commercial venture than a health enterprise. Anything to fill those slots. Charlene hoped the jury would understand that.

"Did the doctor tell you anything about the risks of abortion?" Charlene asked.

"He gave me something to read."

"What did he give you?"

"A paper."

Charlene went to her counsel table and removed a sheet of paper from a file folder. She placed it in front of Sarah Mae Sherman. "Is this what they gave you to read?"

"Yes."

"I would like to mark this as Plaintiff's Four for identification," Charlene said. It was a double-sided, single-spaced form that said, across the top "Things You Need to Know About Your Reproductive Choices."

"You were given this by Dr. Sager?" Charlene asked.

"Yeah."

"And what did you do with it?"

"Looked at it."

"Did you read it?"

Sarah Mae shook her head. The judge said, "You must answer out loud for our reporter."

"No," Sarah Mae said.

"And why didn't you read it?"

"It . . . I couldn't understand it. I don't read good." Sarah Mae tugged at her dress.

"There is a place at the bottom where you are supposed to sign this form. Is that your signature at the bottom?"

"Yeah."

"So you signed this form even though you did not read it?"

"Yeah."

"Why, Sarah Mae?"

The girl's eyes were full of regret. "'Cause that's what I had to do to get it."

"The abortion?"

Barely audible, Sarah Mae said, "Uh-huh."

Charlene took the form and walked it to the clerk. As she returned to the witness box she stole a quick glance at the jury. Their faces melted together into a blank canvas. She saw features, but no expressions.

"Did Dr. Sager go over this form with you?" Charlene asked.

"No, ma'am."

"Did he inquire into your health history?"

"No, ma'am."

"Did he ask you how you were feeling about the procedure?"

Sarah Mae hesitated a moment. "He said something like that," she said.

Like what? Charlene had no idea what Sarah Mae was referring to. They had gone over her story in Charlene's office, and in the hotel last night. Her answer was out of the blue. And the worst thing that could happen to a lawyer in trial is one of her own witnesses saying something that scuttles the case.

This was a crucial moment, because the doctor's conduct was at the very heart of this malpractice suit.

Worse, Charlene could not just skip to another question. If she did, Winsor would get the information for himself on cross-examination. That would look horrible to the jury, as if Charlene wanted to hide an answer.

What have you done this time, Charlene? She heard the phrase her mother used to say when Charlene got into serious trouble. *What have you done this time?*

"He did not get into any detail with you, did he?" Charlene said.

Winsor was on his feet. "Objection! That was clearly a leading question, Your Honor. Miss Moore is trying to lead her witness out of a situation she herself has—"

"That's sufficient," Judge Lewis said, cutting Winsor off from making a speech in front of the jury. "I will sustain the objection."

Charlene knew she had blown it. Winsor had managed to convey clearly enough that she had asked an improper question, and the judge had backed him up. Now she was in a corner. There was no way out.

"What was it that the doctor said to you, Sarah Mae?" Charlene asked.

Suddenly looking confused, Sarah Mae struggled to say, "Well, I can't exactly remember, exactly . . ."

"As best you can."

"Well, he did say something like if there was anything I wanted to say to him before we went in."

This was the first Charlene had heard about it. Why hadn't Sarah Mae said anything about this before?

"Did he say anything else to you before you went in?" Charlene said.

"I can't remember."

"The point is, he—"

"Objection. Argumentative."

"Sustained."

Charlene cleared her throat. "When you went into the procedure, Sarah Mae, did you feel satisfied that you had been able to communicate to the doctor your feelings about what was about to happen?"

Sarah Mae shook her head with a slow, mournful look, as if she were lost in the woods. "I don't rightly, exactly, remember." Her eyes told Charlene she had no idea what she had done. And then those eyes gushed with tears.

Charlene looked at the judge. "Perhaps now would be a proper time for a break, Your Honor."

Lewis nodded. "We'll recess until ten-thirty," he said. It sounded like he was announcing the time for an execution.

3

"Mom!"

Ethel was sprawled motionless on the kitchen floor.

"Mom, please, Mom."

Millie knelt. Ethel was facedown, her left arm folded awkwardly under her body. Millie put her hands over her mother as if she wanted to do something, but could not figure out what. For an excruciating moment she felt as if she alone could determine whether her mother lived or died, yet at the same time her mind was a blank. Her hands trembled over the unmoving body of her mother.

Phone. Millie clambered to her feet and grabbed the kitchen phone. She punched 911. It took less than thirty seconds to give the dispatcher the information. But in this small town, how long would the ambulance take? The nearest full hospital was Bakersfield. Would her mother make it?

Returning to Ethel, Millie knelt and put her hand on her mother's arm. It was so frail. Her skin felt like silk.

Millie saw the faint throb of a pulse in Ethel's almost translucent neck and heard herself cry out, "Oh God, oh God, oh God."

The words triggered her next desperate act. Grabbing the phone, she dialed information and got the number of the church. Then she called, hoping—praying—that Pastor Holden was in.

4

President John Warrington Francis took the cigar out of his mouth, looked at Senator Sam Levering, and said, "What would you do in this situation?"

Levering smiled, his lips curling around his own cigar. "I'd quit, go home, lick my wounds, admit I'm not the man I used to be."

Francis said, "You know what crow tastes like? 'Cause that's what you're about to eat."

The president leaned over to his golf bag and selected a five wood. His ball, a Slazenger 1, was embedded in the deep rough that lined the right side of the fairway. Levering knew full well that Francis was not going to quit. Francis was a three handi-cap, one of the benefits of growing up rich in the northeast, with a father who held two country club memberships.

Levering, on the other hand, was the typical weekend hacker. He hadn't even taken up the game until he came to Washington. He was lucky to shoot in the nineties.

Francis inserted the smoldering cigar into his mouth as he approached the ball. No wonder this guy was president, Levering thought. He was handsome, trim, athletic, and smart. And he knew how to get out of a jam.

After two practice swings that scattered tufts of grass like flushing quail, Francis hit one of the best golf shots Levering had ever seen. The white ball flew up onto the green, rolled, and stopped about five feet short of the pin.

"And that," the president said, "is how it is done."

"Pretty good," Levering said.

"Pretty good? Tiger would kill to hit a shot like that." Francis led the way to the golf cart. Levering got in, shooting a quick glance at the secret service detail in the golf cart behind them. They did not smile. They did not golf.

"The secret to golf," Francis said as he drove toward the green, "is to stay out of trouble. You know? Just stay away from the trouble areas. Which is one of the things I wanted to talk to you about."

The scent of cigar smoke mixed with freshly mown grass was the scent of power. Levering breathed it in deeply, appre-ciatively. "You have something in mind?"

"Hollander," the president said. "She stable?"

"As near as we can tell."

"That's not near enough." Francis brought the cart to a stop on the path next to the green. Then he faced Levering, flicked a bit of ash onto the grass, and said, "I had a meeting with Helen Forbes Kensington yesterday. You know her?"

Only from what Anne had told him. She was Hollander's good friend, and a pretty hot-looking divorcee. "Not person-ally," Levering said, "though I wouldn't mind."

"You and me both," Francis laughed. "Anyway, she was doing some lobbying, wanted me to put reproductive rights further up on the list. Plus she was all in a lather about a case down south, a trial in federal court about informed consent."

"I think I read about that."

"Yeah, well she thinks it's a hydrogen bomb on the whole women's rights movement."

"How so?"

"If the plaintiff wins based on the fact that she should have been informed about the mental health risks of abortion, what happens?"

Levering shrugged.

"Class action lawsuits," Francis said. "If they win, the abortion providers go bankrupt, my friend. Then the anti-abortion crowd won't have to worry about *Roe v. Wade*. They'll have effectively shut down abortion through the back door."

Levering had fought all of his political life for the rights of women, from the days of ERA to the cause of the right to choose. Was this concern real? If it was, then having Millie Hollander under his wing, as chief justice, was even more important than he had at first supposed.

"I'm going to need a strong chief," Francis said. "Someone who can hold the delicate balance up there. And I want your assurance that Hollander is still your first choice."

Of course she was. His little tryst with Hollander had been—through Anne Deveraux's alchemy and his limo driver's loyalty—transformed into a weapon of almost unbelievable potency. Levering knew how much Millie Hollander wanted to be chief justice, how much her reputation meant to her. Sam Levering knew how to use the ambition of others to his own ends. That was politics.

"Yes," Levering said as he and the president headed for the green. "I know she's the right choice."

"Fine," Francis said, getting out of the cart and grabbing his putter from the bag. "Then I want to talk with her as soon as possible. A nice chat before I make the announcement. And I want to run it by Graebner."

"That's a good idea," Levering said.

"Those are the only kind of ideas I have," Francis said. "Now take a look at this putt. You think it breaks left?"

Levering laughed. "Everything you do breaks left, Mr. President."

5

Millie quivered. She was not used to raw emotion unfiltered through careful analysis. But her mind seemed paralyzed; it rang with the words she hadn't had a chance to say to her mother.

Jack Holden had arrived just behind the ambulance. The paramedics said they'd be going to Kern Medical Hospital in Bakersfield. Holden offered to drive Millie. She gratefully accepted, and appreciated that he wasn't feeling chatty. After about twenty minutes on the highway he gently asked, "How you feeling?"

Millie looked at him, wondering for a moment if she might be able to open up a little. What she said was, "I'm a little upset right now." It was a cold, antiseptic description.

"You're very close to your mother," Holden said.

"I haven't had a chance lately to be close," Millie said. Something cracked inside her. A small fissure, and out of it came a warm stream of tears. She swiped her index finger under both eyes, embarrassed.

Holden, if he noticed, did not react. He kept his eyes on the road ahead. "Almost there," he said.

The gray concrete hospital was just off Mt. Vernon Avenue. At emergency receiving Millie gave them as much information as she could. Then she was told to wait. A doctor would be out soon.

Soon stretched into sometime. The TV in the waiting room was tuned to a soap opera vacantly eyed by a scattered few. A boy of about five played with some plastic toys on the floor under the TV.

Holden said, "Can I get you anything? Something to drink?"

"Water," Millie said. "Thanks." She watched as he got up and noticed how solid he looked. He must be a real comfort to people at moments like this. That was the important thing, perhaps. Not all the theology or the preaching or the arguments for God. Maybe all that mattered was what you did when people needed you.

Holden returned with a Styrofoam cup of cold water. It tasted metallic.

"I appreciate that you're here," Millie said.

"Glad to be," Holden said. "I love your mom. She's a great lady."

And then, needing a change of pace of any kind, Millie said, "You write a pretty good brief. Thoughtful."

"Thank you." His gratitude seemed genuine. "Coming from Justice Hollander, that's high praise indeed."

"Want to talk about it?"

"I'm always game. But what about you?"

"Please. Anything's better than just sitting here, waiting."

Holden seemed pleased. "Funny word, *better*."

Millie looked at him questioningly.

"Do you know the term *tertium quid*?" he asked.

"That's Latin for 'third thing.'"

"Exactly. Any moral argument needs a *tertium quid* that stands outside two competing positions. It's like an umpire in baseball or the rule book. Without that third thing, you and I might never agree on what is good, better, best. Or even a moral standard. We always fall victim to the Grand Sez Who."

"Come again?"

"If I say racism is a good thing, and you tell me it is not, I can answer, *Sez Who?* You? I can be a racist if I want to. There is no *tertium quid*."

The intellectual give-and-take was indeed a pleasant diversion. She dove in. "But I can gather the community to denounce you as an ignorant outcast."

"Doesn't mean I have to agree. If I have guns or bombs, I can make an even greater statement."

"And I can lock you up."

"And so we get to the conclusion. Morality on this stage equals power. Might makes right."

Feeling a bit testy now, Millie said, "Where is the doctor?" She started to stand up, then sat down again.

"He'll be here soon," Holden said. "More water?"

"No, no." Millie pushed a strand of hair out of her eyes. "Let's keep talking. It helps." She settled back to talk. "Okay, tell me how the 'Sez Who' theory proves the truth of Christianity."

"Our moral sense is just one bit of evidence to consider," Holden said. "That's the mistake people make. They assume that because one line of argument can't prove the case alone, it is of no value. Not so. What do we do in court? We let the jury look at all the relevant evidence and then decide which way the scales of justice should fall."

"I'll grant you that, Counsel, but . . ." She stopped. "I just called you Counsel."

"I haven't been called that in quite some time. Been called a few other things." His smile was warm.

"Nevertheless, there is still much of the case that's missing," Millie said.

"That's because you haven't reached the killer argument yet."

"Okay"—she let her voice become spooky—"what's the *killer argument*?"

"C. S. Lewis wrote about it in a book called *Surprised by Joy*," Holden continued. "One day he felt that an open door was presented to him. Nothing like light or fire from the sky. Just a door. Beyond that door was joy, not the transient kind, but the answer to the deepest longings of his heart. That's the killer argument."

"It doesn't really sound like an argument," Millie said. "What is the logic?"

"The longing of the heart for something beyond," Holden said, "is proof that our world cannot satisfy us. The fact that we experience thirst shows that we are creatures for whom drinking water is natural. In the same way, our longing for something beyond us is proof there is something beyond. 'Our hearts are restless until they rest in God,' Augustine said."

"But desires come and go," Millie said.

"Not this one. This one stays. Lewis recognized that, and one day he found the door was open. He knew then he could walk through or turn away."

"And he walked through?"

"Yes, though he described himself as the most reluctant convert in all of England."

"Why?"

"He said he would have been happy to remain an intellectual atheist. But his heart was set free when he heard the call. He had to respond. I heard the same thing one night in the lobby of the Nazareth Hotel. It was like beautiful music, not something we rationalize, just something we hear."

Holden paused a moment, his eyes looking at a secret place. "I've heard it described this way. Once your heart hears the music, it is never really happy unless it is dancing."

At that declaration Millie felt something open inside her. Since she'd known him, Jack Holden had laid bare his whole life, all of his feelings, openly. She had held back. No more.

"Jack," she said. "I will admit there have been some moments recently when I've thought about these things. But I'm just not there. I don't know if I ever can be."

"Deadlock," he said.

"What?"

"You're deadlocked, like a 4–4 split on the Court. What you need, it appears, is a swing vote."

"Oh? And where might I find one of those?"

The minister smiled. "Just listen for the music. Then you can decide what to do about it."

"Yes, well, it's all very interesting to kick around, but—"

She stopped when she noticed Jack looking past her. She turned and saw a young doctor striding toward them. "Ms. Hollander?" he asked.

Holden stood and helped Millie to her feet.

"I'm Dr. Weinstein," he said.

"My mother?" Millie asked.

"Come with me, won't you?" He led them through a door to a quiet hallway. "I wanted to give you an update."

Millie found herself taking Holden's arm. The way the doctor spoke gripped her with dread.

"Your mother has had a stroke. We've stabilized her . . ."

Millie squeezed Holden's arm and felt his hand on hers.

". . . and of course we are going to do everything we can. We still need to run some more tests. She is comatose, Ms. Hollander. I understand you are her closest family member?"

"That's right," Millie said, her voice sounding distant and fragile.

"We are probably going to need some guidance here soon," he said. "And you'll need to begin thinking about that."

"Guidance?"

"Heroic measures," Dr. Weinstein said.

6

Washington, D.C., was Anne's world. But New York City was her kind of town. She spent almost as much time there as she did in the Beltway. Even more of late, because her lover was there.

As she sat across from Ambrosi Gallo at Ruby Foo's, their favorite place in Times Square, she couldn't help but wonder at the whole thing. Then again, maybe it was inevitable. She needed *edge*. Life was a big, fat farce without edge.

She had learned that from her stepfather. He used to whisper in her ear, when he did things to her at night, when Mom was away on her business trips. She learned what life was really like in the places you thought were safe.

She never thought anything was safe again, and had come not just to accept that rock-hard fact of life, but to embrace it. That was how you lived and stayed alive. The edge worked magic. It was, after all, what led her to Ambrosi Gallo.

"You finished with that?" Ambrosi asked, pointing a chopstick at her shrimp.

"Go ahead," she said, and watched his graceful moves. Ambrosi Gallo gestured like a symphony conductor. Italians spoke with their hands. Ambrosi sang with them.

Soon they would be in bed, and his moves would continue to sing. Anne would make her own music, the kind that drove him wild. She had never met Ambrosi's wife, and never would. But she was sure Mrs. Gallo would never mean what Anne meant to Ambrosi.

They'd met at a club in the Village. She'd seen this dark stranger circling her from across the dance floor. Just after midnight the move was made. The man slid next to her at the bar and immediately whispered in her ear, "You been scoping me. You serious about it?"

It was no secret who Ambrosi was, a made guy for the Calibresi family, which had moved into the five-borough vacuum created when the feds put Gotti away. The feds knew who he was—Anne knew the people to ask—and they suspected him of eight murders. But they'd never been able to put a case together. Ambrosi Gallo had beaten two raps. Nobody, but nobody, would testify against him.

"You want to go see a show or something?" Ambrosi asked.

"I don't want to go to a show," Anne said, feeling heat building in her. "I want to go to our place."

"You got it, babe," Ambrosi said.

They had a studio apartment in Gramercy Park, the place Ambrosi crashed when not at home in Queens. He was not often home. His wife, he assured Anne, was like all Mafia wives. She knew, she accepted, and she got nice things. No questions asked.

Outside the restaurant window, Anne could see a portion of the passing parade that was the foot traffic in Times Square. She couldn't help wondering how easy it would be for Ambrosi to dispose of any one of them. And then she thought, what he did with guns she did with political clout. They weren't really so different after all.

"What's it like?" she asked.

"What?"

"You know. *Whack*."

Ambrosi's eyes darted toward the adjoining table. "Hey, keep it down, will you?"

That only made Anne smile. "You like to live dangerously, don't you?"

"I also like walking around."

"So tell me."

"What do you want to know for?"

"Part of my education."

"I don't want to talk about it."

"Plus it will make me very excited, if you know what I mean."

Ambrosi's straight white teeth gleamed between his lips. *"Siete del diavolo."*

She frowned.

"You little devil."

Anne suddenly felt oddly upset. Something about the word *devil* as applied to her. She shook it off.

"It's no big deal, after the first time," Ambrosi said. "You ever see that movie, the one where DeNiro plays a Mafia guy and that other guy, what's his name, the little comedian, plays a shrink?"

"Analyze This."

"Yeah, that's it. And the shrink says it's good to hit a pillow when you're feeling stressed out, so DeNiro whips out his gun and shoots a pillow. And the shrink says, 'Feel better?' and DeNiro says, 'Yeah, I do.' I cracked up. But that's what it's like."

"Really? Shooting a person is like shooting a pillow?"

"Once you get used to it." Ambrosi nabbed another piece of shrimp and sent it into his mouth.

"Don't you ever worry about someone finding out?"

"How would they?"

"What if I was wearing a wire?"

Ambrosi looked at her, unconcerned. "You wouldn't be alive if you were," he said, as smoothly as if ordering Peking duck.

Anne's body filled with electricity. There it was. The edge. She realized at once she and Ambrosi were truly one. Killers both, in their own way. "Let's get out of here," she said, tingling all over. "Now."

CHAPTER EIGHT

| 1

Charlene watched as Beau Winsor circled her client. People sometimes called lawyers *sharks*. In Winsor's case, it was apt, though he did not once raise his voice or seem upset with Sarah Mae. It was not the sort of cross-examination one saw on TV shows. This was a surgery in which the patient hardly notices both legs being amputated.

"Now, Sarah Mae," Winsor said, sounding like he was addressing his own daughter, "when you went into the clinic that morning, you knew they performed abortions there, didn't you?"

"I guess so," Sarah Mae said.

Winsor gave a quick glance to the jury. "Now, we don't want you to guess, Sarah Mae." Her name dripped like molasses off his tongue. "You need to tell us what you know for certain. Now, did you know they performed abortions?"

"Yeah." In her innocence, Sarah Mae did not look overly frightened. In fact, she seemed almost trusting of the man in the blue suit with the fatherly gray hair.

"You had been thinking about having an abortion, hadn't you?"

"Yeah."

"And that wasn't an easy decision, was it?"

"Oh, no."

Charlene watched and listened carefully. Winsor was spreading some sort of net, and priming Sarah Mae to stroll right into it.

"So would it be fair to say, Sarah Mae, that you had really gone over and over this in your mind?"

"I didn't want to," Sarah Mae said, her eyes suddenly wide.

Winsor put his hand up, as a comforting uncle would. "We'll get to what you wanted in a moment, Sarah Mae. I understand you're nervous. So I'll ask my questions really simply, and you just do your best to answer them, okay?"

"Uh-huh."

"We're just interested in the truth here," Winsor added. Charlene almost objected, but didn't. How could anyone object to that? While it was technically an improper use of cross-examination—Winsor was simply making a statement for the jury—it wouldn't look good. The man was an absolute master.

"All right, when you went to the clinic," Winsor said, "how did you get there?"

"Walked."

"How long did it take you?"

"I don't rightly remember."

"Was it a half hour or so?"

"I think."

"So you had that time all the way there to think about where you were going, right?"

"I guess."

"We don't want you to guess, Sarah Mae. You just do your best to tell us rightly the way it was, okay?"

"Uh-huh."

"Now when you got to the clinic, you didn't hesitate, did you?"

"Huh?"

"You walked right in, didn't you?"

Sarah Mae swallowed. "I think I did."

For a moment Beau Winsor looked confused. Charlene realized immediately it was an act. He knew exactly what he was doing.

"Sarah Mae, do you remember giving a deposition in this case?"

"I think."

"You think? Don't you remember that you and your lawyer came to my office, and I asked you questions, and a reporter, like the one sitting over there, took down what you said. Do you remember that?"

"Yeah."

"And then your lawyer got a copy of that, what we call a transcript, and went over it with you, correct?"

"Yeah."

"And you had a chance to make corrections at that time."

"I think."

"Well, I'm looking at the transcript here." Winsor slipped on some reading glasses and flipped open the document. "I'm looking at page 34. Now, Sarah Mae, do you recall my asking you this question: *Did you hesitate before you went into the clinic?* And do you remember giving this answer: *No.* Do you remember that, Sarah Mae?"

"I guess."

"You don't remember?"

"Uh-uh."

"I guess it's pretty difficult for you to remember what happened that day, isn't it?"

Sarah Mae started to speak, but her mouth got stuck on open.

"Pretty difficult, isn't it?" Winsor's voice was like warm honey. Sarah Mae seemed drawn to it, almost stuck in it, and she began to tremble. Judge Lewis said, "You'll have to answer the question, Miss Sherman."

Shaking her head, Sarah Mae said, "I don't know. I don't!"

Charlene could not object to this. She could ask for a break, but that would look even worse.

"It's all right, Sarah Mae," Winsor said. "Just catch your breath for a minute. You need some water?"

Sarah Mae shook her head.

"Now, when Miss Moore over there was asking you questions, do you remember her asking you about meeting with Dr. Sager?"

"Uh-huh."

"And there was that one question where she asked you if Dr. Sager had inquired about your feelings. Do remember that question?"

"I think."

"And you said, let me see here, I jotted it down. You said this: *He said something like that,* meaning he asked how you were feeling, isn't that right?"

"I guess. Yeah."

"Now I was a little confused about that. I think the jury would like to hear a little bit more."

Sarah Mae looked at him with saucer eyes.

"What exactly did you mean by that?" Winsor asked.

"I . . ."

"If you remember."

"I don't remember. Rightly."

Winsor put his hand to his chin and studied the witness. "Now this is a pretty important matter, Sarah Mae. Think real hard for us, will you do that?"

"I am," she said.

Winsor stepped to the side of the podium and looked at Sarah Mae. His demeanor changed ever so slightly—from benign consideration to the start of annoyance. Charlene was almost certain that annoyance was a reflection of the jury reaction.

"Sarah Mae," Winsor said, "the fact is you really don't remember much about that day, and that's a real problem, isn't it?"

"I don't rightly know everything. I was so, it was so . . ."

"Did you discuss your testimony with Miss Moore during the break?"

"Objection," Charlene said. "Privilege."

"I'm not asking about the content of the conversation, Your Honor. I'm just asking if they discussed it."

"Overruled."

"Answer the question, Sarah Mae."

"Did I what?"

"Discuss your testimony with your lawyer at the break."

"Discuss?"

"Did you talk about it?"

Now Sarah Mae's face reflected a fear born of confusion and guilt, the kind of guilt a child feels when confronted with a charge she does not quite understand. She looked at Charlene, asking with her eyes what she should say.

"You don't have to look at your lawyer," Winsor said. "Just tell us the truth."

Charlene jumped up. "Your Honor, I will testify to the fact that I did what any lawyer does with a client. During the break—"

"Now I object," Winsor said. "That's a self-serving statement."

Charlene turned on Winsor. "Your whole cross-examination is self-serving, Mr. Winsor, and—"

She was brought up short by the banging gavel of Judge Lewis. "Miss Moore," he said sharply. "You will refrain from addressing opposing counsel. We'll just stop it right here. Mr. Winsor has asked a question and I've ruled that he may ask it. I want the witness to answer. Will the reporter please read the question again?"

The court reporter, a young woman, pulled up the steno paper and repeated the question for Sarah Mae.

"So you went over your testimony with your lawyer, correct?" Winsor clarified.

"Yeah."

"And still you are conveniently remembering some things and not others."

"Objection." Charlene was operating on pure instinct.

"Sustained," said the judge, surprising her.

"Your Honor," Winsor said, his voice theatrical, "I have no more questions for the witness."

2

"I can't stand this waiting!" Millie said. She and Holden were in the hospital parking lot, getting air. The afternoon was hot, dry, just like Millie felt. As nice as Holden had been, she was beginning to want to be alone. She stared blankly at the high school banner across the street. *Home of the Blades.*

"I know how hard this must be," Holden said.

"Do you?" The words came hard and fast. "I need to talk to her."

"You'll get your chance."

"How do you know that?" she snapped. And she knew several things at once—that he didn't deserve her tone, that he was comforting her as his profession demanded, but that she didn't care to hear platitudes at this moment.

"Just believe it," Holden said.

"It's not that easy."

"No, it's not easy," he said.

She looked into his eyes and saw some long ago darkness there, shadowy and shapeless.

"I'll call Royal," Holden said. "The folks at the church will want to be praying."

"Not yet," Millie said. It sounded selfish. It was, partly. "I don't want anyone coming up here. I want my time with her."

"Sure. Will you excuse me for a little while? I'm going to the chapel."

"Chapel?"

"I want to do some praying myself. You know where to find me if you need anything."

She watched him go. When was the last time she had prayed? Millie remembered praying for kids to stop teasing her. Didn't happen. She hadn't taken prayer seriously since.

But then it occurred to her she *had* prayed recently, in a way. In her vision. Hadn't she spoken God's name?

And when her mother was sprawled on the kitchen floor, hadn't she called the name of God over and over? She had been crying out for help. Now, on reflection, it seemed simply irrational. A product of stress.

Still, Millie looked up into the blue sky, as if seeking an answer. None came. The sky was just there, hot and oppressive. And never-ending.

3

On his way up to his office, Lawrence Isadore Graebner paused in front of the twelve-foot sculpture of the judge and bowed slightly, ironically. The limestone figure with a stern expression and a full British wig presided over the main courtyard of Yale Law School. His Honor always appeared ready to declare a cosmic mistrial.

Larry Graebner, however, liked to think of him as merely waiting for the right man to come along and take the law into new venues of justice. Graebner, ever since joining the Yale law faculty in 1975, considered himself that man.

At sixty-one, a time when many of his colleagues were looking toward retirement, Graebner was at the peak of his career. He was on the short list of every Democratic administration for appointment to the Supreme Court. Unfortunately, he was also at the bottom of that list. He knew why. He was a "lightning rod of controversy" according to the *New York Times*. He had simply said and written too much. If and when the Democrats commanded a larger majority in the Senate, and the right president was in place, he just might make it through.

Until then, he was content to offer advice and step into legal challenges he found stimulating.

One of his stimulants called just after five.

"It's Winsor."

"How'd it go today, Beau?" Graebner put his feet up on his African mahogany desk.

"Beautiful," Winsor said. "The plaintiff wilted under the heat."

"How is that young lawyer doing?"

"She's lost. Young and lost. I tried to talk sense into her, but you know these crusading types."

"Hey, never underestimate the power of ideals, even if we think they're wrongheaded."

"Ideals don't win cases. Good lawyering does."

"Since you are on the scene, sanity will prevail?"

"One never knows what a jury will do, but this jury looks pretty solid."

Graebner reached for his espresso, fresh from the gilded machine on his credenza. "I've been doing some thinking about that, Beau. And I think it would be best if we took it out of the jury's hands altogether."

"Why?"

Noting a hint of wounded pride in Winsor—*I am a great trial lawyer, let me handle it!*—Graebner spoke with modulated patience. "Juries get publicity. It's a media fascination. And then they get interviewed. They show up on network news or *O'Reilly*. Win or lose, it's publicity."

Winsor cleared his throat. "But how do we do it?"

"I've got it all worked out. I'll e-mail you the details. You have a little work to do."

"What are you e-mailing?"

"A little bombshell we're going to hand your opponent."

4

Charlene Moore looked out at the lights of the big city. From her room it almost looked like a theme park. Some magical kingdom. But this was no fantasy place. This was an impersonal world that didn't care about what happened to a teenager in an abortion mill.

She wanted them to care. They had to care. If they didn't, the world would continue to spin out of control, downward.

Lord, give me strength for the rest of the trial. I am your woman! Go before me in power!

She heard a soft knock on her door. It was Sarah Mae. Her eyes were red. Charlene brought her to a chair and sat her down.

"What is it?" Charlene asked.

"Sorry I messed it up," Sarah Mae said.

"You didn't mess anything up. You were fine."

"No I warn't. I seen your face. Did I make it bad for us?"

Charlene knelt and patted the girl's knee. "God is in this with us. Do you believe that?"

Sarah Mae nodded. But it was a weak nod. "Mama says we should stop now and make that settle . . ."

"Settlement?"

"Yeah. Like we almost did."

"I thought you didn't want to."

"I don't know no more. What if we lose?"

Charlene felt like someone had kicked her. That was, of course, the big question in any trial. You could do everything right, the evidence could be on your side, and still a jury could do the opposite of what you expected.

"No," Charlene said. "We're not going to lose. Not with God on our side."

Sarah Mae looked at her with eyes that wanted to believe it.

"Trust God with me," Charlene said. "He has called us to this trial." She could feel tears of passion coming to her eyes. For two years she had lived this case, day in and day out, losing sleep, putting up practically all the money she had in costs.

"You crying, Miss Moore?" Sarah Mae said.

"I'm all right."

"You sayin' God'll do right by us?"

"He does right by those who trust in him."

"What's gonna happen tomorrow?" Sarah Mae said, heaving a deep breath.

"The defense will put on its case. Then we'll have a chance to put on what's called a rebuttal. I'll call your mother to the stand for that."

"Mama's nervous. Think you should?"

"Yes."

"I'm still scared."

"You're not alone in that, Sarah Mae. Trust me, will you?"

Charlene took Sarah Mae's hand. It was soft, and so like a little girl's.

5

It was nearly eight o'clock at night when Dr. Weinstein returned, motioning to Millie and Jack Holden, who sat in the waiting room. Millie moved faster than she had in weeks, ignoring the shooting pains, to get to the doctor.

Dr. Weinstein smiled and said to Millie, "Let's go in here," motioning toward the double doors leading to a hallway.

It was ominously quiet, like a morgue. "What is it?" Millie asked. "How is my mother? What's happening?"

"Justice Hollander," he said, "your mother is awake."

Millie couldn't find a response. Her hand went to her mouth.

"You can see her now," Dr. Weinstein said.

Without thinking, Millie found herself turning to Jack Holden. He squeezed her arm and smiled. Then they turned and followed Dr. Weinstein to Ethel's room.

Ethel was on a bed, a tired smile on her face. When she saw Millie she put up both arms. One had a tube taped to it. Ethel seemed completely unconcerned.

Millie wanted to fall into her mother's arms. She contented herself with a kiss to her cheek. "Mom . . . ," she whispered.

"Scare you?" Ethel said, her voice thready.

Millie drew back her head. "Yes," she said. "I thought I'd lost you."

"No, no," Ethel said.

"I'm sick with worry."

Ethel smiled a little then. "Let it roll off your back, like a duck," she said slowly.

"Sure, Mom."

"We still have time."

The words hit Millie with an odd resonance. Where had she heard them before? And then it struck her. The homeless man, just before her accident. *You still have time.* Weird coincidence.

"Yes, Mom, we do," Millie said.

Ethel motioned to her to lean over close, like she wanted to whisper something. Millie bent over, turning her ear toward her mother's mouth.

"I'm proud you're my daughter," Ethel said.

Millie did not move, warmth from her mother's cheek filling her, holding her there. To hide her tears, Millie buried her face in the side of Ethel's pillow.

6

Millie finally allowed Holden to drive her home to Santa Lucia around midnight. Only the promise that he would bring her back in the morning got her out of the hospital.

"Tell me about near-death experiences," she said, to break the silence. He had talked about them in his sermon, and she had wondered if she would ever let him know about her vision. Now, she thought, she just might.

Holden kept his eyes on the highway. "What do you want to know?"

"Isn't it just a psychological response? Something the brain does in a certain state? Like a dream?"

"Some people believe that. Most, probably. Within the Christian community there is some skepticism, too."

"Why?"

"Theological issues. The Bible says it is appointed for a man once to die, and then to face the judgment. Having this so-called near-death experience could be viewed as contradicting Scripture. I don't see it that way."

"But people do report seeing Jesus, don't they? Or some white light?"

"True. But we have to be careful. There are those who claim to have received special revelation from Jesus, or God, and then want to spread that information around. That I do think is a contradiction of Scripture."

"So do you or don't you believe in these reports?"

"Oh, I do believe it happens. Have you heard of D. L. Moody?"

"Vaguely."

"He was an evangelist in the 1800s. The Billy Graham of his day. A great man of God. He had two little grandchildren who died. One was a boy named Dwight, who died in infancy. The other was a little girl, Irene, who was three years old or so. Their father was Moody's son, Will."

Millie listened attentively, as if receiving the facts from a new case to be considered.

"When Moody was on his deathbed, his son, Will, heard him mutter, 'Earth recedes, heaven opens before me.' Then he looked at Will and said, 'It is beautiful. God is calling me and I must go. Don't call me back.'"

The hum of the car was smooth and calm, like they were riding on air. The stars were particularly bright in the desert sky.

"Moody's wife was summoned," Holden said. "Moody was able to tell her she had been a good, dear wife. And then he seemed to fall into unconsciousness again, but as he did he whispered, 'No pain, no valley. It is bliss.'"

"Who recorded all this?" Millie could not help delving into issues such as witness accounts.

"Several family members," Holden said, "most notably his wife. In fact, she set down the facts the same day they happened. Moody came out of sleep and saw the people around him. And then he looked at them and said: 'What does it all mean? I must have had a trance. I went to the gate of heaven. It was so wonderful. I saw the children!'"

"Children?"

"Irene and Dwight. He told Will he saw them in heaven. Will began to cry. Moody comforted him. Will said he wished he could go to heaven to be with his children. And Moody told him, 'No. Your work is before you.' A short time later, D. L. Moody died."

Millie looked at the headlights, illuminating just enough of the highway to see a short way ahead, but no more. "May I ask another question?" she said.

"Of course," said Holden.

"What do you make of the experiences of the other sort?"

"You mean a vision of hell?"

"Are there many of those?"

"Oh, yes. Experiences of demons and fire and things like that."

"So what do you think?"

"Same as with the white light. I believe that there is such a place as hell, though I don't know the exact nature of it. I do believe it is separation from God, and some people who have almost died have been given the gift of seeing how horrible it will be."

"Gift?"

"Sure. The gift of time. In most cases these people become believers in God. I think God is in control. The Bible makes it abundantly clear that God rules over everything, including death and hell."

Millie tried to make sense of that, tried to allow for a new reality, but her mind simply did not allow it. It was too big a jump.

"Do you want to tell me about your death experience now?" Jack Holden asked.

Millie's chest tightened. "Am I that transparent?"

"You don't have to."

Millie felt that if she did, she would be opening a door she would rather keep closed. But another part of her prodded her on. If she didn't say something now, she might never have the courage to do it.

"I'm claiming clergy privilege now," she said.

"I consider all of our conversations privileged," Holden said.

She knew she could trust him. "I did have a vision," she said. "It was like a very vivid nightmare. It was not the good kind of vision, but the bad kind." She described in detail what she had seen.

When she finished, Holden was silent for a moment. Then he said, "I have no reason to doubt that what you experienced was real, and that when you called out to God to help you, it was a real prayer. A prayer that was answered."

"But people in distress are bound to call on God. It's a reaction."

"God does not turn a deaf ear just because it's a reaction."

"There is one other thing," Millie said, looking out into the desert darkness. "This vision, if that's what it was, happened at exactly the time you and my mother were praying for me. Exactly the same time."

Jack Holden's face, even in the darkness, seemed to open up with intense curiosity. "How do you know?"

"The doctor told me the time at which I flatlined. Then Mom told me what time it was when you were praying. Accounting for the time difference, it was on target."

"Well now."

The car hummed along in silence for a while. Exactly what she needed then, silence. Millie had unloaded more of her inner life in the last few minutes than she had in the last ten years.

Then Holden said, "For a long time I've felt that God is weaving a pattern for something big."

"What do you mean by weaving?"

"There's a verse in the Bible," Holden said. "Romans 8:28. I've memorized it in several translations, but my favorite is from a man named J. B. Phillips. His version goes like this: 'We know that to those who love God, who are called according to his plan, everything that happens fits into a pattern for good.' I always liked that. God weaving a pattern. We can't see the final product from here. But God can."

"All right," Millie said. "I'll bite. What's this pattern?"

"I'll be blunt here. I think our country has fallen into spiritual darkness over the last fifty years. A large part of that has to do with our courts, I'm sorry to say. Do you want me to continue?"

Bristling, Millie said, "Go ahead."

"You know, of course, that it was Justice William O. Douglas who wrote, in a 1952 opinion, that we are a religious people whose institutions presuppose a Supreme Being."

Millie knew that to be true.

"But the courts have systematically removed that central tenet from public life. It is the crux of the Declaration of Independence. This country was founded on the belief that our rights come from the Creator."

This was a familiar argument, though Millie had not heard it for some time. "What Jefferson meant by that has long been debated."

"Debated by those who don't wish to acknowledge its truth," Holden said. "And when people say, well, it's just an appeal to reason in deistic terms, that betrays an ignorance of the rest of the document."

"How so?"

"In the last paragraph, Jefferson says America is appealing its cause to the Supreme Judge of the world. Capital S, capital J. And he asserts in the last line that the country is relying on the protection of Divine Providence. Capital D, capital P. No one then, absolutely no one, could have doubted that this was the God of the Bible. Now fast forward to 1980, and the Court holds that public schools cannot post the Ten Commandments. Does that make sense?"

"The development of Establishment Clause jurisprudence, as you know—"

"Forget the legal jargon. Does it *make sense*?"

"With all due respect, First Amendment law is not jargon. And how can you possibly know if God is weaving anything?"

"I can't know for certain," Holden said. "But I'm willing to make you bet."

"Bet?"

"Friendly, of course. Are you game?"

The hum of the car filled the silence between them. Millie said, "What's the bet?"

"That God is not going to let you off the hook."

Millie felt a jab to her insides, as if the car had hit a bump. But it hadn't. "I don't want to be on anybody's hook, thank you. Nor do I wish to be a thread in some cosmic pattern. I just want to . . ."

Silence. What *did* she want? If nothing else, to get back to work. This desert communion was starting to unnerve her.

CHAPTER NINE

1

Millie jerked to consciousness and for a moment did not know where she was. Or the time.

The phone. It rang again.

Her mother's house, of course. Her head throbbing, Millie scrambled off the sofa—now she remembered falling asleep there last night—and made it to the kitchen by the fourth ring.

"Justice Hollander?"

"Yes?"

"Hold for the president."

President?

"Hello, Justice Hollander?" She heard the familiar Bostonian accent of the leader of the free world.

"Yes, sir."

"John Francis."

She knew that! "Yes, sir."

"How you doing out there in the Golden State?"

He couldn't know the half of it. "Fine."

"Feeling better, are you?"

"Almost as good as new."

167

"Great to hear it."

She sat down to steady her nerves. She knew what was coming next, and felt oddly ambivalent about it. What a time to feel that way!

"I'm going to send you up as my pick for chief justice," Francis said. "I don't think that's a shock to you."

It wasn't, but it felt the same. "I am ... honored, Mr. President."

"Well, you deserve it. You've been rock solid on the Court for ten years, and it's about time we had a woman in charge of things over there. When will you be coming back to Washington?"

"I don't really know."

"All right. We'll do some prep with you for the hearings, but those will just be going through the motions. You'll have the usual conservative outrage, but we have the majority on the committee and in the Senate. *No problemo*, as they say down in Mexico."

Millie closed her eyes. She was talking to the president of the United States. He was telling her she was going to be the chief justice. It was a waking dream.

"You do want the job, don't you?" Francis added.

God is not going to let you off the hook.

Holden's words bounced off the walls of her mind. She gritted her teeth against them. "Oh, yes, sir. Of course I do." That had not changed. This opportunity was the culmination of everything she had worked for. What was changing, though she didn't yet know how, was *her*. Surely getting back to Washington, back into the swing of things, would settle her down.

"Excellent," Francis said. "Everything is falling into place nicely. The most important thing is that we keep our slim majority on the Court."

"Sir, I—"

"I know, I know. Ethics and all that. That's why you're the right person for the job. Now I have to go do a little soft shoe for the Sultan of Brunei. Nice talking to you, Chief. Congratulations."

He hung up before she could say thank you.

She sat in amazed silence until the phone signal angrily told her to hang up. It had finally happened. The big dream she had dared to dream back in law school. *Chief Justice Millicent Mannings Hollander.*

Her body suddenly felt renewed. No miracle healing here, just a heightened sense of physical well-being.

She made coffee. It was nearly nine, and Jack Holden would be coming over soon to drive her to the hospital.

She had just stirred some cream into her coffee when the phone rang again. The president calling her back?

"Justice Hollander?"

"Yes?"

"Dr. Weinstein." His voice was low, and Millie's entire body tensed. "Are you coming up here?"

"Yes, what is it?"

"I'm so sorry," he said.

2

As she passed through the rail at the front of the courtroom, Charlene saw Beau Winsor talking to someone who hadn't been in the courtroom before. At first she thought he must be an associate from Winsor & Grimes, but then the face suddenly became familiar. It wasn't quite the same as it looked on TV.

Winsor saw Charlene and motioned her over. "Charlene, do you know Larry Graebner?"

Graebner smiled and stuck out his hand. Charlene shook it.

Lawrence I. Graebner. Here. She knew he had been advising on this case. But she never thought he would make an appearance. Why would he? He wasn't a trial lawyer. He was the brain. And if Charlene prevailed, he would be the counsel on appeal.

Why was he here today?

"I hear you've been giving Beau all he can handle," Graebner said with the ribbing lawyers sometimes threw at their opponents.

"I hope so," Charlene said.

Winsor said nothing. Charlene could almost smell the power, mixed with a generous dose of testosterone. They were two of the keenest legal minds in the country. And they were against her.

When Judge Lewis entered the courtroom and called the case, he smiled faintly at Graebner. And then it hit her. Lewis and Graebner had been classmates at Yale.

"Is the defense ready to proceed?" Lewis asked.

"We are, Your Honor," Winsor said. "May I state for the record the appearance of Lawrence I. Graebner, who will be arguing the motion this morning."

Motion? Charlene had not received anything in writing.

"Very well," Lewis said. "It's a privilege to have you here, Professor Graebner."

"I thank the court," Graebner said.

Charlene watched the judge's face closely, searching for bias.

"We are moving for a directed verdict," Graebner said.

Was that all? Motions for directed verdict were *pro forma*, nothing else. The defense always made such motions at the close of the plaintiff's case. They were hardly ever granted. The moving party would have to show that, taking the evidence and all reasonable inferences in the light most favorable to the opposing party, a reasonable jury could not reach a verdict favorable to the opponent.

In other words, looking at everything Charlene had presented in the best possible light, Judge Lewis would have to rule that the jury could not possibly rule in her favor. It was a virtually impossible burden to meet.

But then again, Larry Graebner was arguing. He wouldn't have flown down here unless he had some reason to believe the motion would be granted.

"As we all know," Graebner continued, "motions for directed verdict have a very heavy burden to overcome. And that well should be, for if it were easy the right to a trial by jury would be undermined."

Pausing, Graebner slipped his thumbs into his vest pockets. It was the homey pose of the country lawyer, but Graebner, speaking without notes, did it naturally.

"On the other hand, Your Honor, the proper separation of powers is likewise undermined when a jury is charged to decide that which is not authorized by law. In this case, a law duly enacted by the legislature of this state. Such an occurrence would be the death knell of the little experiment we call democracy."

He was the Yale law professor now, the classroom pundit. Judge Lewis appeared to be entranced by his classmate.

Classmate. Charlene stood up. "Your Honor . . ."

Every head, it seemed, whipped her way, every eye throwing darts.

"Miss Moore," Judge Lewis snapped, "you will have your chance."

"Your Honor, I have a small point to make before we take up more of the court's time."

"I would like to finish," Graebner said, his voiced tinged with professional impatience.

"Your Honor," Charlene said, "would it not be proper to recuse yourself from this?"

Charlene thought she saw red blotches break out on Lewis's face. "Recuse myself? What possible basis do you have for this objection?"

"With all due respect," Charlene said, "Professor Graebner and you were classmates at Yale. Might there be the appearance of bias in this?"

"Your request is denied," Lewis said. "I am able to weigh the merits of this argument in an objective fashion, and your attempt to influence the court is duly noted for the record."

"I have the right to—"

"Sit down, Miss Moore. You may address the court when Mr. Graebner is finished speaking."

What have you done this time, Charlene? Alienated the judge before he has ruled on the motion. Great move.

Graebner made a grand motion of gratitude to the judge. "I thank the court. I'm sure Miss Moore meant no offense."

By which, of course, he meant she did.

"As I was saying, our democratic form of government must never be undermined by the usurpation of power by any branch against another. What I fear happening here, Your Honor, is that very thing.

"If we take all of the evidence in the light most favorable to the plaintiff, what have we got? A young girl enters a family planning facility seeking an abortion. The clinic, which has been in operation many years, follows to the letter the informed consent law that has been promulgated by the legislature."

"Isn't that the issue here?" Lewis said. "Whether the clinic indeed followed the letter and the spirit of the law?"

"No indeed, Your Honor. The spirit of the law is not for you or a jury to decide. The legislature alone must define the law, within the text. It has done so, in quite specific terms. It provided a document to the plaintiff, which the plaintiff signed."

"What about duress, or incompetence?" Lewis said.

"There is nothing in the statute about any such matters," Graebner said. "Indeed, if one looks at the legislative history, the chief concern of the legislators was to keep those sorts of matters from ever becoming an issue. It made the text of the statute clear. Nor does the history say anything about mental health concerns. In short, Your Honor, this case never should have reached this stage. For a cause of action such as this, the legislature may amend the statute. But a trial court may not."

Graebner waited for the court to ask him a question. Lewis seemed deep in thought. Then he said, "Thank you, Mr. Graebner. Miss Moore?"

"I hardly know where to begin," Charlene said. "I believe we have presented enough evidence for the jury to consider this case. Professor Graebner talks about the right to a trial by jury, but in the next breath seeks to take that away from my client."

"But your client," said the judge, "must have a basis upon which to make this claim."

Then why had the judge allowed her to get to this point? This matter should have been considered before trial. Or had Winsor and Graebner been waiting to sandbag her?

"The basis is the common sense application of the will of the legislature," Charlene said. "It is clear they want all women who are about to make one of the most important decisions of their lives to have all the information they need. That would include, naturally, an inquiry into mental health history."

Lewis shook his head. "But as Professor Graebner says, that is not in the statute. Does this court have the power to give the jury something that the legislature has decided, to this point at least, it should not consider?"

This was like tag-team wrestling, only it was Graebner and Lewis against Charlene. "I appeal to Your Honor, in view of all that we have been through, the time and expense to my client, to the court, to the jurors, that you not dismiss this case. Rule, Your Honor, on the basis of fundamental fairness. Justice is also in the hands of a trial court in its discretion. Mr. Winsor and Professor Graebner can take the matter up on appeal if they lose."

"You have the same prerogative," Lewis said.

Yes, but not the same pockets. Not the same unlimited funds.

"I urge Your Honor to allow the case to continue to verdict," Charlene said, unable to hide the desperation in her voice.

Judge Lewis looked at the clock. "I will take the matter under advisement. The court will recess until one-thirty."

Sarah Mae was shaking as she took Charlene's arm. "What's that mean?"

"We'll know at one-thirty, Sarah Mae." But Charlene had a sick feeling that she already knew.

3

Millie stood in an empty space in the hospital parking lot. She herself was empty. Only a dull reverberation inside her reminded her she was alive, but it was a distant sound—a fading echo, like the rolling of thunder after it has crossed the valley. She held her tears back; it was not easy. Her mother was gone. And Millie had not been there when she died.

Jack Holden, who had been silent beside her, finally said, "I am so sorry."

Millie nodded, wishing he would go away and knowing he wouldn't, wondering if she was grateful or not, finally deciding she didn't care one way or the other.

"There's an old saying," Holden added, "they don't say it much anymore, but it seems so appropriate for your mother. She's gone to her reward."

Millie shook her head.

"That's what she believed with all her heart," Holden said.

"I don't care to hear it."

"I think she would want you to know."

She turned to him. He seemed, somehow, not real. A mannequin. "It's so easy to say." She hadn't meant to be nasty, but it helped in one small way. It dulled the grief, if only for a second or two.

"Not always," he said.

"I don't want to be comforted right now, okay?" she said. "I know it's your job, and you're good at it, but just, for now ..."

"You'll need help—"

"I know what I need! Yes, you can do the funeral. Of course. Take care of it. Make it happen. This week. I'll hire a lawyer to take care of the estate. I'm not going to stay here. After the funeral, I'm going home. Thank you very much for everything."

Jack Holden did not leave her alone. "It helps to talk."

"I already did. Please."

He turned toward the hospital. She felt a little guilt, but only a little. She did not want to feel anything. She wanted to shout at Jack Holden, ask him why God did not answer prayer, and was this the killer argument he had to offer? Where was his music now?

She hated herself, but did not care. Hate dulled grief, too. But only for a moment. The waves were too big. Grief was not a stream. It was an ocean.

4

The usual afternoon crowd was in License, the hot upscale bar in D.C. that had become a regular hangout for Anne. She knew most of the faces at the zinc-topped bar, and they certainly knew hers. She could smell the envy in the air. It was as thick as L.A. smog, and twice as toxic. She had come here to meet Cosmo.

Jill "Cosmo" Hannigan was so named by Anne because she looked like the quintessential *Cosmopolitan* cover model. Impossibly skinny, but dressed to show off her assets without apology. She was an associate at a D.C. firm specializing in international contracts.

Usually she was perfect company for Anne, a picker-upper for tired spirits. Cosmo had a biting sense of humor, almost a match for Anne's. Getting tipsy with her was one of the pleasures of Anne's life.

Now, sitting over her Tanqueray martini—up, with a twist—Cosmo was uncharacteristically down.

"What's going on?" Anne asked. "You seem a little out of it."

Cosmo looked up from her drink. "I was in the kitchenette at the office on Friday. One of the partners came in, Mr. Baer. Does that name mean anything to you?"

"No."

"It should. He's about sixty, and he's been a player in the firm for thirty years."

"Wait, wasn't he one of the Clinton lawyers in the Paula Jones thing?"

"He's the guy. Well, anyway, we're alone in the kitchenette. He comes in, and his tie is loose. But Baer's tie is never loose. He's always perfectly dressed. He had this faraway look on his face, too. I say hello to him, and he doesn't look me in the eye. He doesn't say hello. What he says is, 'What am I doing?'"

"And you said what?"

"I asked him if he was looking for something. That's when he looks at me and says, 'What am I doing here, in this office? I should be with my family.' And then he walks out."

Anne shrugged. "So, the guy spends too much time at the office. Big deal. He goes home, buys his wife dinner, all is well."

Cosmo said, "No. He hasn't got a family. His wife divorced him years ago. His grown kids hardly talk to him. That was the freaky part."

"Why freaky?"

"Just that he was thinking out loud, like he had regrets or something."

"Middle-aged angst."

"No, it was more than that. It was like he was calling everything he'd done into question. But as long as I've known him, he's never had any doubts. Always hard driving, hard charging, great at what he does. It got to me. Because the way I'm going, that's where I'll be someday. And I don't want to have the same regrets."

"You won't."

Cosmo reached out and squeezed Anne's arm, hard. "I'm not sure! That's what gets me. What happens when it's all over? Who cares about what we did? Why should we do anything?"

"Look, I thought about that once. When my folks died I had a couple of days there. But I got over it. You just have to keep moving so they can't hit you. And there are no answers. Life is pretty much absurd. The existentialists had it right. So what do you do? You just do your own deal, that's all. It's a game, and you try to win."

"What is winning, though? That's what I'm asking."

"It's just what it is. Getting what you want before the other guy gets it."

"And then what?"

"Man, you're cheery today. Did you watch *Old Yeller* or something?"

"No," Cosmo said. "I went to church."

Anne almost slipped off the bar seat. "You did *what*?"

"I just wanted to go," Cosmo said. "I hadn't been since I was a girl."

"So what did you find out, Joan?"

"Joan?"

"Of Arc."

"Very funny."

"I'm in a funny mood. What church was it?"

"Methodist. Down the street from me."

"So? Did you get saved or what?"

"I just listened. I listened to the singing. I listened to the words of the songs."

"Hymns. They're called hymns."

"I know that. And I listened to the sermon. I don't know, I just felt like doing that."

"Please," Anne said, "don't go crazy on me. You're my best friend."

"Then why can't I talk about this?"

"Finish your drink," Anne said. "This calls for a rich dinner and gooey dessert. Wanna?"

Cosmo thought about it, then smiled. "You drive."

At least they laughed out on the street, where Anne had parked her red Audi. It was martini laughter, light and funny, and it got them off of all that heavy stuff they'd been talking about. Anne was almost teary eyed with Cosmo's imitation of Rosie O'Donnell when her laughter stopped cold.

Standing right next to her car was the homeless guy. The one who had looked at her on her balcony.

His dirty beard and face were unmistakable. And he was looking at her again, like he'd been expecting her.

"What?" Cosmo said. Then she turned and saw the guy, too.

"You got some spray?" Cosmo whispered.

Anne reached into her purse and put her fingers around the little canister of mace. Cosmo said, "Let's go back inside, then come out again."

The homeless man said, "You work for him, don't you? You work for Senator Levering."

His voice was remarkably clear. Not the guttural sound one associated with denizens of the street.

Anne stood as if cemented.

"You do, don't you?" the man repeated. He took a step forward.

"Stay there," Anne ordered. She brought the mace out. Maybe he'd see it. She felt no hesitation about spraying him in the face.

"You still have time," the man said.

"What's he talking about?" Cosmo said.

"How do I know?" Anne said.

"How does he know you?"

Good question. He took another step. Anne sized him up. He could be taken down. Easy. But how *did* he know her?

"Listen to me," the man said. "It's not too late." He took two steps now.

"Back off," Anne said.

The man did not stop. He walked slowly but steadily toward her. His face, dirty as it was, was pleading with her.

"Do you hear me?" the man said. "It's not too late!"

"I said back off." Anne held the mace ready, and with her other arm reached out for Cosmo.

"Let's go," Cosmo said.

But Anne was mesmerized, like a bird in front of a snake. She felt her hands trembling.

"Not too late!" the man said, and charged.

The next few seconds were like a slow-motion dance with death. Later, Anne would think that the face of the man was more horrifying to her than anything she had ever seen in any nightmare or horror movie. But it wasn't because the face was grotesque—in fact, it was a reasonably pleasant face. No, it was what she saw in his eyes that terrified her. They burned with such intense focus, looking into her, as if he knew her better than she knew herself.

In those few seconds, though, she had no time to reflect, only to react. She pressed on the nozzle.

Nothing happened.

The man was now so close she could smell him. She heard Cosmo scream.

She depressed the nozzle once more, and this time an acrid hiss of mace spray shot out. The jolt hit the man full in the face.

He screamed. His hands shot to his eyes. He gouged at them wildly. He dropped to his knees and screamed again.

Anne grabbed Cosmo's arm and pulled her around the man crying on the sidewalk. By the time they drove away in Anne's car, a small crowd had gathered around the homeless man. She glanced quickly at the scene and saw someone in the crowd pointing at her car.

4

Charlene took Sarah Mae's trembling hand in her own. They stood as the judge entered, then sat at counsel table when he called the proceedings to order. He had not asked for the jury.

"Back on the record in *Sherman v. National Parental Planning Group*," Judge Lewis said. "I have given due consideration to the arguments of counsel in this matter. I find both to have made excellent points."

Excellent? Charlene thought. *Even her?* There was hope. She had a very small burden to carry in order to defeat the motion.

"I have spent the last two hours poring over the legislative history of the informed consent statute," Lewis said. "And while there is plenty of ambiguity about the intentions of the drafters, there was a very clear consensus about what this statute was supposed to accomplish. While it was meant to give a certain amount of added information to a class of people, namely women seeking abortion, it was also clearly intended to provide a barrier in the area of litigation."

Lewis paused and looked at Charlene. His look made her stomach drop.

He was *preparing* her.

"And while this court believes strongly in the jury as finders of fact, I am mindful of my role as the interpreter of the law. In that capacity, I find I am in agreement with the argument of counsel for the defense."

Charlene's heart joined her stomach in free fall.

"Therefore, the defense motion for a directed verdict is granted. The case is dismissed."

For a moment silence prevailed. Then Winsor was standing, hugging Graebner and a representative of the NPPG. They slapped each other on the back.

Then she heard Aggie Sherman's anguished, angry wail. Sarah Mae's mother slammed her hands down on the railing and shouted, "No!"

Charlene took a step toward her to comfort her, but Aggie pointed directly at her and screamed, "You stay away from us!"

A bailiff rushed over and warned Aggie to quiet down. Sarah Mae slumped in her chair. Charlene stood clamped to the floor, unable to move, watching the aftermath of the destruction of her world.

But worst of all was not what the decision meant for her. No, she could somehow recover from this. The worst thing was seeing Sarah Mae's head fall into her hands and her small, girlish body begin to shake.

Charlene put a hand on her shoulder. Almost immediately she felt a hand on her own. Aggie was pulling Charlene away. "Don't touch her," she said.

"Please—"

"No! Sarah Mae, come along. Now."

Helpless, Charlene watched as Aggie yanked Sarah Mae up like a sack of linens. Sarah Mae's eyes flashed at Charlene, a mix of confused emotions Charlene could not read. Following her mother through the railing, Sarah Mae Sherman disappeared from view, and for all Charlene knew, from her life.

She fought back tears. She would not cry, not here. But she longed for someone to talk to.

Anyone except Beau Winsor. He offered his hand to her. "Don't feel too bad," he said. "There will be other fights."

Charlene opened her mouth, and there it stayed. Open and without speech.

"You're young. You're talented. Ever think of joining a firm?"

Slowly Charlene shook her head.

"Give me a call. Let me take you to lunch."

All she could do was shake her head.

Winsor said, "If you change your mind . . ." And then he nodded and walked away.

Larry Graebner also offered his hand, and Charlene felt compelled to take it.

"I'd consider his offer," Graebner said. "It's a good one."

"This isn't over," Charlene said weakly. "I'll file an appeal."

Graebner glanced at the courtroom doors. "If you do, and you lose, our position will become precedent in this circuit. Would you want that?"

"Has it occurred to you we might *win* on appeal?"

"It really hadn't," Graebner said. "But anything's possible." Larry Graebner smiled. "Good luck, Ms. Moore. You did a fine job."

CHAPTER TEN

1

Millie was beginning to hate the word *hope*. Jack Holden had used it several times already in the eulogy. And each time he said it, she heard a few mumbled "amens" behind her. She felt herself wanting to sear these people with a *don't you understand?* look.

Hope was in the casket, about to be buried. The hope that she would get more time with her mother. The hope that had been waved in front of her when her mother had managed to talk to her at the hospital.

"'Therefore, since we have been justified through faith'"— Holden was reading, and she heard the words as if outside the building—"'we have peace with God through our Lord Jesus Christ, through whom we have gained access by faith into this grace in which we now stand. And we rejoice in the hope of the glory of God.'"

This was how her mother would have wanted her funeral, and for that she could endure it. But not the word *hope* anymore. Please.

"'And hope does not disappoint us, because God has poured out his love into our hearts by the Holy Spirit, whom he has given us.'"

More amens. Holden had asked her if she wanted to say a few words, and she had declined. What did she have to say to these people? She was an outsider. She had once been one of them, but she had left long ago. In body and in spirit.

She dutifully stayed for the meal that had been prepared by several in the congregation. She dutifully shook hands and received condolences. She dutifully said what needed to be said without sounding rude.

They were good people, and they had been her mother's family. Millie hated the way she felt about them now. She was jealous—of the times they'd had with Ethel that Millie had not. Her smile felt forced. But she smiled. Mom would have wanted it that way.

She was grateful for the job Jack Holden had done. But she was also jealous of *him*. He had had time with her mother, too.

He approached her at the back of the fellowship hall, where Millie had sought some respite from talk.

"You'll be going back to D.C. soon?" he asked.

"Two days," Millie said.

"May I say something?"

"Of course."

"Even though the circumstances are not the best, it's been good to talk with you. You know. About all the things we talked about."

"My mother thought highly of you," she said. "You were a great comfort to her."

"You have her qualities."

"I wish." Ethel Hollander was so unlike her daughter. Or was it the other way around?

"I'll be here if you need anything," Holden said. "Arrangements with the house, that sort of thing."

"I appreciate it."

"And I'll be praying for you."

She felt a scream welling up inside her. It did not issue, but the pressure was intense. "Why wasn't I there?" she said suddenly. Loudly. "Why wasn't I with her?" She wanted to grab Holden's shirt and shake him, shame him out of his assurances, force him to join her in guilt and doubt.

Her mother was *gone*. There would be no more words. Ever.

2

Anne was starting her second espresso when she heard a knock. She looked through the peephole and saw an African American man in a sharp brown suit looking directly at her.

"Ms. Deveraux?" he said.

He must have been waiting for the light to change in the hole when she put her eye to it. She still didn't say anything.

"Detective Markey, D.C. police," he said. "Can I have a moment of your time?"

Police? "No," Anne said. She watched him through the fish-eye glass.

"Are you refusing to speak to me?" he asked.

"Yes."

"That is quite unusual."

"I'm busy. Slip your card under the door. I'll call you."

"It concerns your boss."

Anne paused, then thought she'd better get this over with. If he had something on Levering, she had better get it.

"Let me see the badge," she said. Markey held his shield to the lens. Anne unlocked the door.

"Careful, aren't you?" Markey said, stepping inside.

"You have no idea," Anne said. "I'm in a hurry. Can you make this quick?"

"Certainly. You had a run-in with a man yesterday."

"The homeless guy? He reported it? I can't believe this. He was ..."

"He was what, Ms. Deveraux?"

"He was approaching me in a menacing way."

"So you maced him?"

"That's why I carry it. Is this some major case? The guy want money?"

"The guy you took down is a street person. They call him Elijah."

"Who does?"

"The other street people."

"Okay, so his name's Elijah. What do you want from me?"

Markey said, "Well, Elijah is not someone unfamiliar to us. We've talked to him before."

"About?"

"Your boss."

Anne blinked, feeling very annoyed. She'd been around cops many times, for various reasons, and usually got what she wanted from them. Now this guy thought he could play detective with her, like he was in some bad HBO movie, doing the cat-and-mouse thing. Anne did not do mouse.

"Detective," she said, "I've got a full schedule. Just give me the whole thing in one gulp, and let's get on with it."

"Where was Senator Levering on the night of June fourteen?"

Anne felt her throat clenching. "Why?"

"Do you know where he was?"

"Senator Levering has a busy schedule."

"You know his schedule, you probably tell him where to go and when. You troubleshoot. All the usual stuff. It wouldn't be hard for you to check your book, or your palm thing, whatever it is you keep a calendar on."

"Detective, I'm not inclined to check anything until I know the relevance. And what does any of this have to do with that guy on the street?"

Markey said, "You assaulted a witness."

"Witness?"

"You remember that on June fourteenth, Justice Hollander was hit by a car?"

"Of course. Everybody knows." Anne tried to keep her voice even.

"She was with someone right before it happened but won't say who."

"So? Maybe she wants to save a friend embarrassment or something."

"Like the senator?"

Anne swallowed. "Come on."

"About a week after it happened I got a call from the desk that somebody wanted to talk about the accident. Somebody who was probably nuts. It was a slow morning, so I took it. Turned out to be our friend Elijah. And he had a very interesting story to tell."

"A street person," Anne said, making it sound as ridiculous as possible.

"That's what I was saying to myself. He said he was out by the Lincoln Memorial when he saw Senator Levering with a woman in some sort of wrestling hold, and then the woman ran off. He followed the woman. And he saw what happened."

"Wait a minute here. Are you trying to tell me some street bozo sees Senator Levering in the dark and can identify him?"

"Who said it was dark?"

Anne put her hands on her hips. "I'm assuming."

"I try never to do that. "

"Still, you're taking this guy seriously? Where's the credibility?"

"You're right. We didn't take him seriously. He had kind of an odd way about him, you know, that crazy kind of look."

"That's what I'm saying."

"But then yesterday, somebody sprayed Elijah. A witness wrote down the license plate number of the person who did it. The guy in dispatch who ran the plates crossed it in the computer with Elijah, and sent it to me. So now it looks like Senator Levering's number-one aide sprayed mace at a potential witness, one who IDed the senator. Suddenly, I'm interested again."

This isn't happening, Anne told herself. The potential damage was huge. "Senator Levering was not out wrestling with Justice Millicent Mannings Hollander," she said. "That much I can tell you. But even if he was, why are the D.C. police interested? Would that be a crime?"

"Maybe."

"That's not what this is about, is it?" Take the offensive. "It's about some low-grade detective trying to notch a prominent politician."

He looked at her evenly.

"I've seen this before," Anne said. "You're not kidding anybody. So why don't you go get some real bad guys for a change?"

"You are not being very cooperative. It would help your own situation, you know."

"I don't think I follow you."

"You maced a guy. That's an assault, too."

Anne felt frozen in place, as if a police officer had asked her to assume the position. "You cannot be serious."

"I'm afraid I am, Ms. Deveraux," Markey said.

"Then you can contact my lawyer. Our interview is over."

Markey took out a pad. "Who is your lawyer?"

Anne glared at him. "You're the detective. You find out."

3

Aggie Sherman angrily shook her head. "You shouldn't of come here."

Charlene stood in the doorway of what could only be described as a shack. A bare yellow lightbulb on the porch gave a strange circular glow in the night. Facing Aggie Sherman through the screen door, Charlene looked past the huge mosquitoes hovering around the mesh and said, "Please. I need to say something."

"Say nothin'. You lost us a load of money and we don't need to hear you say any more! Now get off my porch afore somebody sees you."

"I need you to forgive me," Charlene said.

In the long silence that ensued, Charlene felt as much as heard the din of the cicadas in the night. What would be her fate? Thumbs-up or thumbs-down? Then Aggie Sherman wordlessly unlatched the screen door and opened it.

"Thank you," Charlene whispered as she stepped inside.

"Just so you know," Aggie said, "Sarah Mae's been crying ever since we got back here."

Charlene's heart cracked. "I'm so sorry."

"Sit down then."

Charlene sat down on the sagging brown sofa. Aggie lit a cigarette and sat opposite Charlene in a faded recliner. "You like my place?" Aggie asked with bitter sarcasm.

"It reminds me a little of the place I grew up in," Charlene said.

A look of curiosity came to Aggie's face. "That right?"

"We didn't have much," Charlene said. "We had each other. Same way you have Sarah Mae."

"That's all I got. That girl. I wanted better for her than this. Her daddy run out on us when she's ten year old. You think that don't hit a child?"

"I know it does," Charlene said, remembering her own father. The warmth she felt in his arms, the security. That Sarah Mae was denied this hit Charlene personally. This whole matter was hitting her personally. That was why she was sitting here.

"That's why I wanted that settlement money," Aggie Sherman said. "Look at this place, will you?"

Charlene took a deep breath. "I talked you into going forward with the case. I told you God wanted us to do it. I made you believe you would get more money if we kept going. I did that because I wanted to win this case. I hate what happened to Sarah Mae. I wanted to win for her. But I also wanted to win for me."

Aggie Sherman sat silently behind thin wisps of smoke.

"I got to thinking I was God's special woman," Charlene continued. "I guess I found out I'm not so special. I could have had help on this case, there were groups that offered, but I wanted to do it alone. I wanted to be the one who did it, who won it all, and then maybe the people who told me I'd never make a good lawyer would see me. But I failed to be a good lawyer. A good lawyer looks out for her clients first and always, and that's why I came here tonight."

Aggie took a puff on her cigarette and brushed some ashes off her lap. "You tried," she said. "No one's takin' that away from you."

"I've been on my knees asking God what to do, and all I keep hearing is that I need to be broken. I need to get myself out of the way. But I don't need to quit, either."

"What's that mean?" Aggie said.

"An appeal."

Aggie Sherman shook her head. "Can't afford it."

"I wouldn't ask you to pay anything."

"You'd do that for us?"

"Yes," Charlene said.

Aggie Sherman looked at Charlene, long and hard. Outside, the moan of a cat sounded like a creaking door.

"I hated you," Aggie said. "I hated that you made me want more money. And I hated you cause you're black and we needed your help. Guess I need forgiveness, too."

Charlene Moore had heard the word *grace* countless times in church. But she knew at that moment that she had never fully understood it. And the feeling that she had let God down, let Aggie and Sarah Mae down, gave way to a sense that, at last, God's will might truly be done in her life. She did not know how, could not see it yet, but she trusted it would be. And she was ready for it. For maybe the first time in her life, she was really ready for God's will to be done.

4

Anne Deveraux could tell Senator Levering was in a foul mood. Really on edge. His drinking was not doing him any good, either, but Anne was not a nursemaid. She was a highly paid aide, and as long as he was well enough to authorize her checks, she'd let him do what he wanted with his personal life.

"This Unborn Victims Act they're trying to get to the floor," Levering said the instant Anne sat down. "It could be dangerous. They think they get that language in, *unborn child*, then they have ammo to go back to the Supreme Court and overturn *Roe*."

"That bill won't pass," Anne said. "Let's be realistic."

"I'm just tired of dealing with it. I've got some crazy minister back home on his radio show calling me a Nazi. After all I've done for the state! You know how that grates? I work my whole life for the rights of women and children and the poor. And this is what I get for my troubles. So, please, have some good news for me."

A vein stood out in Levering's forehead. Anne looked at it with fascination. It did not look healthy.

"Sorry my news isn't better," Anne said.

Levering rubbed his head, reached into a drawer, and pulled out the largest bottle of Bayer aspirin she had ever seen. "All right, let's have it. Is it a report on Hollander?"

"Not exactly," Anne said.

"What does that mean?"

"It has to do with your little tryst."

Levering stared at her, then popped a couple of Bayer in his mouth and downed them with a glass of water.

Anne waited until his eyes returned to hers. "The cops have a witness," she said.

Levering's face screwed into disbelief. "Of what?"

"You and Justice Hollander doing a dance number by the Lincoln Memorial."

"Who is this witness?"

"That's the only good part of this. He's a street person. But . . ."

"But what?"

"I had a little run-in with this guy."

"Run in?"

"I sprayed mace in his face."

Levering's disbelief morphed into something like shock. "Let me get this straight. You sprayed a police witness, someone who says he saw me with Justice Hollander?"

"It was a total coincidence. I can't explain it. The odds have to be astronomical. But it happened, and there's a detective who's got starch in his underwear over it. He questioned me; he's probably going to want to question you next."

The senator stood up, his face looking beefier than usual. Part of it was the stark light of the office. The other part was his obvious pique. Anne readied herself for a diatribe.

Levering paced to the window, looked out at the dull Washington day, and then turned back to Anne. "How bad is this?"

A wave of relief washed over Anne. He was in damage control mode, and she was his machinery. Things were getting back to normal.

"Worst case the press picks it up, gets this guy to talk to them," Anne said. "They play it up from some sort of sympathetic angle. Here's a lowly street person and one of the most powerful men in the country. Then they press you to affirm or deny, you deny, and they get to your driver, or this Helen Forbes Kensington, and one of them cracks. Then you've got a situation where everybody knows you're lying to the cops and the country."

"Great," Levering said. "For a moment I thought it was bad."

Anne waited for instructions. She had a few ideas of her own, but wanted to get the word from the senator first. Give him a feeling of being in control.

Silence stretched on. Levering became motionless at the window, his back to Anne. He kept his hands clasped behind him, his fingers wiggling as if to indicate brain function. Then, without turning around, he said, "We're sure he's homeless?"

"Yeah."

"If we went further with this, what would be the downside?"

Anne knew what he meant. Early on in their association, when they were dancing around each other, testing limits, they had come to a meeting of minds. Levering's goal was the presidency, and no effort would be spared in his getting there. Any obstacle would be removed. The only limitation would be the downside risk.

The means for dealing with situations beyond the norm had never been explicitly stated. Anne had been the one to suggest they base their relationship on "plausible deniability." Levering would never issue directives that could later come back to haunt him. Anne would be given a free hand, so long as Levering didn't know the details.

What surprised Anne at the time was how easily they both had accepted the parameters.

Anne calmly replied, "The cops know this guy is a potential witness against you. On the other hand, he isn't much of one. It's a really weak case. I don't think the public would buy it."

"But there's a chance," Levering said. "I mean, I've got a little bit of a reputation in that area."

Boy howdy. "This guy might take off, hit the road. They're not going to hold him."

"How do we convince a crazy homeless person to leave town?"

"I'll handle the details."

"Right," he said. "I don't want to know anything specific."

"Of course," Anne said. Then she added, "When you get to the White House, you will need a chief of staff."

Levering smiled wryly at her. "You have anyone in mind?"

"Maybe."

He nodded. "You make this little problem go away, and the job is yours."

5

The plane rose into fog, a gray netherworld. Millie took a deep breath and looked out the window.

In so many ways this day should have been a relief. She'd spent precious hours with her mother, seen her before she died. That wouldn't have happened if she hadn't had her accident. And she was going back to Washington to assume the job of a lifetime—chief justice of the Supreme Court.

So why the feeling that her whole life was about to change?

She put on the earphones the flight attendant had passed out earlier and clicked the dial until she got classical music. The recording was right in the middle of Beethoven's Symphony no. 9, *The Ode to Joy.*

She put her head back, letting the music wash over her. Then she looked outside again. Bright sunlight streamed through her window as the ascending plane topped the fog. Suddenly, there was clear sky, the bluest of blues, and soft clouds seen from above, like an angel's playing field.

The music swelled.

Inside her something opened up. There was a flooding in, an expansion, as if she were a sail filling with wind. And it terrified her.

She put her hands on the earphones, pressing them in, making the music even louder to her ears, as if she could crowd out all thought, all sensation.

But she could not. For one brief moment of almost unendurable intensity she felt like a door was opening, and thought she might go crazy.

PART
TWO

Whenever you put a man on the Supreme Court
he ceases to be your friend.

HARRY S. TRUMAN

CHAPTER ELEVEN

1

By mid September, Washington was buzzing again.

Anne Deveraux could feel it in the air, the way a ballplayer must feel when the new season is about to begin. Time to play hardball.

First order of business in the new season involved two games at once. One was keeping Dan Ricks, sleaze reporter, off balance. The other was using him for the essential information on Millicent Mannings Hollander. Her hearing before the Senate Judiciary Committee, which would vote on her nomination to be chief justice, was coming up. Should Hollander suddenly veer off her liberal course, she and Levering would be ready to leak embarrassing material.

So she was ready for the first pitch. But Ricks was late.

He had insisted on meeting her in the parking garage of the Marriott. He joked about it being like the scene in *All the President's Men*, that he was Deep Throat and she was Woodward and Bernstein. But Anne was convinced it was not really a joke with Ricks. He loved this cloak-and-dagger stuff.

He thought he was into big-time investigative journalism, when really he was a weasel in a coat and tie.

Anne checked her watch. 12:30. Lunchtime. That was the other absurdity about this. If he wanted to do the Deep Throat thing, why had he chosen the afternoon?

Maybe the guy was just nuts. But if he was any later, Anne was going to make sure he was dressed down, too.

She thought of calling Ambrosi, but remembered him telling her never to call him on his cell. She could understand. What if she got him while he was whacking some guy? *I thought I told you never to call me at the office!* Funny.

The stifling air smelled of gas and tires. Anne sat back in her car and listened to rock music. She closed her eyes and immediately heard a tap at the window.

It was Ricks.

"You took your sweet time," Anne said.

"Traffic," Ricks said. He was sweating. His forehead looked like it was speckled with rock salt.

Anne opened the door of her car and got out, making Ricks do a little backwards dance. "You could have called," she said.

"Hey, I'm here," he said, a little too aggressively for her taste. He held a ratty briefcase, the kind with a foldover flap. He opened it and pulled out a file folder. He did not immediately hand it to Anne. "You have something for me?" he asked.

"Anxious, aren't we?"

"Just doing business."

Anne reached in through the open window of her car and snatched an envelope. It was filled with cash. She had counted out the five thousand herself.

"Perfect," Ricks said, taking the envelope. He handed Anne the file.

"Detail me," she said.

"Everything's in there we talked about. I have a copy on disk."

"Copy?"

"Sure."

"You aren't supposed to have a copy of any of this. That wasn't part of the agreement."

"Way I remember it, we didn't have anything in writing."

"Writing? Listen, you work for me, you do what I tell you to do, you get paid, and you shut up."

"Hey—"

"This is for Senator Levering, not for your rag."

"We didn't say anything about that."

"It was understood."

"By you maybe."

Ricks had wet pit stains starting to show through his light brown coat. Anne thought she could smell him. Or was it exhaust fumes?

"This is extremely sensitive material," Anne said. "If any of it should get out without our authorization . . ."

"Not to worry, okay? Let's just call it insurance."

"Insurance?"

"Sure," Ricks said. "As long as we're all on the same page, I'm happy, you're happy."

Anne waited for him to say something else. Instead he smiled. She could not stand smugness, especially from a guy like Ricks. "Don't think you can mess with me," she said. "That wouldn't be very smart."

"Is that supposed to be a threat or something?" Ricks said.

"Gee, you *are* a good investigative reporter."

With a slight recoil, Ricks said, "I've been threatened by better people than you and your boss. I don't rattle."

Anne wondered if she should tell him about her boyfriend, about his way of rattling people. But no. Let it be a surprise if need be.

"Besides," Ricks said, "you need me."

"What would I need you for, Mr. Ricks?"

"I got poop that's a scoop. News you can use and won't make you snooze."

"Just what is it?"

"I get paid for my scoops, don't you remember?"

"Not interested."

"Okay," Ricks said. "I'll give you something because I like you, Anne. I see a little of me in you."

Anne almost gagged. "What have you got?"

"Oh, just a little something from Mr. Burrow."

That got Anne's attention. Biff Burrow was the owner and operator of the *Burrow Bulletin*, the Web's most popular political gossip site.

"You know Burrow?" Anne said.

"Know him? We are like two peas in a pot."

"Pod," Anne said.

"So you want to know what's up or not?"

"Go ahead."

"What's all this about a homeless man who saw your boss and Millicent Mannings Hollander doing a grope session?"

Anne told herself to stay cool. "Are you serious?"

"He asked me about it," Ricks said. "The cops ever question you about this?"

"No."

"Never?"

"Never."

"Why do I get the feeling you're holding out on me?"

"What's Burrow going to do with this information?"

"Nothing yet. He wants to talk to the guy himself. But the cops are not saying anything. And now you're not saying anything. Looks like a job for Superman." Ricks opened his coat, as if to display a giant S on his chest.

"This is so absurd," Anne said. "Burrow is crazy."

Ricks's teeth disappeared behind his lips. "Remember this," he said. "You owe me." He turned and walked away, almost bumping into a Mercedes. That would have left a stain, Anne thought. On the car.

2

The Judiciary Committee of the United States Senate convened on a hot September Monday in room 226 of the Dirksen

Senate Office Building. Millie sat at the witness table, alone, a solitary microphone in front of her. Beyond that, as if across a wide expanse of sea, sat the nineteen members of the committee. Behind her were the media and interested others, filling the austere chamber. A camera was set up behind Senator Hal Killian (D-Wisconsin). It would be the unforgiving eye that piped Millie's face across the country.

She tried not to look at it. Her hands, one on top of the other in front of her, trembled slightly. She breathed in and out, in and out. This was it, the last wall of fire she would have to walk through before becoming chief justice of the Supreme Court.

Committee chairman Sam Levering gaveled the proceedings to order at 10 A.M. He gave Millie a quick nod, just as if nothing had ever happened between them.

Levering read from a prepared statement.

"The Constitution empowers the president to nominate the chief justice of the United States, with the advice and consent of the Senate. That is clear-cut, straightforward language. It does not advise that the process become a protracted ordeal of unreasonable delay and unrelenting investigation. Yet somewhere along the way, Senate confirmations became lengthy, partisan, and unpleasant. They have done enough harm, and that must not happen again.

"I am very glad to welcome Associate Justice Millicent Mannings Hollander, nominated by the president to assume the chief justice position of our highest court. She has served the Supreme Court for ten years with distinction, and I can only hope that my colleagues will move quickly on this nomination. That would indeed be news."

Levering paused to smile for the cameras and the gallery. The ranking minority member, Senator Chuck Gelfan (R-Iowa), scowled. He was known as a relentless questioner with the sense of humor of a board. He had been on the committee during Millie's first hearing, ten years ago, and had thrown a number of verbal darts. She had managed to avoid them, but soon enough it would be round two. Gelfan looked like he couldn't wait.

"Justice Hollander has not prepared a statement," Levering said, "so I will begin by swearing in the witness."

Millie stood, raised her right hand, and was given a solemn oath by the man who had tried to grope her.

Levering began the questioning. "Good morning, Madame Justice."

"Good morning, Senator," Millie said.

"First," Levering began, "tell us how you're feeling. The entire country was concerned when you had that unfortunate accident."

Smooth as silk. Innocent as a lamb. Millie leaned forward a little. "I am doing quite well, thank you. Almost one hundred percent."

"That's great news. Just great. We all welcome you back to Washington."

Senator Gelfan glared at her.

"I have only a few questions," said Levering. "Your judicial philosophy is well known. As chief justice, will you remain the bedrock of common sense and decency you have always been?"

What was she going to say to that? *No, Senator, I plan on running a crap game behind the bench.* "I hope so, Senator."

"Will you continue to uphold the principles we hold dear?"

"I will always try to do so."

"Then I have no other questions," Levering said. "Senator Gelfan, you may proceed. I would like to remind my colleagues that we'll keep the questions to five minutes each this round."

The older senator picked up a paper and began to read what his staff had prepared for him. "Over the past three decades this country has seen an erosion of the dignity afforded human life, most specifically unborn human life. Madame Justice, will you continue to align yourself on the side of those who would allow the taking of unborn human life?"

A few groans came up from the gallery. Senator Levering winced. Millie had been expecting the question, but not her reaction. A sharp pain twisted inside her. Could the cameras see? She fought for calm.

"Senator Gelfan," Millie said, "as you know there are cases dealing with that issue that are, or will be, granted review. It would not be ethical for me to comment beforehand on how I might rule."

Gelfan lowered the paper and directed a choleric gaze at Millie. "This is a question of supreme importance to the majority of Americans. Don't you think they have a right to know what the next chief justice might have in mind?"

"Senator, what all Americans have a right to is an independent judiciary, free of political influence." That had come out sharply, and she was glad. A little fighting spirit to steady her nerves.

"Do you continue to believe the Court's decision in *Roe v. Wade* was rightly decided?"

"I . . ." She stopped suddenly, and there was that pain again. It stitched up from her stomach and burned to the top of her head.

"You were about to say?" Senator Gelfan said, like a cat pouncing on a wounded sparrow.

"My past decisions . . . are a matter of record."

"That's not what I asked you," Gelfan said. "My question was, as you sit here today, do you continue to believe that *Roe v. Wade* was decided correctly?"

"Senator . . ."

"It's a simple yes or no question, Justice Hollander."

Levering leaned into his microphone. "Point of order—"

Like an angry pit bull, Gelfan whirled on the chairman. "I am asking the questions—"

"Point of order!"

"—and I do not—"

"This is not an adversarial proceeding."

"—appreciate the interruption."

Millie sat back, feeling almost surreal, as if she were disembodied and given a seat in the gallery to watch this circus. But she was grateful for the slight pause.

"As chairman, I will have my say," Levering said. Gelfan leaned back in his chair, his weathered face pinched into a scowl.

"When my predecessor was in this chair," Levering said, referring to Gelfan, who was chairman when the Republicans controlled the Senate, "and certain nominees came before us, those of us on this side of the aisle were lectured, over and over again, not to ask questions on specific issues. Not to make these hearings into litmus tests. I now find it quite troubling that, with the shoe on the other foot, my good friend from Iowa wants to change this policy. I will make this short and sweet. Madame Justice, do you believe it would violate your oath and your ethics to answer specific questions about specific issues that may come before the Court?"

"Yes," Millie said. "I do believe that."

"Senator Gelfan," Levering said.

The Iowa senator was being handed a sheet of paper from an aide. He looked at Millie. "But you may answer questions about your judicial philosophy. That is *not* improper, is it?"

Millie took a deep breath. "With all due respect, Senator, my judicial philosophy is evident in my opinions."

"Then I will ask you this. Is that judicial philosophy evolving?"

"Evolving?"

"Changing in any way. Surely the American people have a right to know that."

Millie squinted into the lights. She had always been of the "living, breathing Constitution" school, the idea that changes in society mandated changes in how one viewed the law. For one thing, it sounded right. Who could be against flexibility when it came to justice?

But she was not unaware of the other side, the original intent argument, which said that unless one stuck close to the philosophy of the founders, judges would be free to change the laws according to their own preferences. Nevertheless, she had decided early on in her law studies that the latter school was impractical.

"I would hope," Millie said, "that any judge, indeed any politician, would be open to changing for the better. I hope that I am as well. All I can say is that I take my position as a justice of the Supreme Court with the utmost seriousness. It is an honor for me to serve there, and I will continue to strive to do what is right as . . ." She paused, a word coming to her throat and sticking there. The word was *God*. ". . . as I see it." In that moment an image of Jack Holden flashed through her mind. She wondered if he was praying for her.

Gelfan read a few more questions. Then it was Hal Killian's turn. The handsome Wisconsin Democrat was thoughtful and articulate.

"Justice Hollander," he said, "I've admired your judicial opinions over the years. I find them models of clarity, of principle. I would be interested, do you have any judicial heroes? Anyone you would hold up as a model?"

"Yes," Millie said without pause. "Justice Oliver Wendell Holmes. I believe he brought an integrity and clarity to the Court that has rarely been surpassed."

"I agree with you," said Killian. He engaged her in a range of questions, and then things swung back and forth, between Republican and Democrat. By the time the session ended, Millie felt as if she'd been run up a flagpole in a hurricane. But she had a sense that the hearing had gone her way. In fact, Sam Levering winked at her just before the break.

She was going to be the next chief justice of the highest court in the land.

3

When Millie got back to her chambers, Rosalind Wilkes, one of her clerks for the new term, was waiting. She was a graduate of the University of Chicago Law School, and one sharp cookie. She had Millie's court mail.

"I weeded out most of it for later," Rosalind said, "but there's one letter here that looks like it came from Santa Lucia."

The letter was addressed by hand, in ink. The return address was also in ink. It was from Jack Holden.

"Thank you, Rosalind," she said. "Would you mind closing my door?"

When she was alone again, Millie opened the letter with unexpected anticipation.

Dear Justice Hollander:

I hope you don't mind a real letter. I know email is more practical, and considering your schedule, preferable. But I have never felt I can get to the heart of things better than if I put pen to paper. And I want to get at the heart of things in this letter.

I watched the hearings on TV. It may be presumptuous of me to read anything into what I saw, and I know I have barely come to know you, but it seemed to me there was real anguish inside you as you went through some tough grilling. I want you to know that I was praying for you the whole time.

Praying! She remembered that moment when she was being interrogated by Senator Gelfan, and her mind had flashed to Holden. She had wondered if he was praying for her.

The surprising thing to me was my own reaction. It was more than just a feeling of compassion, as one would have toward a friend in distressing circumstances. What I was feeling was wishing I could be there with you. I wanted to be able to offer a word of encouragement, and

The last sentence did not end with a period. There was white space, and then Holden started again.

Hang it all, I'm not as smooth at this as I thought. Here's the deal. I wanted to be with you because I began to feel more than just respect for you while you were here in Santa Lucia. I began to feel affection.

I hope you didn't drop a volume of Supreme Court Reports on your toes when you read that.

It came as a shock to me. I didn't think I could feel this way again about someone.

I had to decide if I should keep quiet about it, just let it go, or tell you. Well, I'm telling you. And I am inviting you to write back and tell me to jump in that lake after all. I will respect that.

I have nothing against lakes per se, but here is my preference: I would like to continue our conversation. By phone, letter, pony express, whatever. I don't want to stop talking with you.

May we?

There it is. As I write this, I'm wondering if I'll actually put it in the mail. But I had to get my feelings down on paper.

Regardless of your decision, it was an honor to get to know you out here, to have the chance to spend some time with someone I deeply respect.

It was signed, simply, *Jack*.

Millie was glad she was sitting down. Glad she didn't have a heavy volume in her hand to drop on her foot.

She felt her face heating up. She shivered, actually shivered, like a child watching a scary movie. She sat there for a long time.

Then she decided it was time to tell him what had happened to her. She took out several pieces of paper and her favorite fountain pen. And began to write.

4

The demons were active tonight.

They swirled around his head, like dancers of death, jabbing at him. Sam Levering even saw them in the swirls of his bourbon, in the way the light hit the ice. And sometimes he heard voices.

Images came at him, haphazard but horrid, from the past. He saw his son as a boy with flaxen hair and unlimited potential. He saw his own political career devastating his family. And worst of all, he saw himself not caring. Giving everything up to serve his unlimited ambitions and grasping dreams.

He kept the lights off at times like this. Normally his home was fully illumined, and people would be around. Servants. Friends. People to distract him. Even Anne, working her behind-the-scenes magic, would have been welcome.

But when the demons came he preferred to drink them away in the dark, here in the library. And no one else was home.

Had it all been worth it?

Levering forced himself to say yes. He had fought the good fight, for civil rights and the right to choose. For subsidies to help single mothers and laws to keep the wealthiest Americans from enjoying tax breaks while the poor couldn't even get a decent minimum wage. And countless other fights. There had been heartbreaks and setbacks, to be sure. He had been bloodied, but remained unbowed.

Yes, it was worth it, he told himself again. But somewhere, a voice argued with him. It was not worth it, this voice said.

If he could have gone back in time, back to before his first elective office, back to a wife who loved him and a son who adored him, would he do it? Would he give up being just a few years from the presidency of the United States for that?

Senses and sounds from his memory. Smell of ocean. The three of them at the Pacific shore, a little place called Cambria, his wife had found it (she did things like that, and back then she could convince him to go). Tad only three and stark naked, ocean swirling around his feet as he giggled and jumped up and down. Sam with his milk skin (which would burn soon enough) and bathing suit, picking up his son and wading further out.

The smoothness of his son's skin. The laughter. The little eyes widening as the waves came toward them, and Tad clinging tighter to Sam's neck, the only one who could save him.

Levering drank quickly, the bourbon burning in his throat—the burning was the best part—and then up through his nose. And before he could remember anymore, the demon dance was interrupted by the phone. The direct line.

"Catch you at a bad time?" President Francis asked.

The worst. "No, Mr. President. Just enjoying a quiet evening at home."

"Sorry to hear that, if you know what I mean."

Levering could almost see him raising his eyebrows, Groucho Marx style.

"Reason I called," Francis said. "You happy about Hollander?"

"Did you see the hearings?"

"Some."

"What was your take?"

"Frankly, Sam, I got a little nervous. That stuff about being open to changing. What was that all about?"

Levering knocked back the rest of his booze. "Just horseradish to calm the conservatives. Being open to change means hey, I might even slide over to your side sometime. But she won't slide."

"You're still sure about that?"

"John," Levering said with mild reproof, "I've been in this game a long time."

"All right," the president said. "Just keep your eyes wide open. This is a delicate balance we got going here. I don't want to lose the presidency over this."

"That would be tragic, John."

"I better keep my eye on you, too," Francis said with a laugh.

You got that right, Levering thought.

After the call Sam Levering poured himself another drink, a stiff one, no ice. He killed it in less than a minute. He wanted sleep now, wanted the demons to quit for the night, and alcohol was the only way he knew to do that.

He was stumbling out of the library when he lost his balance. He fell, and as he did he reached out with his arms, flailing stupidly, grabbing for anything to prop him up. All he could reach were books, and they fell on top of him as he hit the carpet.

Cursing, he clambered to his feet and felt for the light switch. His vision was blurry, the room angling at strange degrees according to his pickled brain. He leaned over to the four volumes that had landed on him, cursing some more, and then he stopped cold.

One of the books was a crisp, black, leather-bound Bible. The one his son had sent to him years ago. He had not noticed it since. He'd just shoved it in the stacks and forgotten all about it.

Now it had jumped out at him, like an accusation.

He picked it up at once, ran his thumb over the leather cover, hefted it. It hefted back, the weight of its pages heavier than he remembered.

For a moment he thought he might cry.

Instead he grunted. Carrying this Tad-thing, he felt his way through the darkened house to the back door. He staggered outside into the stillness, down the steps, and onto the grass. He found the trash bin, opened the lid, dumped the Bible inside it.

Then he slammed the lid down with all his strength.

5

A little old woman who might have stepped out of a Frank Capra movie answered the door. "Hello, Millie," Dorothy Bonassi said, as if eight years hadn't passed since they'd seen each other. "Come in. Bill's expecting you."

The house was large, but not ostentatious. Books were everywhere. A grandfather clock tick-tocked in the large hall.

Dorothy Bonassi showed Millie through the kitchen and out the back door, which opened to a commodious verandah. It overlooked a green lawn, with a large dogwood in the middle.

At the bottom of the stairs, Millie saw a gardener fiddling with some dirt near the house. He wore a large sun hat and gloves, and worked a trowel like a pro.

Dorothy paused and shook her head. "Bill, did you forget she was coming?"

The gardener said in a familiar voice, "No, Mrs. Bonassi." And then William T. Bonassi looked up from his garden and smiled. "Welcome, Millie. Nice to see you again."

"I'll just go and make some iced tea," Dorothy said.

Bonassi took off his gardening gloves and offered his hand to Millie. His grip was firm and sure. Like the man himself, Millie thought. Here he was, eighty-nine years old, and looking as full of life as he did when he'd retired. She remembered his vibrancy from those days, his prodigious memory and his sense of humor.

"I'm getting ready for the fall planting," Bonassi said. "Trying to bring in Black-eyed Susan this year. You know Black-eyed Susans?"

"I'm afraid not," Millie said.

"*Rudbeckia fulgida*. Nice, hardy flower, grows in sun or shade. What I like about them is they're tough and easy to grow in almost all types of soil. Except soggy. Soggy soil isn't good for the Susan."

He looked at her as if expecting a response. "No," she said with half a brain. "Soggy soil isn't good."

"Always thought the Susan was what a Supreme Court justice ought to be like."

Millie cocked her head, seeing a little glint in the eyes of her former colleague.

Bonassi said, "Firm, ready for any weather. But not soggy in his philosophy. A soggy philosophy makes a soggy judge."

Mrs. Bonassi played the perfect hostess, as Millie remembered her. In fact, she did not seem to Millie to have aged so much as . . . fulfill. That was an odd word, but the only one Millie could think of. Dorothy set the tea out on a silver tray on the verandah.

"I won't say I wasn't surprised when you called," Bill Bonassi said. "We served, what, two years together?"

"Two, yes."

"And I don't remember that many conversations, outside the normal small talk. I do remember two words you used to say to me all the time, however."

"Really? What were they?"

"*I disagree.*" And then he laughed. Millie could not help but laugh a little, too. In this setting he seemed more like a favorite grandfather than an esteemed former justice.

"I must admit I was a little intimidated," Millie said.

"By me?" Bonassi said.

"By Bill?" Dorothy said at the same time.

Millie nodded. "The Lion of the Court, after all."

"Ah," Bonassi waved his hand in the air. "Twaddle. Who makes up those names?"

"I do remember something about you," Millie said. "Your faith. Bill, you never talked about your religion around us and I respected you for that. You didn't want it to become the thing that defined you on the Court. And I—"

"No, no," Bonassi gently corrected. "On the contrary, my faith defines me in every way. But then again, everyone has faith."

"How so?"

"Well, we have faith that there is such a thing as existence. And that we are rational creatures capable of finding answers. We have to make that leap of faith or there's nothing to talk about, is there?"

"I suppose not," Millie said with a slight laugh.

"Faith precedes knowledge. It makes knowledge possible."

"But how did your faith influence you on the bench?"

Bonassi thought about the question, his fingertips touching in steeple fashion. "It certainly influenced my view of the basis of law. I believe the principles of justice to be real, not merely man-made ideas. May I inquire, dear Millie, why you are asking?"

Millie took in a deep breath. "I didn't know who else to come to. I had an encounter with God—" *Does this sound stupid?* "I mean, I have come to believe in a God. I hadn't thought about him for a long time, but I'm thinking about him now and I'm pretty shaken up about it."

Dorothy Bonassi immediately put an understanding hand on Millie's arm. She said nothing, only smiled. "Tell us about it," she said at last.

Millie did, starting from the accident all the way through to the moment on the plane when she felt like a door was opening for her.

When she finished, the Old Lion had a sparkle in his eyes. He seemed fifty years younger. "I didn't embrace Christianity until I was out of law school. It threw me for a large loop, too. Changed the way I looked at the law, that is for certain."

Yes, and that was what terrified her. The law, for her, had been a solid piece of ground for over thirty years. It was shaky now, and she could not see the sinkholes. "Tell me how," she said.

"I started thinking about the rights of people," Bonassi said. "That's what the law comes down to. It's about people. What gives people that sort of dignity, I started to wonder. And I decided that it was God. I came to see that without principles of law firmly rooted in a source outside of ourselves, the very idea of law becomes an absurdity. That's what Jefferson said in the Declaration of Independence, after all. We are endowed by our Creator with certain inalienable rights. Without that source, where do rights come from? It can only be from the subjective preferences of whoever happens to be in power, including judges."

Millie had, of course, heard that argument many times before. "But I have always believed that the principles in the Constitution itself bind us."

"What are those principles, Millie?"

"Equal justice under law, to start."

"And how do we define justice?"

"That's always the question, isn't it? Each case is different."

"The principles, however, are not. The founders set this country up on a foundation of biblical metaphysics."

"On what?"

"They were steeped in the Bible. It was the one book that everyone knew. The Bible teaches this: that nature is intelligible, the product of a loving Creator. It teaches the dignity of every man. It was Jefferson who said, 'The God who gave us life gave us liberty at the same time.' He really believed this, contrary to what some revisionists claim."

"Jefferson wasn't a deist?"

"There's a lot of flapdoodle taught about Jefferson. Just read what he wrote. In his *Notes on the State of Virginia*, he said"—Bonassi closed his eyes, finding the words—"'Can the liberties of a nation be thought secure when we have removed their only firm basis, a conviction in the minds of the people that these liberties are the gift of God? That they are not violated but with his wrath?' That is what I'm talking about."

"Jefferson wrote that?"

"And Madison, father of the Constitution, said the belief in a 'God all powerful wise and good is *essential* to the moral order of the world and to the happiness of man.' As Casey Stengel used to say, you could look it up."

Millie lifted her glass. It slipped out of her hand, slamming hard on the glass table.

"I'm sorry," Millie said quickly.

"Think nothing of it, dear," Dorothy Bonassi said. "Bill sometimes has that effect on people."

Millie saw William T. Bonassi give his wife a look of such deep love that her heart filled with something like music. In that instant she thought of Jack Holden.

"Sorry about the lecture," Bonassi said. "I could go on."

"But you won't," Dorothy said.

"I won't," Bill Bonassi said obediently. "How about I give you some books instead? They're less crotchety than I am."

"Yes," Millie said, "I'd like that."

"You have a Bible?"

"I think so."

"Good. Remember what old John Adams said in 1807. 'The Bible contains the most profound philosophy, the most perfect morality, and the most refined policy, that was ever conceived on earth.'"

Millie shook her head. The Old Lion's memory, at eighty-nine, was still absolutely amazing.

"This is a strange feeling," she said.

"I know," Bonassi said. "Use your noodle, Millie." Bonassi tapped his head with his index finger. "I've always considered you one of the sharpest tacks on the bench. If you'll pray and read, the answers will come."

"Prayer," she said. "I've forgotten how."

"Start with an easy one. *Help me.*"

"I think I can handle that." Millie realized the feeling of disquiet she'd had when she first got here was suddenly gone. "May I come again?"

"Please come down here and argue with me anytime." Bonassi added, "It'll be just like old times."

CHAPTER TWELVE

1

Jack Holden slipped the letter from the envelope and, his heart pounding like a basketball on asphalt, he began to read.

Dear Jack,

I have to start out by saying I'm sorry for not writing sooner. There is a reason for that, and now is the time to tell you.

On the plane back to D.C. I was thinking about many things. About my accident, that vision I had when I almost died, about Mom, and a lot about what you had to say in that legal brief of yours. It was getting under my skin, and I was a little angry at you about it. I did not want to think about those things because I was coming back here to assume the most important responsibility of my life.

But I could not stop thinking about what you wrote. I think I know now what was happening. God was not letting me off the hook.

Then there was this moment, I was listening to Beethoven on the headphones, and the plane broke out into this lovely sky, and light was everywhere, it seemed.

Not just light, but the essence of all light. Am I making sense here? I don't know ... think about the most beautiful light you've ever seen.

I said to myself, "Watch it, Millie. Watch out!" Because I knew the door was opening and I was going to go through it. Behind the door I heard the music. My heart wanted to dance. But my mind didn't want to.

I know now I went through the door, kicking and screaming. I could not *not* believe in God anymore.

And I kept thinking about what you told me about Moody. I believe he saw those children. I believe my vision was from God, too. It was his gift, as you said.

I want to see Mom again. That's all part of this, too. I can't deny that, nor would I want to.

But fear is here as well. What is all this going to mean? How is it going to change me? How is it going to change the way I work? Will my opinions on the law change?

Well, I've been trying to figure all that out! But I've been trying to do it like I always have—alone. Think it through. Figure out the best course of action to take. All before the first Monday in October when I go back to work!

But the only thing I've figured out so far is that I can't do this on my own. So last night I called Bill Bonassi. Yes, William T. Bonassi, the retired justice. I served my first two years with him, almost always on the opposite side of the decision. We all knew he was a Christian. I have to find out what this faith I've so tentatively embraced actually means. He has given me some books and the offer to talk more. I feel like this is the most productive step I've taken since I got off the plane.

Please forgive me for waiting so long to tell you. But until now I didn't know if these thoughts of God would last. I really didn't want it to last, to tell you the truth. It has thrown me for a loop.

But I know one thing for certain: the door has closed behind me, and I am on the other side, and my heart is learning how to dance.

Please don't stop praying for me. And for the Court.
I love this institution and want to serve it so much, so well.

I promise I will call soon to talk with you. I know right
now you must be rejoicing. I join you in that. For the
moment, at least, I feel more joy than I have ever felt.

Stay out of the lake. Write to me again. Thank you for
everything.

Millie

Jack Holden put the letter on his desk. He closed his eyes
and breathed in deeply. Then he went outside and with thank-
fulness overflowing in him, shot hoops for an hour, his longest
stretch in a long time.

2

Anne Deveraux met Cosmo for drinks at License at five-
thirty. Her friend was already at the bar nursing a martini.

"I want two of those," Anne said over the loud music. They
were blaring classic rock today. Jethro Tull.

"Tough day?" Cosmos asked.

"Usual. Had to bust some chops."

"Ooh, you sound like Joe Pesci or something."

"Joe Pesci?"

"You know, like some Mafia guy."

Anne said nothing, motioned for the bartender, pointed at
Cosmo's glass. He got the message.

"So, are you some Mafia guy?" Cosmo asked.

"You're weird."

"Or are you dating some Mafia guy?"

Anne looked at her. Cosmo's eyes were full of mischief.
"What brought this on?" Anne asked, trying not to sound like
she was a kid with a hand in the cookie jar.

"I don't know, your mysterious boyfriend and all. It's like a
movie. I was trying to think, why won't she tell me? It's because
he's Mafia, or a Republican, or something like that. Maybe
you're seeing a Catholic priest, I don't know. You won't tell me."

"Fine, I'll tell you."

"I thought so."

"He's in construction. In New York."

"Construction?"

"Buildings. He builds buildings." It was better that Cosmo didn't know. Someday, maybe.

"Like a Donald Trump?"

"Sure, like Donald Trump."

"The guy loaded?"

"He's got some money."

"When can I meet him?"

"Sometime. Enough about him. What about—" She stopped when someone dropped onto the chair next to her. She gave a quick glance and saw a man staring at her. Markey.

She almost slipped off her chair.

"Hi," he said.

"Who's this?" Cosmo asked.

"Detective Markey," he said. "Glad to know you."

Anne felt her stomach twist around like one of the bar pretzels. "Who said you could sit here?"

"This is a public place."

"I'm having a private conversation."

"I just need a minute or two," Markey said. The female bartender asked him what he'd like. "Ginger ale," he said.

"Maybe I should go," Cosmo said.

"No," Anne said. "You don't have to go anywhere."

"Maybe that would be best," Markey said. "Just for a minute or two."

Something in Markey's look told Anne this was not going to be a casual conversation. "Give me a couple of minutes," she told Cosmo.

"Just call me later," Cosmo said. She dropped a five dollar bill on the bar and walked off.

"Thanks a lot," Anne said to Markey. "You're a real social asset."

"Just doing my job."

"As what? Keeper of the cop cliché book?"

"I don't want this to be unpleasant."

"It already is. Detail me."

He looked at her quizzically.

"Tell me what this is all about," Anne said slowly.

"Your boss, Senator Sam Levering. A year and half ago there was talk about a bimbo eruption. Remember that?"

Anne was silent. He obviously knew the facts.

Markey went on. "Three women were supposedly going to come forward and make statements about Levering and his, well, his peculiar tastes in the bedroom. I've got the names written somewhere. Want me to find them?"

"Just go on," Anne said.

"Anyway, there was noise made about these three going on Larry King and spilling their guts. It was apparently the work of a very conservative lawyer out in Tulsa who did not like Levering one bit. But the story never got on the air. Remember why?"

Anne returned his look with iron resistance.

"This lawyer was suddenly caught with a sixteen-year-old prostitute out on Highway 20. And then the women clam up."

"The guy was trying to make money and a name for himself," Anne said. "Sham artists are all over the place."

"And three women change their stories?"

"Happens."

"Sure it does. When somebody gets to them."

A woman screamed from across the room. Anne's heart almost jumped out of her chest. She looked and saw the woman, her head thrown back, dissolving into a huge, obnoxious laugh.

"Must have been a funny one," Markey said.

"This whole conversation is a funny one," Anne said. "Why don't you get to the point and then leave me alone?"

"I always wondered about that lawyer," Markey said. "It wasn't my jurisdiction, of course, but I take an interest in things. I make connections all the time. It just happens. And this morning I'm thinking to myself, what has become of our witness? The one I told you about. Remember?"

"No," she lied.

"The street guy. Elijah."

"Oh, him. What about him?"

"We can't find him now."

Ever since she could remember, Anne Deveraux had worked hard at perfecting the art of the lie. She had to. Her stepfather had made it plain what would happen to her if she told her mother what he did to her at night. *Little Annie, you know what I can do to you if you tell, don't you? Don't cry, little Annie. I'll have to make you stop if you do.* She had no choice. Out of fear she had learned to deceive. To keep a straight face when backed up against a wall.

This detective had no idea who he was dealing with, and little mind games weren't going to get to her.

"That's too bad," Anne said, giving her voice the perfect tone of unconcern.

"You wouldn't happen to have any information on where he might be, would you?"

"Of course not."

"I mean, the guy you spray has a connection to your boss—"

"Oh, come on, Detective," Anne said. "Not only is that the weakest witness I've ever seen, he couldn't possibly be right."

"Why not?"

With a perfectly calm voice, Anne said, "Because Senator Levering was with me that night."

Markey frowned. Perfect.

"I went back, as you suggested, and checked my book and Senator Levering's. We had a strategy meeting at his place. We ate pizza and drank Diet Cokes, although I will admit to you the senator gave his a little dash of bourbon every now and then. We watched *Nightline* and then worked until about two in the morning. Any further questions?"

Markey blinked at her a couple of times. "Yes," he said. "What was on *Nightline* that night?"

Anne smiled. She almost felt sorry for this police hack. "The Pentagon budget," she said. She had looked it up a couple of nights ago in preparing the alibi. Then she added with just the right touch of uncertainty, "At least I think that's what it was."

"I'll check on it," Markey said.

"You do that."

He drained his ginger ale and left, looking, Anne thought, a little rattled.

3

"Like the bartender said to the horse," Helen said. "Why the long face?"

"Is it that long?" Millie asked.

"Like a list of crooked congressmen."

"Sorry. I haven't been good company so far, have I?"

"This is a time to celebrate," Helen said. The exclusive restaurant Helen had chosen was just over the Virginia line and had the flavor of the Old South.

When Millie did not say anything, Helen added, "You are ecstatic about this, aren't you? I mean, as if Mel Gibson walked up to you and asked you to model lingerie?"

Millie looked at her oldest friend in D.C. *I don't know her at all, really,* she thought. How many times had they ever talked about their deepest concerns and desires? Helen was in many ways a private person. She let people in only a little, and then only when it seemed to serve her purposes.

But then, that was how Millie was too, she realized. Now, those barriers needed to be broken. "Something has changed for me," Millie began carefully.

Helen peered at Millie over her raised wineglass, which she held in the fingers of both hands. "Changed?"

"Yes."

"We talking menopause here?"

"No, not that, I—"

"Because if we are I have some drugs that—"

"That's not it." Millie felt suddenly reluctant, but the boat had left the shore. She had to go with it. "I had some time to think in Santa Lucia."

"Thinking is what you're good at, girlfriend."

"Sometimes."

"So what are you thinking about now?" Helen sipped her chardonnay, waiting.

Go for it, Millie thought. "God."

Helen paused, the glass at her lips, her eyes narrowing slightly. "God?"

Millie nodded.

"As in?"

Suddenly Millie's tongue was doing back flips. "God . . . you know . . . as in . . . God." *What a fabulous and eloquent judge you have become,* she thought.

Helen tapped her glass with a fingernail. "Tell me more, Igor."

Millie didn't know what words she would use so she just let them pour out. She told Helen everything—the near-death experience, Santa Lucia, her mother's death, Pastor Jack Holden. Helen sat through it all with an expression half bemused and half—what? Troubled?

"And I've been meeting with Bill Bonassi," Millie concluded.

Helen's eyebrows went up. The restaurant seemed suddenly still. Helen herself seemed frozen, as if in a state of emotional shock. Millie prayed silently her friend would remain that, a friend, and understand. And accept.

Helen began tentatively. "Frankly, Watson, this is troubling," Helen said. "Bill Bonassi? Do you know how bizarre that sounds?"

"I suppose."

"The biggest right-wing justice of the last fifty years?"

"It's not a political thing," Millie said. "Bill has been answering a lot of my questions about Christianity."

"Yeah? Whose brand of Christianity? His? Falwell's? What is up with this?"

Millie closed her eyes a moment. "I'm not thinking about it in those terms, Helen. A lot has happened in the last few months."

"I guess!"

"I can only tell you I had been saying no to God for many years, and then I realized I was saying yes."

"Wow," Helen said with a faraway look, as if she were gazing upon some strange new thing.

"I know," Millie said.

Helen waited a long time before putting her wineglass down and reaching for Millie's hand. "Hey, kiddo, you went through a terrible thing there. I understand that. Of course I do. You got shaken up. It's natural to think about these things—you know, religious things."

"Thank you, Helen."

"For what?"

"Listening."

"Hey, it's me. So, you are looking at Christianity." Helen paused, as if a new thought had snuck up on her. "What do you think it means?"

"Means?"

"You know, for the future."

"My future?"

"Yeah. As chief justice and all."

Millie saw the look of incipient concern on Helen's face. "You worried I'm going to go off on some odd angle?"

"Bill Bonassi," Helen said with a shrug. "It at least raises the issue."

"Helen, I'm going to do what I've always done, okay? One case at a time."

"I just don't want to see you get hurt."

"Hurt? How?"

"You know, if the press gets hold of this."

Millie had thought about that. She was not so naive as to think that the hungry sharks of Washington media wouldn't try to make a big deal out of her spiritual quest. If they found out.

Helen squeezed Millie's hand. "We can handle this thing together, kiddo," she said.

CHAPTER THIRTEEN

| 1

On October 8, a cool Wednesday afternoon in Washington, Chief Justice Millicent Mannings Hollander presided over the first judicial conference of the new term.

She felt like she was made of warm jam. That was partly due to her initial trepidation—the new-kid-at-school syndrome, even though she'd been here ten years—but mainly because she knew, when the discussion began on the first case, there would be a judicial firestorm.

For conference, the nine members of the Court met in the large room next to the chambers of the chief. They shook hands with each other before taking their seats at the large rectangular conference table, under the watchful portrait of the famous chief justice, John Marshall. Only the nine justices would be present—no clerks, secretaries, staff assistants, or anyone else allowed.

Justice Riley gave Millie's hand an extended shake. He smiled at her and said, "I know you're ready to run this ship."

Millie felt her face strain to smile in return. She almost felt like a traitor. Riley had no idea what was about to happen.

She only knew what experience had taught her. Each justice would have considered the cases to be discussed and formed preliminary opinions. As chief, Millie's job was to state the facts of the cases and begin a round where each justice would state his or her opinion on the matter. That would give them all a sense of where each justice stood, and how strongly they believed in their positions.

Then a give-and-take would ensue. Sometimes it would be brief, if the case was simple; for complex cases it could get rather lengthy. And for volatile cases, things could get heated, in a mannerly sort of way.

Considering this first case and her take on it, Millie knew there would be flames. "Good afternoon, everyone," she said.

Eight heads nodded at her, with a few "good afternoons" thrown in.

"Let us get right to it," Millie continued. "Our first case today is from the Sixth Circuit Court of Appeals," she said. "*American Civil Liberties Union of Ohio v. Roland Tate, Governor.* The facts are as follows.

"In 1959, three years after President Eisenhower signed legislation making 'In God We Trust' the national motto, the state of Ohio adopted a similar motto, 'With God All Things Are Possible.' Last year the Governor of Ohio approved a bronze flatwork, twelve feet by ten feet, with the state motto inscribed, to be placed outside the statehouse in Columbus, Ohio. The ACLU of Ohio, joined by a taxpayer in the state, filed suit to stop this action. A divided three-judge panel of the Sixth Circuit held that the action violates the Establishment Clause. That is the issue we must decide. I will defer my own comments for the moment."

She noted a few bewildered looks. It had long been a tradition in conference for the chief to begin with a position statement. But Millie wanted to see where everyone else stood before weighing in.

As the senior associate, Thomas Riley had the first word. "Well, this is a clear Constitutional violation," he said.

No surprise there, Millie thought.

"The motto comes from a Bible verse, Matthew 19:26. It's a verse where Jesus Christ is talking about the salvation of souls. Well, if the Establishment Clause means anything, it means the government should not align itself with Jesus Christ, or any other religious figure. That's what Ohio is doing with this motto. It should be struck down."

Simple, clear, to the point. Millie had expected no less.

On Riley's left sat the next associate in seniority, Raymond Byrne, a twenty-three-year member of the Court and a consistent textualist. Naturally, the press always put his name on the conservative side of the ledger.

"Surprise, surprise, I disagree," Byrne said. There was good-natured laughter all around. Byrne, a glinty-eyed, third-generation Irishman, had the best sense of humor on the Court. "It seems to me that there is no difference between 'With God All Things Are Possible' and 'In God We Trust.' If the second passes Constitutional muster, then so does Ohio's."

And so on around the table they went. Millie kept track in her mind, and when all was said the view of the case split perfectly, 4–4, among the so-called conservative bloc and what the press called the moderates.

Justice Byrne, along with Justices Facconi, Johnson, and Parsons, were for the acceptability of the motto. Riley, joined by Weiss, Velarde, and the new Justice Atkins, thought it violated the Establishment Clause.

Then all eyes turned to Millie.

There was no avoiding it now. No place to hide. No bookcase that spun around into some secret chamber through which she could make an escape. Millie thought she could read the faces clearly. Riley looked especially gratified. He was a staunch separationist. He did not want any government, state or federal, to have anything to do with religion. He was clearly expecting Millie's vote to be a favorable tie breaker.

On the other side, Ray Byrne looked as he always did in years past when religion cases came along. He would be on the losing side, and set to write another of his lengthy dissents. His face was set in anticipation, his pugnacious jaw thrust out.

For a moment that hung heavy and silent, Millie did not speak. She felt nerves exploding up and down her arms. She took a lingering sip of water.

Finally, she spoke. "The Establishment Clause says 'Congress shall make no law respecting an establishment of religion.' It seems to me we have to understand what that meant to the framers of the Constitution."

She paused, flicking her eyes around the room. Already she could feel the thin tendrils of disquiet undulating from the moderates. She could understand the reason. No one had ever heard her say anything like this before. Going back to the framers' intent was what a conservative judge would do. Indeed, Ray Byrne was leaning so far forward that his fighter's chin almost touched the table. In keeping with tradition, however, no one interrupted her.

"I went back to some historical cases and materials," Millie said. "I began with James Madison and Thomas Jefferson, worked up to our decision in *Town of Pawlet v. Clark,* from 1815, written by Chief Justice Marshall, and all the way to *Zorach v. Clauson* in 1952. You remember that Justice Douglas said there, 'We are a religious people whose institutions presuppose a Supreme Being.'"

Justice Riley's face was beginning to turn pink. Normally, the justices would be making casual notes on their vote sheets or legal pads throughout the conference. Now, not a single justice held a pen or pencil.

Millie felt lightheaded. Was it hot in the room? No, the air was cool, the circulation perfect. But the future of the Court hung in the balance, and Millie held the deciding vote.

"What is clear to me now," Millie said firmly, "is that the original intent of the Establishment Clause was to prevent the institution of a national church. It was to prevent coercion. James Madison so understood it. But the clause was never intended to take out the expression of religious sentiment from the public square. Therefore I must conclude that the state motto 'With God All Things Are Possible' does not violate the United States Constitution."

Thomas Riley slapped the table with his open palm. A resounding *whap* bounced off the burnished walnut walls of the conference room. It was like a shot, the bullet ripping into Millie's chest.

Byrne, on the other hand, had a smile as broad as his chest. If eyes could dance, his were doing a jig with full orchestra.

"I must say," said Riley, his tone civil but cool, and undergirded by a smoldering intensity, "that this is a rather drastic departure from your previous Establishment Clause position."

Millie nodded.

"Might I remind you," Riley said, "that for you to take this stance you must renounce all your previous opinions on the subject?"

"Of course I understand that," Millie said.

"May I ask for your reasons then?" Riley snapped.

"Certainly," Millie said. "This is not a question that can be decided without looking at the original intent of the Establishment Clause. In 1798 John Adams said, 'The Constitution is made only for a moral and religious people. It is wholly inadequate to the government of any other.' Justice Douglas echoed that sentiment in 1952."

"Yes, yes," Riley said, "but Justice Black wrote about the wall of separation in 1947."

"In *Everson*," Millie countered, "relying on a phrase in an obscure letter from Jefferson. Erecting a view of establishment based on such minor dicta was not good Constitutional law. It does not even reflect what Jefferson really meant. That can only be discerned by what he actually did. As president, for example, he used federal money to build churches and sponsor Christian missionaries. He established religious requirements for the University of Virginia. He was not a strict separationist by any means."

"It's a policy that *works*," Riley said.

"Tom, our Establishment Clause jurisprudence has been pretty messy. We all know that. Maybe the founders had it right. In any event, can you honestly say any of them would have objected to a state having the motto 'With God All Things Are Possible'?"

Millie paused, and Riley smoldered. She had not seen him this way in years. It troubled her. But she had to continue. "I must hold that it is time to move back to the original understanding of the Establishment Clause."

Justice Byrne, who had been hanging on every word, shook his head. "I never thought I'd say this in a religion case, but Chief Justice Hollander, I agree with you."

For a protracted moment silence was heavy in the conference room. The other justices seemed too stunned to say anything. They appeared to be calculating the effects of this development.

"I want a break," Riley said, standing. Before Millie could say anything he was heading for the door. He slammed it behind him.

All of the justices looked at each other. In ten years Millie had never seen a justice storm out of conference. Ever.

"Well," Justice Byrne said, "this has been an interesting afternoon."

2

Will God kick thinkin' in the pants? Charlene Moore thought.

He would have to if she was going to win this argument. But she had truly left it to him. She no longer cared about winning the case for herself. It was for Sarah Mae. And Aggie.

The judges—two men, one woman—sat like statues waiting for Charlene, as petitioner, to make her case.

"May it please the court," she began, "I am Charlene Moore on behalf of the petitioner, Sarah Mae Sherman. We are here to ask for a reversal of the district court's decision to—"

"Counsel," a judge interrupted. It was Foster Lucas, a Clinton appointee. "Isn't the issue here one of changing the law? The district court judge, as I read the record, interpreted the statute. Are you here to tell us he was wrong?"

Bam. Right to the point. Charlene looked up from her carefully organized notes.

"We are saying he was wrong," she said. "In interpreting the statute too strictly, the very intent of the law was frustrated."

"And you can tell us the intent of the law?" Lucas said.

"Yes, Your Honor."

"How, pray tell?"

Pray and tell, Charlene thought. "It is clear from the text itself what the intent is. The law means to protect pregnant women. That protection means nothing without full disclosure of all medical and psychological effects of a—"

"Let me stop you there, Counsel," said the woman. She was a Reagan judge, Deena Lynn Caplin. "Where is the psychological aspect of this? What sort of harm are we talking about?"

"Your Honor, when a woman terminates a pregnancy, she is taking a life. She is—"

"That is a religious statement," Foster said. "It has no bearing on this issue."

"I disagree, Your Honor. It is not a religious statement. It is a medical one. Despite how the fetus is characterized, all sides must agree we are dealing with a living thing."

"But the question of humanity," Foster said, "is one for philosophers or theologians. Not judges."

"But the state of mind of Sarah Mae Sherman is the issue," Charlene said. "She believes her baby existed at one point in time. Now, the baby does not exist. That has had a devastating impact on her because the respondents did not disclose all of the relevant information about fetal development. They should have, because it impacted her mental state. Thus, they violated the intent of the informed consent statute. That is why I am asking this court to remand this case for trial."

And so it went for twenty more minutes. Charlene clearly read Foster. He was opposed to her position. Judge Caplin seemed conflicted. She was most troubled by the silence of the statute on the subject of psychological harm.

The third judge, Gregory Knight, was another Clinton appointee, but something of a maverick. At least that was his reputation. Charlene could not read him at all, and he asked no questions.

Then it was Larry Graebner's turn to argue. As he spoke, Charlene noticed the judges asked no immediate questions. Apparently, they were deferring to the great legal mind of the Ivy League. Graebner's argument was no different than that in his brief. But at the very end he dropped his bomb.

"Finally," Graebner said, "my opponent has tried to open the door on the matter of the humanity of the fetus. This is a code word for personhood, Your Honors, something the anti-abortion forces have been attempting to get the courts to rule on ever since *Roe v. Wade.* Well, I ask this court not to take the bait. A decision to do so will just add another layer of chaos to what should be a settled area of the law. This case never should have gotten to this point. I urge you to affirm the decision of the district court."

Charlene wanted to shout. She wanted to scream. She wanted to get up and ask if all sanity had been removed from the justice system. This case was about the nature of Sarah Mae's harm, and what she was not told about her pregnancy. You could not separate this issue out, like some chef dividing egg whites.

But she did not shout. Instead, she fought to remain calm as the judges filed from the bench.

And then she saw one of them, Knight, glance down at Larry Graebner and smile.

3

Millie found Riley in his chambers. "Can we talk?"

Riley motioned for her to enter. She did and closed the door, as his two law clerks watched with somewhat bemused expressions.

"I guess I owe you an explanation," she said.

His eyes were indeed full of expectancy, though it was of an angry sort. "I guess maybe you do."

"I did a lot of thinking this summer," Millie said. She paused, looking at him, wondering if he might say something. Some word of encouragement perhaps. He was as silent as stone. "I found occasion to reassess a number of things," Millie continued.

"Apparently so," Riley snapped.

She reached down into her heart, heavy inside her like a wet rag, for the affection she had for him. "Tom, I value our friendship. I always have. I don't want anything to interfere with that."

"We're talking justice to justice now. Put personalities aside."

"All right."

"What on earth has caused you to change your mind so radically on the Establishment Clause?"

With her palms Millie smoothed her skirt. "I thought it through again, Tom. Believe me. I've spent weeks poring over the cases."

"But you're a ten-year veteran, with a record that is clear and consistent. You don't just wake up one morning and say, 'Gee, I guess I've been wrong all these years.' Do you?"

"Perhaps I do."

Riley waited for an explanation.

"Tom, I have become a Christian."

The austere silence of Riley's chambers seemed suddenly ominous. Only the muted whir of the air system tethered Millie to an outside reality. The old justice sat frozen for an extended moment, and then said, "This is rather stunning news."

"I know. I—"

"Christianity? At your age?"

"It's not an age issue," Millie said. "It is a matter of seeing things in a different way."

"But why now?"

"I suppose the accident started it. It caused me to reflect on things. And on it went from there."

"Your mother dying, which we were all sorry to hear. Maybe that had something to do with it."

Millie nodded. "No doubt."

"Have you thought," Riley said, "that such a traumatic event may have ..." He waved his hand in the air, diplomatically.

"Caused me to break down mentally?" Millie finished for him.

"No, not that. But these things can throw us off."

"Tom," Millie said, gathering all the earnestness she could. "I don't feel *off*. I might have thought that once. But I've been approaching this like I would a case that comes before us. I've been reading and analyzing and taking notes. But I've also been praying and trying to listen. I know how odd that may sound to you, but I just believe it, Tom. I am a Christian because I believe it."

Riley said nothing. If he was reflecting on anything, Millie thought, it was probably his sudden demise into the Court's minority on religion cases.

"And now you're suddenly what?" Riley said. "A Bill Bonassi-type justice?"

"I am not a type," Millie said.

"Don't be naive, Millie. You know how it is. People depend on the Court. They sense what it is doing and adjust. You have been the swing vote on many crucial occasions. We all know that. The people know that. If you veer off in another direction all of a sudden, it's going to wreak havoc."

"I don't see this as veering off."

"Why not? You've done a 180 on Establishment. A complete turnaround. What are you going to do with, say, abortion? You've always supported a woman's right to choose. Do you still?"

The directness of the question hit her hard. "Just because I am a Christian doesn't mean I am going to change my approach. I always take any issue as it comes up, case by case."

Silence for a moment, then Riley's tone became fatherly. "Millie," he said, leaning forward the way a concerned counselor would. "We've known each other a long time. You know how fond I am of you. And I understand what it's like to go through difficult, confusing times in life. When my wife died in '92, it was terrible. But I got through it. And I didn't drop off the face of the earth. I didn't change my entire life. I went on, the way I always had. And you can do the same."

"I can only promise," she said, "that I will take great care how I decide cases, as always. I will not change the way I approach research and deliberations. But"—she looked at Riley, into the blue, intelligent eyes she knew so well—"we may not always agree like we used to."

"I hope," Riley said without hesitation, "it won't come to that. But if you suddenly throw this Court off in the opposite direction . . ." He shook his head. "I don't want to have to fight you, Millie."

His words, almost whispered, hit her like a car slamming into her. Yes, that was it. Like her accident all over again. Her throat tightened. "I would hope there won't be a rift," she said.

But there was. She knew it.

4

Fall storms pummeled the east for four days after that. But on Monday the sky was clear and blue, as if to signal a fresh start for the business of the Court.

By the time Millie was in her chambers, ready to engage in legal research on an issue of interstate commerce, she felt she was coming out from under a dark cloud. Perhaps the storm of Tom Riley's reaction would also blow over, and she could get back to business as usual.

She began the morning at her desk with a new habit. She had a brand new Bible, a gift from Dorothy Bonassi. Each morning for the last two weeks she had opened to the Psalms and let them pour into her. There was no agenda, none of the anxious striving she had experienced during her conversion. It was the living Word of God, and she soaked it up like the desert soaks up rain.

Today she was on Psalm 19. She read the first verse slowly, whispering the words. "'The heavens declare the glory of God; and the firmament sheweth his handiwork.'"

She realized she finally believed that. The music of it filled her. And she felt, at last, that she had climbed to another height. Not near the peak, not yet. But up from where she had started, where she had spent years. And she was safe here. She would not fall.

She closed her Bible and picked up her work. Turning to the draft opinion on interstate commerce that one of her clerks, Paul, had prepared, Millie knew she would make use of the blue pencil. But it would be a pleasure to edit this one. It had nothing to do with the Establishment Clause, and she could use a break from *that* section of the Constitution, thank you.

Her other clerk, Rosalind, knocked on her door and entered. Her face had an ashen, faraway look.

"What is it?" Millie asked.

"You'd better come," Rosalind said.

Both of her clerks had workstations in the antechamber. Paul, the bespectacled *Law Review* editor from Stanford, sat before his terminal in silence. The glow from the screen reflected off his glasses. He did not look up to make eye contact with Millie. His blank stare made her think of an accident scene, as if he were seeing a dead body sprawled on a patch of asphalt somewhere.

"Did somebody die?" Millie asked. Perhaps the president? A fellow justice? She felt her heart quicken.

Rosalind shook her head, her blond hair framing her concerned face, and indicated Millie should take her seat in front of Rosalind's screen.

Millie sat and looked at the screen. Big block letters spelled out the *Burrow Bulletin*. And just below that a headline read "Supreme Court Chief Gets Religion!"

Millie read the article in silence.

Gimme that old-time religion! That's a song you may hear coming from a most unlikely place—the chambers of a certain chief justice of the United States Supreme Court!

Did I say chief justice? Yes, I did. Looks like the cat's out of the bag, the chickens have flown the coop, the bloom is off the rose. Somebody stop me!

The *Burrow Bulletin* has learned that Millicent Mannings Hollander, the recently enrobed chief of our highest court, has seen the light!

Not only is she now a professing Christian, but she's already reversed herself in the first major case of her tenure, soon to be decided! The case involves the Establishment Clause and government interference in matters of religion.

Insiders tell the *Burrow Bulletin* that Hollander is going to rule that the government of Ohio can go holy roller and inject God right into their public life! This is a complete reversal of how Hollander has ruled in the past!

What next? This reporter is betting abortion will be the next domino to fall. With Hollander now the fifth in a conservative majority, the whole balance of the Supreme Court has been thrown off! Never in our history have we seen a Supreme Court justice change so completely in one fell swoop.

Your intrepid correspondent is in touch with some members of Congress, who are vowing to look into this. One even called it a "fraud" on the American people!

Stay tuned! In the next few days, you are bound to see the reverberations of this bombshell across the nation!

Burrowing . . .

As if from a distance, Millie heard Rosalind's voice. "Justice Hollander, are you all right?"

Millie did not answer. The inside of her head felt like a collapsing building, a chaos of rubble and dust, imploding upon itself. For a long, sickening moment she thought she might stop breathing.

"Madame Chief Justice?" Rosalind said.

"I'm sorry," Millie said.

"Is it . . ."

Millie looked at Rosalind. Her face was like that of a child whose mother has just been accused of a terrible crime. Now she was asking, not wanting to believe it.

"Rosalind, Paul," Millie said. "I need to tell you what has happened."

Rosalind still looked like the waiting child. Paul, in contrast, was the petulant one. He did not look up from his screen.

"Paul?" Millie said.

Finally, he looked at her. His eyes were almost tearful.

"Please," Millie said. "Let me tell you both what this is about."

The phone on Paul's desk rang. Millie waited as he picked up and inquired.

Paul's eyes shot to Millie while the receiver was still at his ear. Then he put the receiver to his chest. "It's ABC News," he said. "They want to have a word with you."

5

For Senator Sam Levering, breaking news was like Prozac—an instant respite from depression. He was, in fact, a news junkie.

That was why his limo had not only two TV monitors, but also a special remote so he could jump immediately to any of five news outlets—CNN, Fox, ABC, NBC, and CBS.

This morning he was concentrating on ABC. The reporter was standing in front of the White House delivering his report. The "strange conversion" of Chief Justice Hollander had reached the top of the Washington news food chain.

When the limo phone rang, Levering knew exactly who it would be.

"Good morning, Mr. President," Levering said.

"What's good about it?" Francis said.

"You've heard."

"Of course I've heard. It's all over the place. You'd think we'd had a terrorist attack with all the reporters."

Levering mused that this felt very much like an attack. Surprising, potentially debilitating.

"What are you going to do about it?" Francis demanded.

"I'm on it."

"Were you on it when you forced Hollander down my throat?"

Levering felt like cussing out the president of the United States. Instead he said, "I will take care of it."

"Get her off the bench," the president said.

"She's a Supreme Court justice," Levering snapped. "She either has to retire, die, or get impeached."

"Choose one," Francis said.

Was he serious? "Mr. President, let me assure you. I can deal with Hollander. I will get her to play ball, as they say, or force her to resign."

"How?"

"Leave that to me."

"I already did that," Francis shot back. "I just better not see a rollback on women's rights, gay rights, every other kind of rights. What a nightmare. You know what they'll say about me? That I made the worst pick for chief justice ever. Should have seen it coming. This could change the Court for twenty years."

"Shall we meet?" Levering said. "I'm free this afternoon."

"No," Francis said. "I'm golfing with the CEO of GE. Just do something and get back to me."

Click.

Levering looked out the window and saw the Washington Monument rising into a fog.

He poured himself a shot of bourbon and called Anne Deveraux.

CHAPTER FOURTEEN

1

Charlene woke up just before the train hit her.

The locomotive bore down on her, its horn blaring. She was stuck on the tracks, unable to move. No restraints held her. Her feet simply would not take her away from certain death.

The nightmare ended, as they most often do, before impact. But the train whistle sounded again, and this time Charlene recognized it. It was the prolonged beep of her fax machine.

She had fallen asleep on the couch. Last night she could not sleep at all, her stomach in a knot. The decision from the Court of Appeals was late, and there was no word from the clerk when it would come in.

No matter how much Charlene prayed for sleep, it was denied her. She took that as a sign that God did not want her to sleep, but to continue praying. She did so, starting with prayers for Sarah Mae and Aggie Sherman, then for the case to be resolved in their favor.

But that was not all. Charlene found herself praying for Millicent Mannings Hollander.

She had been stunned by the news. A Supreme Court justice coming to know Christ as Savior while actively serving? That was definitely a first.

But would Hollander's faith lead her to adopt a different view of the law than she'd had before? What would that do to the balance of the Court?

Charlene had a sudden wild thought. What if Sarah Mae's case actually got to the high Court? How would Hollander rule? Graebner and Winsor believed strongly she would be on their side, and Charlene had to agree. But what now? She prayed for God's will, not her own, and finally fell asleep around four in the morning.

The fax beeped again. Charlene rubbed her eyes and checked her watch. 11 A.M.

She jumped up and snatched the page that had just been cut from her ancient thermal-roll machine. The cover page made her heart jerk. It read "United States Court of Appeals, Eleventh Circuit." Ten pages to come.

It was the decision.

The first page was squeezing out slower than cold molasses. "Come on, come on!"

The page was a third of the way out of the machine. Charlene craned her neck so she could look at it. She could only read the caption, the case name, and the introductory gobbledygook that was part of every printed decision.

"Hurry up!"

With the first page halfway out, she saw the names of the three judges who had considered the case. She remembered their faces, heard their voices again as they asked questions of counsel. She heard Graebner's confident answers, and her own stumbles as she tried to remain calm and clear.

What was the decision?

When the page was almost out she was at last able to read the first lines of the first paragraph. It gave an overview of the proceedings and the decision of the district court judge. Then the last line of the paragraph came into view: "For the reasons stated herein, we . . ."

The first page spat out.

"Move it!" Charlene railed at the fax machine. Page two was barely showing its top edge as it emerged.

Charlene gripped the edge with her fingers, as if she could coax it to go faster. The machine kept its own pace.

Her neck was starting to ache with the craning.

Finally, the next line came into view, and the first word was *reverse* . . .

Breath left her.

. . . *the decision of the district court and remand for further proceedings.*

Hot tears came much faster than the fax paper. Sarah Mae had won.

2

The media camp outside Millie's home was like a Russian circus. She herself had become the dancing bear. The story. Not her opinions, but her. It was the nightmare she had never wanted to happen in real life.

Now she knew what it felt like to be a prisoner in her own home. She'd seen the way politicians had to deal with reporters on their front lawn. Walking out with forced smiles. Trying to get in cars while cameras rolled. Putting up a false front.

She could never do that. What were her alternatives? Find a way to sneak around town? Ask, respectfully, for privacy? Fat chance they'd give it to her.

She was not going to watch television. She couldn't stand hearing her name on the news.

She was about to burst. Helen hadn't called since the bomb had exploded. Millie had left a message, but maybe Helen was out of town.

Millie walked to her front window and peeked through the blinds. The media camp was there on the street. A camera aimed at her from a van seemed to be looking right into her eyes. She quickly drew back.

Now what?

The phone rang. It seemed like the millionth time. She let her machine pick it up again. It hadn't taken long for her private number to fall into the hands of the news outlets.

Then she heard a familiar voice.

"Millie, it's Jack Holden. I'm here at the church. I just—"

Millie snatched the phone. "Jack!"

"I'm so glad I got you. What is going on?"

"Oh, nothing much," Millie said. "Just a replay of the invasion of Normandy out in the front yard."

"That all?" Jack said. "Then I feel sorry for the other side."

His light touch was comforting. She felt herself holding on, trying to stay rational.

"I don't suppose you've been watching the religious stations," Jack said.

"Unless Dan Rather is the pope, no."

There was a pause. "A guy who has a network here is calling you a miracle from God. Says *Roe v. Wade* is finally going to be overturned."

"Oh, no." Millie's stomach went into freefall.

"Looks like you're getting it from both sides."

"Why can't they just let me do my job?"

Jack said, "Can I read something to you?"

"Please."

"'Blessed are you when people insult you, persecute you and falsely say all kinds of evil against you because of me. Rejoice and be glad, because great is your reward in heaven, for in the same way they persecuted the prophets who were before you.'"

"I wish I felt blessed," Millie said.

"It's not a feeling. It's a promise. 'The God of all grace, who called you to his eternal glory in Christ, after you have suffered a little while, will himself restore you and make you strong, firm and steadfast.'"

"This is good stuff. You got more?"

"A whole bookful. You have anybody you can talk to back there?"

"Justice Bonassi. I've been meeting with him and his wife. They've been great."

"That's a godsend," Jack said. "I've prayed you would find good support." Then he added, "How are you doing, really?"

Millie thought a moment. "It's hard, but I keep remembering what Mom used to say. Just let it roll off your back like a duck."

"She was a wise woman."

"What I don't like is that it is such a distraction to the Court's business. So I hope this blows over soon."

"And when it does," Jack said, "maybe I can come out there. And take you to dinner. That'd give the reporters something to talk about, wouldn't it?"

She laughed, suddenly wishing he were here now.

3

The barbershop for members of the House of Representatives was in the Rayburn House Office Building. A throwback to someone's idea of a small-town hair salon, it sported a barber's pole outside the door and three chairs. Since it had been privatized, the House barbershop had lost more barbers than it kept.

Sam Levering did not get his haircuts here. The Senate had its own, nicer, salon. His mission in the House shop was to find the House Speaker, Representative Brian Kessler. Kessler's office had told Levering where he was, though that was no guarantee Kessler would actually be in the chair. House members were notorious for demanding an appointment with the barber, and then being late, often hours late, or not showing up at all.

But there he was, in the middle chair, being snipped by a short black-haired man.

"Hello, Brian," Levering said.

"Sam," Kessler said. "You slumming?" A fifty-year-old red-headed freckle face, Kessler was the quintessential boy next door. That was how he kept getting reelected. Only Levering and a few other insiders knew about certain practices that might have scandalized Kessler's constituents.

"Can your man here take a break?" Levering said.

The barber shot a hard stare at Levering.

"Can't this wait?" Kessler said.

"Knowing you, it can't," Levering said. Kessler was always doing three or four things at once. Levering wanted his undivided attention.

"Ermanno," Kessler said. "Why don't you give us a few minutes, huh?"

With an Italian version of *humph,* the barber walked out of the shop. Kessler spun around in the barber chair. Levering parked himself in the adjoining one.

"I want you to start thinking about impeaching Hollander," Levering said.

Kessler remained impassive. He was a cool one. One didn't get the speakership without developing an iron poker face.

"That's pretty extreme, don't you think?" Kessler said.

"Just start thinking about it, that's all."

"Are you nuts?" Kessler said, his cheeks starting to show the first blossoms of pink. "I don't like the idea of messing with the Supreme Court."

"What if the Supreme Court, by a slim majority, starts messing with our issues?"

Kessler shook his head. "Sam, you're talking about the third arm of government. I don't want to lead our party down that path."

"Do you have any idea what might be at stake?"

Kessler pulled the apron off his chest and leaned forward. "Sam, listen. That's going way too far. There would have to be a big public outcry for impeachment first."

"You watch," Levering said calmly. "There just might be."

"There's more to this?"

"I said watch. And be ready."

Kessler ran his fingers through his incomplete hairstyle. Soon it would be lacquered down so even a typhoon couldn't damage it. Levering had always admired Kessler's hair.

"Look," Kessler said, "I'm not going to make any commitments. At the most, I'll wait and see."

"You don't have to wait to see. I'll tell you how to proceed."

A thin smile came to Kessler's face. "You wouldn't be trying to put the Arnold on me?"

The Arnold was code on the Hill for strong-arming. "Let's just say the president and I would much appreciate this little act of kindness." Levering felt like Marlon Brando in *The Godfather.* It almost made him laugh.

"What if I refuse?" Kessler said.

"You won't."

Kessler's soft cheeks became hot pink. "You think I'm going to sit here and let you—"

"How's your wife back in Sioux Falls?" Levering said.

Kessler's eyes opened a little wider.

"Still in the first stages of Parkinson's?" Levering asked.

"You slime." Kessler said it softly, haltingly.

"Your social activities never need to get back to the old hometown," Sam Levering said. "We'll be in touch."

On his way out, Levering dropped a dollar in the barber's tip tray.

4

Friday's conference with the justices was like watching a slow, virulent cancer take hold in the body of the Supreme Court. Millie managed to make it through, but strain was clearly seeping into the chamber.

So she was more than grateful when Helen called, inviting her to lunch. She said she would come around with a driver and they'd go out to a secluded place by the Potomac for a picnic. It was the perfect plan.

The car entered the Court garage at one o'clock. It was a large black limo with tinted windows. Helen certainly knew how to do a D.C. power picnic, Millie mused as the driver opened the limo door. For a moment she thought she recognized him from somewhere.

When she got in, she knew. Seated next to Helen was Senator Sam Levering.

"What is this?" Millie asked. The door slammed behind her.

"Millie," Helen said, "we have to talk."

Speechless with shock and anger, Millie glared at the senator. The last time she had been in a limousine with him had not exactly been a pleasant experience.

"Madame Chief Justice," Levering said with a nod.

"Helen, what is going on?" Millie asked.

The limo started up and Millie practically fell back into the seat. Outside the sun was shining. Inside the air was foul and close.

"We need to talk," Helen said. "Sam—Senator Levering— and I are really concerned about what's going on."

Levering folded his ruddy hands across his stomach. "Madame Justice, do you know what Ambrose Bierce once said about politics?"

Millie just looked at the senator, anger rising in her like a flame.

"He said politics is nothing more than the 'strife of interests masquerading as a contest of principles.' A wise man, Bierce."

"That politics should be without principle?" Millie snapped.

"You miss the point," Levering said in his smooth, practiced manner. "We are awash in a strife of interests, that's all, and you're right in the middle of it. I want to see if I can help you out before the politics gets to the Court."

Millie felt the tone switch to mild threat. She was livid. Threaten the Court itself? She would fight to the bitter end to protect the honor of the Court. "Just what is it you are suggesting, Senator?"

"A chance," Levering said softly.

"A chance for what?"

"To survive."

"The Court is strong enough to survive," Millie said, "and so am I."

The phony congeniality melted off Levering's face. "Look, Madame Justice, what I'm talking about here—"

He stopped as Helen put her hand on his leg. "Let me," she said to the senator. Then to Millie: "What Senator Levering is trying to say, Millie, is a concern I share as well."

"Why didn't you come to me first?" Millie asked.

"It's all bollixed up," Helen said. "So much has happened. The point isn't the past, though—it's the future. Yours and the Court's."

Millie felt like screaming at them both to leave the Court alone. "Why don't you both come out and tell me what you want?"

"I'll take it," Levering said firmly. "Many of us in Congress are very uncomfortable about you mixing religion and politics and the law. Very uncomfortable. Especially after a bunch of us went to bat for you. Not only to be CJ, but when you first came up as a nominee. You made certain assurances—"

"No, Senator," Millie said. "I never locked myself into a position on any issue."

"Don't quibble with me," Levering said, pointing his finger at her. "You know what I'm talking about. You indicated to me in private, and to the public at large, that you were going to continue your course as it had been in the past. Nobody ever thought you'd go . . ."

"What, Senator?" Millie said. "Were you going to say crazy?"

"Actually," Levering said, "I was going to say nuts."

Millie felt lightning flash inside her head. She wanted out. Now.

"That's a little harsh, don't you think?" Helen said to Levering.

"Millie," the senator said, giving her an I-feel-your-pain kind of look. "No one wants this to be hard on you, or the Court. And no one is denying you the right to think about life, make some personal changes. But you need to step back and look at the big picture. The picture of this country of ours, of the rights and laws that we've built up painfully over the last hundred years."

What was this, his Fourth of July stump speech?

"You are in a position, not only as chief, but as the key vote, to tear down that delicate edifice," Levering continued. "Wouldn't you agree that this should be a matter of sober reflection? Of patience? I understand you had a law clerk resign over this."

How did he know that? The idea of leakage from within the walls of the Court filled Millie with a sickening dread. "That happened," Millie said. "So?"

"Don't you see the danger?" Levering said. Helen, looking at Millie, nodded in agreement, as if Millie should see it, too. Levering leaned forward, his elbows on his knees. "You take the angry resignation of one clerk and you expand the reaction over an entire nation. You'll have civil strife like we haven't seen in a generation. All because of religious f—"

Millie thought he was about to say *fanaticism.*

"—fervor," Levering said.

Millie felt all of her muscles tensing, especially her hands, which she opened and closed in front of her.

"We just want to know," Helen said, "if you'll think about it, talk to us, talk to me. We can get through this, Millie. We can."

"Get through it *how,* Helen?" Millie said.

"We have someone you need to meet," Helen said. "Trust me."

Millie felt the last reserves of any sort of trust for Helen nearly canceled out by the presence of Sam Levering. But this was not just about trust, or about one justice. The integrity of the Supreme Court itself was involved. For that, she would stay, if only to figure out how to keep the senator's creeping tentacles out of the sacred chamber.

5

Anne wasn't sure of the precise moment she decided to take up smoking again. It just happened.

She stood outside the Plaza Hotel in New York and lit up. Why Ambrosi had chosen this place to meet was beyond her. It was so public. So old-style gentility.

Inhaling the smoke as if it were life-giving oxygen, Anne watched the upscale afternoon crowd milling about. A hansom cab pulled up in front with a giggling couple in their early thirties. They seemed blissfully happy. Anne immediately hated them.

Why wasn't *she* happy? Everything was going her way, wasn't it? She was taking care of business for Levering and she was good, so good. That weasel of a detective, Markey, had no idea what he was up against. He'd fade out soon enough.

So why should she be smoking as if her life depended on it? She laughed at that. A life lived in dependence on tobacco products? Well, why not? She remembered a bumper sticker she saw once: "Everybody has to believe something. I believe I'll have another beer."

I believe I'll have another smoke.

One of the Plaza doormen looked at her with a leer. Anne shook her head, as much to herself as to the doorman, and turned back toward Fifth Avenue. At the same time, she fished out another cigarette and turned her thoughts toward Levering.

He was losing it, whatever "it" was. His general anxiety level seemed to be growing by leaps and bounds. If it wasn't for the paycheck, she might have considered leaving his employ.

Was she losing "it," too? She shook off the thought. Losing was not in her program. Ever since her parents had died, she had trained herself to win at all costs. All costs.

She took a few steps down the sidewalk, just to get moving. The steamy air of the New York street was, in its own way, bracing for her. She breathed deeply of its mix of smoke, fumes, and dust.

She was just about to turn back toward the hotel when she saw Elijah.

Her jaw dropped. The burning cigarette in her fingers fell to the sidewalk. Had Ambrosi shipped Elijah to New York?

Anne didn't even glance down. She couldn't. Elijah was walking straight toward her.

She felt a scream rising in her throat, but even then her mind said something about being in front of the Plaza Hotel, idiot, and do you want to make a spectacle?

Her mind zipped back to the last time she'd seen him, when he'd told her that it wasn't too late. Like some ghostly herald from Shakespeare.

Should she run? That would be an even bigger spectacle, some crazed chick in heels tottering down the street.

Or she could mace him again.

She reached in her purse, fumbled around. It was in there somewhere. Where?

He was within ten feet of her, looking past her, when she realized her error. It was not Elijah. It could have been his brother, though. The similarity in build and bearing was striking. But it was definitely not him.

Anne felt chills run through her body as this New York version of the crazy prophet passed her without a glance.

Oh, she was closer to losing it than she thought. What was going on with her? She dug in her purse for another cigarette.

"Hey!" Ambrosi's voice. The word came out like a hard *A*. She dropped her purse.

"What is up with you?" Ambrosi said. He was dressed all in black, a silky black suit with matching shirt and tie, and dark glasses. He looked like midnight on two legs.

Anne let fly a few choice words as she gathered up the things that had spilled out of her purse. Ambrosi watched.

"You could help me," Anne said.

"You look like you could use a drink."

"Did you hear what I said?" She was crouched down, trying hard to keep her tight dress from tearing and, at the same time, keep her undergarments from being exposed to the gawking pedestrians.

"Cool off, baby," Ambrosi said.

When Anne finally had her bag restuffed, she stood up and said, "Did you take care of our problem in D.C.?"

She imagined him blinking in mock disgust behind his shades. "Who are you talking to?"

"Just reassure me."

"I already told you."

"Tell me again."

"Yeah."

"Yeah what?"

"Done."

Anne shook her head. "You escorted him where?"

Ambrosi looked at his nails. "Look, babe, I didn't give you the whole thing. We had to go all the way."

Anne looked around, as if FBI cameras were homing in on them. "You killed him?"

"Whacked. Remember?" He laughed.

"We didn't ask you to—"

"You can't do anything now," Ambrosi said. "It's over. Wanna do the Oak Bar?"

Too late.

"Yeah," she said to Ambrosi. "Let's get a drink *now.*"

6

The park faced the Potomac. Its gentle murmur in the October afternoon was in sharp contrast to the jangling alarms inside Millie. Despite Helen's presence and soothing voice, she sensed something was very wrong. And she was determined to find out just what that was.

"Over here," Helen said. She led Millie toward the eastern end of the park. There were a few scattered people around, some lolling in the shade of birch trees, others at picnic tables having lunch. She wondered if any of them had any idea who was here. A United States senator and the chief justice. No one seemed to notice.

Helen stopped at a table where a lone woman sat. The woman looked up at Helen and smiled. It was clear they knew each other.

"Millie . . . I mean Justice Hollander," Helen said. "I'd like you to meet Toni Ridge."

The woman smiled at Millie and extended her hand. She was around thirty-five and wore a conservative business suit. She might have been a lawyer or an accountant. Or an actress playing one. Her hair and eyes were movie star quality.

"I'm very honored to meet you," Toni Ridge said.

Mystified, Millie said, "Thank you."

"I thought you should meet her," Helen said. "She works in one of our NPPG offices in Maryland. Legal counsel." Helen motioned for everyone to sit.

"You know Senator Levering, I believe," Helen said to Toni. The look that flashed across Toni's face suggested to Millie she knew him quite well. But all she said was, "Of course."

Helen took charge, as if running one of her meetings. "I wanted you to see a human face, Millie. Someone whose life you have touched profoundly."

Millie looked at the beautiful young woman. She appeared to be the picture of urban success. She even wore a wedding ring, prompting Millie to imagine a square-jawed husband who also had movie star looks.

"Toni, why don't you tell Millie, I mean, the chief justice, just what this is all about," Helen said.

"I'd be happy to," Toni Ridge said. She folded her hands in front of her, like a guest on a talk show. "Madame Chief Justice, when I was in law school, at Georgetown, I fell in love with your opinions. Not simply because I agreed with your opinions, but because of the writing itself. No one on the Court is a stylist like you."

"Thank you," Millie said quietly.

"I knew then I wanted to follow in your footsteps," Toni said. "I wanted to learn the law and hopefully, someday, become a judge. Who knows, maybe I'd end up on the Supreme Court. It's a wild dream, I know."

"Everything worth attaining starts as a dream," Millie said. Despite the odd circumstances, Millie felt an affinity for the woman. Anyone who loved the law . . .

Smiling shyly, Toni said, "Yeah. I believed that. Anyway, I really took to law school. I made *Law Review*, everything was going great. And then . . ."

The trailing off of her voice was like the change in score in a movie. What had once been a light, airy scene was suddenly ominous, with things lurking in shadows.

"Go ahead," Helen told Toni. "You're among friends."

The young woman looked at her hands. They were no longer folded demurely. Now the fingers squeezed against the back of her hands, bunching the skin.

"Well," Toni said after a long sigh, "it was in my second year, toward the end. Everything had gone along so well. I had a great job lined up for the summer. I was going to be editor-in-chief of the *Law Review*. There was even a chance"—Toni gave a small laugh—"that I might be number one in my class. I was neck and neck with a guy named Harold Rose, and I was determined, boy. I wanted that."

She looked down at her hands, still stretching her skin as if trying to pull some comfort from them. Helen put her hand on Toni's, patted them.

"Anyway," Toni said, "I was going home one night from a long stint at the library, walking across campus. I guess I was stupid. Why did I have to go around by the athletic field? It was a straight shot to my apartment by way of the student union."

She paused, took a deep breath, continued. "He was waiting in the doorway of the women's locker room. I tried to run
the other way. But he got me."

Now Millie started to see. Not only what Toni was going
to describe about that night, but also the effects. It was beginning to be very clear why Helen and Levering wanted Millie to
hear this. She thought of stopping everything right then, but
could not bring herself to interrupt the woman's story.

"He was strong," Toni said. "Massively strong. He got tape
over my mouth without any problem and carried me like a sack
of laundry to the grassy strip between the gym and locker room.
And that's where it happened. That's where he raped me."

Millie swallowed hard, caught between empathy and incipient anger.

"Sure enough I got pregnant," Toni said. "Sure enough they
never caught the guy. That didn't matter. What mattered was
now everything I had worked for and hoped for was going to
be torn down. There was no way I could carry a baby to term.
But I knew I wouldn't have to."

Toni looked at Millie with large, watery eyes. "I knew that
because of your principles," Toni said, "that a woman's right to
choose was safe and strong. I found myself going back and
reading your opinion in the Messier case, where you so elo-
quently defended *Roe v. Wade,* because of how far our country
has evolved in morality and ethics since that time. When I went
in for my procedure, I was actually happy."

A creeping sensation wound its way up Millie's spine, like
curling fingers pushing and pulling at her.

"And that's my story," Toni said.

"Thank you," Helen said.

Millie said nothing, but felt like Helen and Levering were
waiting for her to respond. Give Toni a *Thanks for sharing* or
something, and then a *Thanks for setting me straight.*

Instead, Millie put her own hand on Toni's. The woman
looked at her expectantly. "Ms. Ridge," Millie said, "I know
this must have been hard for you."

"I just wanted you to know," Toni said. "Helen said I . . ." She stopped suddenly.

Millie leaned back. "Yes, what was it Helen said?"

Toni Ridge looked as if she'd been caught stealing files from her law firm. Helen Forbes Kensington looked at the grass.

"I think it's time somebody told me what's really going on," Millie said.

Levering threw up his hands. "I agree. Let's go."

7

"Listen," Sam Levering said. "This whole thing has gone far enough. You want to stay on the Court, you make a pledge right now."

They were in the limo heading back to the Court building. Helen sat silently by, looking out the window.

Millie fought hard to keep from throwing something—a decanter of booze from the bar would be fitting—at the senator's face. "How dare you," she said.

"Oh, please," Levering said. "Spare me your outrage. You've got a decision to make right now. I'm not gonna sit around while you mess up the Court."

Mess up! Getting a lecture on messing up from Sam Levering was too much to bear. *Oh, God, what do I say?*

Helen turned toward her. "Millie, what the senator and I are trying to do is help you remember what it is we've been fighting for all these years, for the right of women—"

"Stop," Millie said. "I don't want to hear it. Helen, how could you?"

"I'll tell you how," Levering said. "The fundamentalists are shouting hosannas about your conversion. Or haven't you heard? They're already writing *Roe* off the books."

"How can either of you think I'd listen to any outside influence?" Millie's heart was making its way to her throat, pounding with outrage. "Including yours?"

Helen sighed. "Millie—"

"Hold it," Levering snapped. "Just hold it now and let me do the talking." His face swiveled toward Millie. "Let's cut to the chase, shall we? Here is the way it is. You will check with me on the big votes, the big cases, from now on. I will tell you what to do."

Millie's hands curled in on themselves, her nails pressing flesh. "Are you insane?"

"Been called a lot of things in my time. *Insane* is pretty tame."

"I would never," Millie said, pausing to choose her words carefully, "ever consider compromising the workings of the Court, or my own independence, for anyone, let alone you. You are a United States senator with an oath of office. How do you look at yourself in the morning?"

"With these eyes," Levering said, passing his fingers in front of his face. "I can see things, you know. I can see the future. Want me to tell you yours?"

Anger kept Millie's mouth closed while she waited.

"You refuse to take my direction," Levering continued, "and I walk over to the House and get a little investigation going. Impeachment, Madame Justice." He drew the last word out so it sounded like *Just-ess*.

He *was* insane. Threatening impeachment as a form of extortion? Right here in his own limousine, with Helen sitting in silence, without protest.

"You can't possibly succeed with an impeachment," she said. "The country won't stand for it. Congress won't stand for it."

"Don't you remember what Bierce said? The Congress is a masquerade of principles, Madame Justice, and I can manipulate that particular masquerade."

"You have no grounds for impeachment."

Levering's smile was sickening. "You have no idea." He leaned forward, raising a warning finger. "This is a promise. You give me your answer by tomorrow. You don't, and I will rain fire and brimstone on you. And you can take that to the bank, Saint Millicent Mannings Hollander."

8

Millie's head was practically bursting with anger when she got to Bill Bonassi's house. Night was hovering over D.C. and several times she thought she'd faint in the taxi. The world was spinning out of control, out of the realm of reality. She needed Bonassi's counsel now.

They met in his study as Dorothy went to brew some tea. The room was primarily floor-to-ceiling bookcases, the Old Lion's den.

"Tell me about it," he said.

She managed to tell him everything without breaking down. He sat, listening patiently, not interrupting her once.

When she finished Bonassi took a long pause before answering. "Mark Twain said there is no distinctly American criminal class, except Congress."

It was the right comment, lightening the pressure just a bit.

Millie blurted, "I never thought I'd be in a position like this. What do I do?"

"Get a lawyer," Bonassi said.

"Do you know anyone?"

Bill Bonassi raised his hand. "Why not let me take a crack at it?" he said.

"You?"

"Dottie says I'm spending too much time with my garden. I'm driving her nutty."

"But I couldn't ask you . . ."

"You don't have to," Bonassi said. "I'm signing up. *Pro bono publico*. We can't let the Leverings of this world spread their poison, not on the steps of the Court. I want in, Millie, if you'll have me."

Now there were definite tears in her eyes, and she didn't stop them. "Thank you. I don't know what else to say."

"No need to say anything." Bonassi stood up, and suddenly looked twenty years younger. Excitement seemed to pour out of his skin. "Here are the ground rules. We'll do everything by prayer and the law. In that order. Agreed?"

A rush of relief came to Millie like a cool breeze. "Agreed."

Bonassi rubbed his hands together. "I'll make a little call to our senator friend and let him know exactly what I think of his proposition. I'll do your public speaking. You say nothing until your moment."

"My moment?"

Bonassi nodded. "There comes a time in every trial for *the moment*. It may be on the floor of the United States Senate, when they try your case. Are you prepared to go all the way?"

Her heart was beating rapidly. "All the way, Bill."

"Good. We'll know the time you should speak."

"I hope so."

"No," Bonassi said gently. "You'll pray so. You're a Christian now, with all the privileges of a child of God. One of those is prayer. We'll need it. This is a spiritual battle."

"I have a suggestion," he continued. "Let's pray for Sam Levering."

9

The Senate dining room had two sections. One was for members and guests, the other—called the inner sanctum—was for senators alone. Sam Levering was eating his usual—bourbon and bean soup—when the maitre d' informed Levering a cop wanted to see him.

"Can you make this short?" Levering said to the cop, who said his name was Markey. "I've got an appropriation rider to propose in"—he looked at his watch—"twenty minutes."

"I'll get right to it, then," Markey said, sitting opposite Levering. "There's been a disappearance. I was hoping you could shed some light on it."

"What sort of light would that be?"

"Just the facts."

Levering could not help rolling his eyes. "Don't foul up my air with platitudes, will you, boy?" He hadn't meant it in a racial way, but that's the way it sounded. Well, too bad.

Markey did not look upset. In fact, he looked a little like that actor, what was his name, Denzel Washington. Why wasn't this guy out making movies instead of harassing senators?

"I am conducting an investigation, sir," Markey said, "and I would appreciate your cooperation."

"Ask your questions and then leave."

Markey took out a pad and pen. "Do you know anything about a homeless man named Elijah?"

"Sounds like a Bible story."

"That was his street name, sir."

"Never heard of the guy. Why would I?"

"Your aide, Anne Deveraux, knew him."

Levering's skin began to itch. "What's Anne got to do with this?"

"Hasn't she ever mentioned this man?" Markey asked.

"Some homeless man? No." The booze was helping him keep calm. What did this detective know, anyway?

"She had an encounter with this man," Markey said.

"Look, her private life is her private—"

"I don't mean that kind of encounter," the cop interrupted. "She sprayed him with mace."

Plausible deniability. It would save him again. "I have no idea what you're alluding to. If you're trying to connect me with this man, whoever he is, and something Anne did in her off time, it's just not going to fly."

"Funny," Markey said.

"What is?"

"Oh, just the way Ms. Deveraux spoke about your working relationship. How close it was. You'd think she would have mentioned an incident like that to her boss."

"Well," Levering said, "she didn't." He looked for a waiter. That second Jim Beam was calling. *Steady.*

"So your official statement is that you have no knowledge of the whereabouts of this man Elijah?" Markey asked.

"You do pretty good cop-speak. They teach you that?"

"No." Markey put his pen and pad back in his coat pocket. "My father did."

"Really now? Your daddy a cop?"

"Preacher."

For some reason Levering felt sweat seeping into his collar.

"Isn't that nice," Levering said. "Your daddy teach you to interrupt citizens with pointless questions?"

The cop's demeanor did not change. "May I have your permission to speak plainly?"

Odd request from a detective. "Sure."

Markey said. "I have a feeling about this case. Maybe it has something to do with you, Senator, and maybe not. Maybe it has something to do with Ms. Deveraux, and maybe not. But if my feeling is correct, some bad things are going down around here. And I will find out what they are."

Levering was brought up short. Not because of his brashness, but because of the seeming sincerity with which this detective spoke. Like he knew things he had no way of knowing. Levering inhaled, trying to keep himself as calm as possible.

"Is that the end of your sermon?" Levering responded.

"Amen," Markey said.

"Then get out."

With a curt nod, the detective turned and walked out of the inner sanctum. Levering waited a moment, then yelled to the waiter for another drink.

CHAPTER FIFTEEN

1

New York Times
Wednesday, November 12

A request for an impeachment investigation of Chief Justice Millicent Mannings Hollander has been officially lodged in the House of Representatives by Congresswoman Leigh Barbaros, a California Democrat.

Rumors of such a move have been circulating throughout the Capitol for days. The investigation seeks to delve into the veracity of Hollander's testimony before the Senate Judiciary Committee in light of recent revelations of a religious conversion that could tip the delicate balance of the nation's highest court.

The request will be reviewed by the House Judiciary Committee and its Subcommittee on the Constitution. If the subcommittee determines there is merit to the charges, Articles of Impeachment will be drawn. The full Judiciary Committee must approve the Articles before they are sent to the full House for a vote. A simple majority is all that is required to approve the Articles and send the matter to the Senate for trial.

"It's not that we're against someone converting," one congressman, who requested anonymity, said. "But if it is in complete disagreement with what you swore to when approved, it bears looking into. Especially if it could mean a completely different Supreme Court."

Since 1936, the House has initiated seven impeachment investigations. Only one involved a Supreme Court justice. In 1970 an investigation into the actions of Justice William O. Douglas fell short of the filing of formal charges by the House. The last House impeachment was against President Bill Clinton, which resulted in a Senate trial and acquittal.

THE BURROW BULLETIN

Hollander to Be Impeached!

The House of Representatives, currently investigating Chief Justice Millicent Mannings Hollander, already has the votes to impeach! While the official request for an investigation is just in a preliminary stage, sources Burrowing in on the story tell me an impeachment (which is just like a grand jury indictment from the House) is a done deal. "This lady's toast," one Burrower said.

"There's a whole bunch of stuff no one knows about yet," this Burrower continues. "It's really going to get hot."

The *Burrow Bulletin* will keep its readers updated. But look out! Gloves are reportedly about to come off.

TRANSCRIPTS/LarryKingLive

KING: Tonight, a distinguished panel discusses the
    impeachment investigation surrounding the Chief Justice of
    the United States Supreme Court. Joining us, from Boston,
    professor of Constitutional Law at Yale University Law
    School, Lawrence I. Graebner. In Washington, retired
    justice of the Supreme Court, the Honorable William T.
    Bonassi; joining me here in Los Angeles is Rebecca
    Margullis, President of the National Organization for
    Women. And they are all next on LARRY KING LIVE.

    Good evening. The impeachment of a Supreme Court
    justice, the chief justice in fact, is a distinct possibility

tonight. Professor Graebner, I'll start with you. What do you make of it?

GRAEBNER: Well, Larry, the Constitution gives the people of the United States, through its representative bodies, the power to impeach federal judges. Since the federal judiciary enjoys lifetime tenure, this is the only procedure for removal at our disposal.

KING: For high crimes and misdemeanors.

GRAEBNER: No, no. That is the standard for the impeachment of civil officers. The president, vice president, and so on. The standard for judges is found in Article III, Section I, and states that judges, both of the Supreme Court and lower federal courts, shall hold their seats during good behavior.

KING: So what's good behavior?

GRAEBNER: The real question is what is bad behavior.

KING: Okay. What's bad behavior then?

GRAEBNER: Well, as Gerald Ford said when he was in Congress, and proposed impeaching Justice William O. Douglas, an impeachable offense is whatever a majority of the House of Representatives considers it to be at a given moment in history.

MARGULLIS: And that's right now, Larry.

KING: We'll get to you in a moment, Rebecca. I wanted to ask Justice Bonassi what he thinks of that. Justice Bonassi, it's an honor to have you on the program.

MARGULLIS: Can I just ask a question?

KING: Rebecca, we'll get to you. Go ahead, Justice Bonassi.

BONASSI: Thank you, Larry. With all due respect to Professor Graebner, the House is undertaking what can only be described as a witch hunt. A person's personal religious beliefs are being questioned, as if they were some sort of crime.

MARGULLIS: When it comes to a woman's right to choose, there is—

KING: Rebecca, just a moment, please.

BONASSI: What? What did she say?

KING: You go ahead, Justice Bonassi.

BONASSI: I was saying that this is not a proper standard
for impeachment. The framers never meant this power to
be abused in this way. They did not want inquisitions for
personal views.

GRAEBNER: If I may, an inquiry into personal views is what
the confirmation process is supposed to be. But when
a judicial candidate lies to the committee, that is surely
grounds for later removal.

KING: Rebecca Margullis, you—

BONASSI: Wait, wait a second, Larry. We've just heard a
scurrilous charge from the professor. You can't seriously be
suggesting that the chief justice was intentionally lying to
the Judiciary Committee. We need proof, Professor
Graebner, as you no doubt tell your first-year students.

GRAEBNER: There's plenty of proof. We have her testimony.
And as the House investigation proceeds, I am sure more
will be coming out.

BONASSI: That is an absolutely outrageous statement—

MARGULLIS: Larry—

BONASSI:—an affront not only to our system, but to the
reputation of a fine justice who has served this country
with absolute integrity and dignity.

MARGULLIS: Larry—

KING: Rebecca Margullis in Los Angeles, what's your take on
all this?

MARGULLIS: Millicent Mannings Hollander must go, Larry.

The National Exposure

Pics Show Justice in Arms of Minister!
Is She Seeking Help with an Alcohol Problem?
by Dan Ricks

There is a "smoking gun" in the House investigation into
Chief Justice Millicent Mannings Hollander.

Smoking gun? Maybe a whole arsenal of hot weapons!

A source close to the investigation says this is "the most
incriminating stuff since Monica's dress."

Included in this pile of inculpatory items are several photographs taken in California during Hollander's supposed

convalescence. Instead of healing her head, she was apparently head over heels . . . with a fundamentalist Christian minister!

The question they're asking on the Hill is this: Do we want the chief justice of our Supreme Court, the one who will be instrumental in decisions regarding abortion, church and state, privacy, and so on, in lip lock with a minister? Especially a minister who is rabidly anti-abortion?

That's right. The Reverend Jack Holden once did time in the clink—after trying to shut down a family planning clinic!

But that's not the worst of the trouble for the chief justice.

According to a reliable source, the accident then Associate Justice Hollander was involved in a few months ago was the result of alcohol abuse! The story is that Hollander was out on the town with a well-known politico, had a bit too much to drink, and ran off from the limo they were sharing—right into oncoming traffic! Apparently no one at the hospital thought to test a Supreme Court justice for blood alcohol content.

The story is confirmed by the driver of this politico's limousine, by the way.

"The House won't stand for this," the source told the *Exposure*. "Nor will the American people. Millicent Mannings Hollander will be gone from the Supreme Court before the first snow falls."

2

Detective Don Markey took a sip of battery-acid coffee and reached for the small Bible he kept in his metal government-issue desk. Markey tried to read at least a little bit from the Word every day. His colleagues knew his practice, and had stopped razzing him about it. His nickname, "Preacher," had been dropped in favor of the whispered sobriquet, "Goose." As in Wild Goose Chase.

Markey knew he took more chances than others on the force, looked under more rocks, around more corners. He even went through more dumpsters. He was relentless when he got a hunch, and for the most part his superiors let him go.

Markey took another sip of bad coffee from a Styrofoam cup and opened his Bible. He had been reading through Proverbs, seeking wisdom. Crying out for it. The whole Levering situation was bothering him to no end.

Elijah's disappearance smelled. The odds that he had left town on his own were small. Homeless people found places to call home and tended to stick to them unless they had a very good reason to leave.

The timing was suspicious, too. No sooner had he put a little heat on the senator's chief aide than Elijah was gone.

He only had a hunch, no hard evidence, so what could he do but ask for wisdom?

He had been quietly reading for five minutes when the phone rang.

"Markey," he said.

"Hey," said Phil Crane. Phil was another D.C. detective. "You need to get down here. I'm out at Key Bridge."

"What's up?"

"Just come down here. We have a body. Dragged out of the river."

"Why do you need me?"

"You'll see."

It took just under twenty minutes for Markey to get there. The scene was taped off and a lone medical examiner waddled around a couple of uniforms, examining a body.

Phil was standing by the body's feet. They were bare, puffy, white. A blue-black ring encircled each ankle. Markey did not see the face as the ME poked at it with something that looked like a knitting needle.

"Know who it is?" Markey said.

"Nope."

"Why'd you want me down here?"

"Because he looks like a homeless guy, no ID, ratty clothes."

Markey stiffened. He bolted toward the ME and put his hand on his shoulder.

"Hey!" the ME said.

"Sorry," Markey said, looking down. There could be no doubt. The bloated face belonged to Elijah.

3

When she could stand the silence no longer, Millie walked, unannounced, into the chambers of Thomas J. Riley.

His clerk, whose name was Russell something, looked as if a terrorist had walked in. His lips moved in a soundless expression of something like shock.

"I'll let myself in," Millie said.

Riley looked up from his desk with a bit of the same expression as his clerk. He held his pen in midair as Millie plopped herself down in a chair. She saw on his desk the Latin phrase he loved to quote: *Vincit omnia veritas.*

"We have to talk," she said.

Riley looked at the clock. "I'm preparing for argument."

"I have to know something."

The justice lowered his pen.

"I have to know if any leak has come out of this chamber," she said.

"Leak?"

"Information. Inside information."

"I don't follow you." He seemed cagey, like he must have been back in the courtrooms of Wyoming.

"Tom, we've been through a lot together over the years," Millie said, her throat tightening. "I hope that counts for something, even though we look to be on opposite sides now."

"Go on," Riley said.

"Someone got to the media with my conversion."

"You think it was me?" Riley tossed the pen on the desk.

"Maybe not intentionally—"

"At all!" he snapped.

Millie paused, sudden regret in her heart. This was a man who had been like a father to her, a mentor, an inspiration. That they were even having this conversation was tragic in a deeply personal way. But she had to ask the questions. She had to clear the air in the Court, or she could not hope to lead it.

"If you are telling me you had nothing to do with it," Millie said, "that's good enough for me."

"I've said all I'm going to. Now if you'll excuse me we both have work to do."

Millie felt dirty somehow. Like filth had been dumped into these hallowed halls, and everyone was walking in it. That saddened her most of all. That the Court, the institution she loved with all her heart, should have come to this.

"I'm sorry," Millie said, rising. "I just hope we can find a way to be civil with each other."

Riley held his pen but did not move it. His eyes bore into her. "Millie, I don't like this any more than you do. But what is happening here is, in my view, a disaster. Impeachment! Do you understand what that means?"

"Of course, I—"

"I'm not sure. And I'm not sure there aren't grounds. Your religion is going to influence your decisions."

Millie rocked back, a little stunned but not surprised. Tom Riley had made his reputation by getting to the meat of the issue instantly. And this was the issue. She knew it.

"It already has on Establishment," Riley continued. "Will it continue on into other areas? If it is, you are not the same justice the Senate confirmed."

"Tom, we both know a judge has to get to the meaning of the law as closely as possible while recognizing his biases."

"Answer the question, please," Riley said.

"It's not that simple, is it?"

"Let me give you a hypothetical then. You have always upheld a woman's right to choose. You know we have cases in the pipeline that will test that. Are you going to rule like a Bill Bonassi now?"

A ripple of anger spread through Millie. "Why is everybody trying to nail me down?"

"Because if you change your mind on that issue, the country will be torn apart."

This truly was the heart of the issue. Millie had known Tom Riley for ten years, had joined him on most decisions, and knew he took the long view of the law. With abortion rights being the central moral question for society, Riley had long argued—and she had agreed—that its threads must be handled gently or there could be social upheaval. If Millie held a different view now, it was possible that the Court could radically alter its past decisions by way of a new 5–4 slant. That was what Riley was asking.

"I haven't seen a specific case yet," Millie said. "The time will come, I'm sure."

"Come on, don't duck this. Do you still believe that right is Constitutional?"

Did she? All of the arguments from her days in law school, on the Court, in briefs and at orals, came rushing back to her. For a moment it all seemed a jumble, a thicket she had no hope of fighting through.

"I'll word my question another way," Riley said. "Do you believe a fetus has the rights of a person?"

"Tom, until I get a case—"

"Let me help you. You know that verse in the Bible, the one we always see in *amicus* briefs. It's from the Psalms, I think. It says something to the effect that God knits babies in the womb. And there are other Bible quotations about God knowing people before they exist. I suspect that's what Bill Bonassi believed."

Millie's head was starting to feel the grip of some huge fist. "I find this offensive, Tom."

"Are you telling me you are the same today as you were last term? Or any previous term?"

"I am a different person in some ways—"

"At the core, Millie. You have had a religious *conversion*. Are you saying that won't affect you at all?"

"I don't know!"

"And if it does, what will that do to our reputation?"

Millie's stomach twisted. Riley's logic was solid, as always. His ability to foresee the consequences of laws made him one of the most insightful of the justices. His insight cut like a knife.

"One thing has not changed," Millie said. "I care just as much about the Court as you, Tom. And I am not going to let politics influence what I do here. I will fight this bogus impeachment business. And I will continue to do what I think is right as a judge."

"I am going to fight back," Riley said. "I—" He seemed then, for the flicker of a moment, to break down. But his face clamped back any emotion. "That's enough," he said.

Millie wanted to say something, but could find no other words. She stood and walked out. The loneliness Millie felt on the way back to her chambers was overwhelming, a cavernous feeling of loss. Even Rosalind, her clerk, seemed to have put up, if not a wall, a veil. And Paul had resigned. At least Rosalind had said she didn't want to leave Millie in the lurch.

"Ready for argument?" Rosalind asked. "I have the briefs and bench memo ready."

"Thank you, Rosalind."

The young woman nipped at her bottom lip with her front teeth. "It didn't help, did it?"

"What didn't help?"

"Talking to Justice Riley. I saw you go in."

"No, not much."

The clerk nodded, concern on her face. Millie put a hand on her shoulder. "I know it hasn't been easy on you," Millie said. "And I am truly sorry. But I want you to know how grateful I am that you've stayed. It means a great deal to me."

Rosalind nodded.

"Come on," Millie said. "It's time to get to the bench."

4

Hardball.

Sam Levering played hardball, played to win, always had.

He was never sorry, though sometimes he felt a little pang when an opponent went down in flames. He felt a little sorry for Millie Hollander. The photos that the smarmy reporter took, and the insinuations about her love life, were almost below the belt. Almost. But it had to be done. And he still had Anne Deveraux to take the fall if worse came to worst.

There was also something arousing about hardball. Whenever he hit one out of the park, as he'd just done with Hollander, he found his libido returning to youthful levels. At such times he wanted two things. A drink and a woman. The former would be sour mash whiskey. The latter could be just about anyone. Tonight it was a blonde named Sondra.

The Capitol building's nearly one hundred "hideaway" offices were virtually unknown by the public, roped off from tourists with snapping cameras. Marked only by door numbers, many of the hideaway offices had gilded crystal chandeliers, floor-length mirrors, fireplaces, and frescoed walls. They were ostensibly for members of Congress to escape the demands of their regular offices. But Levering had discovered the real use was far more personal. LBJ, when he was Senate Majority Leader, had made legendary use of them for his "hideaway honeys." What was good enough for a president, Levering reasoned, was good enough for him.

And room S–326-A, where Daniel Webster had once stored his wine, was his favorite.

Sondra—she must have been about twenty-five—giggled as Levering led her inside.

"Shh," he said. "It's past ten. The walls have ears."

"So do you," she said, playfully biting Levering's right lobe.

"Okay, okay," he said. "But keep it down." The Capitol police were sometimes nosy.

Levering kept a bottle of bourbon in a cabinet near the window. The little minx did not drink anything except wine, but the bottle at dinner seemed to have done the trick.

As he poured himself a bourbon, Sondra snuck up behind him and kissed his neck. She giggled again. That could get old, he mused. Better to drink and get down to business.

His cell phone bleeped in his pocket.

"Oh, no," Sondra said like a pouting coquette.

"I'll turn it off, honey," Levering said. "Just let me take it."

He flipped the phone open.

"Levering."

"This is Detective Markey."

Something like steam heat—part anger, part alcohol, part unfulfilled desire—flushed Levering's face. "How did you get this number?"

"Sir, I have to—"

"I don't want anybody calling this who isn't—"

"Sir, if I may—"

"I'm gonna have a little talk with your commanding officer, boy, you better believe it." Levering waited for an audible show of contrition.

"We found him," Markey said.

"What? What are you talking about?"

"Elijah. The homeless man who was a witness to what really happened that night with Justice Hollander."

The steam was coming out of Levering's nostrils now. "Listen!"

"You'd better listen, Senator. You know this man."

"I don't know anything about him. I told you that."

"We've made a positive ID from the prints."

"I'm hanging up now—"

"It's your son, Senator."

An invisible hand gripped Levering's throat. He held the phone to his ear, as if pressing it against his flesh would erase what was just said.

"I'm sorry, Mr. Senator," Markey said. "The body is that of Tad Levering."

CHAPTER SIXTEEN

1

"They found him!" Anne squeezed the cell phone like an arm wrestler.

"Whoa," Ambrosi said. His phone crackled. He was probably between big buildings in the city.

"In the river," Anne said.

"Don't worry about it."

"He was the senator's own son."

Pause. "So? What do you want me to do about it now?"

"I don't know what I want." And she didn't. The walls were closing in around her.

"Your boss going mental?" Ambrosi asked.

"Oh, yeah. He was on edge before. But this . . ."

"Look, maybe I can help. The both of you."

"Help?"

"I have a sense of pride here."

"What are you talking about?"

"I did a job for you. You didn't like the results. Okay. Happens. You got access to fifty thousand?"

The sudden shift to money talk jolted Anne. "Of course. But why?"

"Let me do another job for you. This one will be clean."

"What sort of job?"

"A biggie."

He seemed to Anne to be smiling.

"Tell me," Anne said.

"I been following the whole thing about the justice. What's her name?"

A prickling came to Anne's neck. "Hollander."

"I could take care of that."

Unthinkable. Absolutely unthinkable. Anne opened her mouth to tell him so. Then stopped. Unthinkable, yes, but in an incredibly exciting way.

"I can't let you do it," Anne said.

"Oh, yeah?"

"Too risky. There's all sorts of security. Especially now."

"Hey," Ambrosi said. "You don't remember what Al Pacino said? Somebody told Al he couldn't whack this guy. Al says if history teaches us anything, it's that you can kill anybody. He's right."

"Look, we better get off now," Anne said. "When can I see you?"

"After."

"After what?"

"I'll let you know."

2

In the moonlight, the back acre of Bill Bonassi's property looked like the realm of a ghost story. There were no colors, only differing shades of light and dark.

Millie and Bonassi sat on the verandah. Millie wondered if this would be the last time she did so as chief justice. Tomorrow, according to new reports, the House committee would release its report, and recommend that the members vote to impeach Millicent Mannings Hollander.

"This is only the beginning of the fight," Bonassi said, trying as always to encourage her. Usually it worked.

Not tonight. Tonight she felt it all slipping away. As if, out in the shadows of the huge lawn, the forces of darkness were gathered to declare victory.

"But the fight is dirty!" Millie said. "They had someone taking pictures of me at the hospital! While my mother was dying some sleazy photographer was snapping away. And the alcohol story! Bill, is it un-Christian to want to claw their eyes out?"

"Righteous anger is allowable, I should think."

"How can they do this to the Court?"

"They can because they want to scorch the earth. If the Court gets burned up, so be it. You're a threat to them now. They'll say anything, do anything."

"I want to talk. I can't stand this. Let's call a press conference."

"I'm preparing a statement," Bonassi said calmly. "It will emphasize that an impeachment is nothing more than an indictment, and that anyone accused in this country is innocent until proven guilty. We seem to forget that sometimes."

"But when do I get to speak?" Millie asked.

"Right now the dogs are barking. They won't hear you."

"But when?"

"We'll know when."

Millie let out a labored breath. Her chest was tight. "I wish I had your faith, Bill. I'm still not there."

"Faith takes time. Instant faith is not very hearty. The Bible says it's the *testing* of your faith that develops perseverance."

"Why?" Millie said. "Why is this happening?"

Bonassi laced his fingers together. "That question is most often answered after the fact. You look back, and you see what God's pattern was."

The word plucked an inner chord in Millie. "My friend, the minister in California, said something like that. God weaving a pattern for the good of those who love him."

"Ah, yes," Bonassi said. "Romans 8:28. The reverse para-noid text."

"Excuse me?"

Bill Bonassi's smile was moonlit. "The Scriptures make an incredible claim that, for those who follow Christ, God arranges things so that *your good* is the final outcome. He is out to get you, you see, but out of love. You are a reverse para-noid if you believe this."

Millie shook her head slightly. "Seems almost too good to be true."

"That's a pretty good definition of God, isn't it?"

"The polls, I'm told, have been running 3–1 against me. And the newspapers and TV news—"

"Forget 'em!" Bonassi said. "We have truth on our side."

Millie flashed to the sign on Tom Riley's desk. *Vincit omnia veritas.* And then, suddenly, she knew what would save the Court.

"Riley," she blurted.

Bonassi looked at her.

"Riley is the key," she said.

3

Don Markey had never interrogated a senator before. He'd questioned a few members of the House, but most of them were as witnesses or sources of information for crimes that did not involve them directly.

This was another level entirely. This time there was a strange link between the murder of Tad Levering, the senator, and Millicent Mannings Hollander.

If one accepted that this was a murder. Markey did without question, but in the interview room, with Levering's lawyer present, that was not a done deal.

"His son was mentally disturbed," the lawyer, a three-piece job named Sugden Bales, said. "That was obvious. And men-tally disturbed people kill themselves."

"By tying cinder blocks to their own feet?" Markey asked.

"Why not? Can you think of a better way to drown?"

"I want to know if the senator thinks that," Markey insisted, looking at Levering. The senator was, Markey thought, the proverbial shell of a man. His whole appearance had changed. Where he had once been almost comically belligerent, he was now folding in upon himself, as if his very bones, like fallen tent stakes, had been ripped out of him.

"The senator is not going to say anything to you," Bales said. "I am advising him not to say a word. You want to arrest him? Be my guest. You'll look like an attention-grabbing fool, but that's your call."

Bales was right, Markey knew. There was not enough evidence to hold Sam Levering. Markey had watched Levering closely when he IDed his son's body. The grief in his face couldn't have been faked, not even by a Slick Sam.

But did he know about the killing at all? If he did, he wasn't talking.

"Look," Markey said to Bales. "We know the dance. We can turn off the music and move ahead to where we'll be in a few weeks anyway. Just have the senator answer a few questions, with you standing here, and we'll be done with it."

"No," Bales said. "Absolutely not."

"Why don't you ask your client?"

"I don't have to ask him, I know what he—" Bales stopped when he turned to Levering.

The senator was shaking, his head buried in his chest. Then he broke out in great sobs, deep and groaning. When he looked up at the ceiling Markey could see his eyes were bloodshot. His cheeks were streaked with wet. "Oh, God!" Levering howled at the ceiling. *"Taaaad!"*

It would have taken an icy heart not to feel for the guy. Markey had seen criminals and con men, faced with overwhelming evidence, crack. Most didn't, but some did. Usually that was sorrow over being caught. But Levering was hurting to the very depths.

Bales, looking as uncomfortable as a bishop in a bar, made a pitiful attempt to pat his client on the shoulder.

"Maybe," Markey said, "we should take a short break."

"Maybe we should just call the whole thing off," Bales said. "And you can just—"

"No," Levering said.

The two other men looked at him.

"Wait," Bales said.

"No, I want to talk."

"My advice is—"

"I don't care about your advice," Levering said, the familiar belligerence flooding back to his voice. "I want to talk."

"Your lawyer has advised you not to," Markey said, even as he readied the tape recorder.

"I said I don't care." Levering smoothed his hair back with his hands, then used the backs of his hands to wipe his eyes. His breathing was labored.

"Sam, please," Bales said.

"Go have a smoke, Sug," Levering said.

"I'll stay."

"Get out of here!"

Sugden Bales looked as if he had been smeared with something foul. He said nothing as he snagged his Givenci briefcase and walked out the door.

"You got that thing ready?" Levering said, nodding toward the recorder.

"Yes, I do," Markey said.

"Okay then."

4

At conference it was clear that the tension had gotten to everyone. Even Ray Byrne, who normally brought a light Irish wit to the discussions, had more lines on his face than Millie could ever remember seeing.

And as the justices made their traditional handshakes around the table, eyes were averted. Especially Justice Riley's. He did not look at Millie. His handshake was weak.

Everyone sat, making little motions with the pens and legal pads in front of them. Justice Atkins doodled, and the normally placid Arlene Praeger Weiss tapped a drumbeat with her pen. Riley and Byrne simply looked at a spot in the center of the conference table, as if waiting for an answer to magically appear.

"All right," Millie said finally. "We all know what's going on. We all know it's affecting us. We also know that the country's business has to continue, and we are a big part of that business. We must not allow anything to distract us."

Riley cleared his throat but did not look up.

"I was named to this position," Millie said, "to lead the Court. That is what I intend to do. We have cases before us right now that need our attention. I suggest we get down to work. Does anyone have anything they'd like to add?"

There was a short pause as the justices exchanged looks. Then Byrne spoke. "Well said, Chief. We're with you."

A couple of voices chimed assent. Millie thought she heard from Parsons and Velarde, and was thankful she had achieved that level of bipartisanship. Her heart ached, however, as Riley remained impassive.

She pushed the feeling downward and said, "Let's start with *United States v. Ferguson.*"

When the conference broke at noon Millie asked Tom Riley to stay behind. The expressions of the other justices reflected that everyone sensed the tension between Millie and Riley.

"We can't go on like this," Millie said when they were alone.

Riley folded his arms and shrugged. "This is the way it is, apparently."

"It doesn't have to be." She suddenly felt the eyes of John Marshall upon her. The great justice peered at them from his portrait, as if his own heart were breaking. "Tom, if you will stand with me and make a statement, along with the others, we can beat this thing back. A Court united, if not in ideology, at least in purpose. We cannot let politics infect us. If it can happen to me, it can happen to any judge, any time. Tom, will you do it?"

She had not wanted desperation to enter her voice, but it was there. And when Tom Riley did not immediately answer, the desperation lodged itself in her, choking off breath.

Finally, Riley said, "Why don't you just resign?"

Resign? Had he really said that? Of course he had. "No."

"Can't you see the horrible damage you've done?"

His words could not have hurt more if they had been knives cutting her skin. Then anger began to well inside her. "I was not the one who leaked the lies to the press."

"It was inevitable," Riley countered. "And the damage might have been greater."

"Greater?"

"How many cases might you decide if . . ."

She looked at him coolly. "If I'm not impeached?"

Riley did not back down. "The Court is what's important."

"No," she said. "The Court is important only if it reflects the views of Thomas J. Riley. That's it, isn't it?"

Justice Riley stood up and started for the door. "I have given thirty years of my life to this institution. The things I have built up . . ."

"The things *you* have built up? This is an institution, Tom. It is greater than any one person."

He glared back at her. "You said it. That's why you should step down."

Riley's face was like winter stillness. His mouth twitched, as if readying to speak of its own accord. But he was silent. It was a silence of finality, like death. He walked out of the conference room.

Millie sat several minutes without moving. She felt as if her body was incapable of emotion, lest it be consumed. And then the grief came, the stark loss, and she bit down hard on her lower lip to keep from crying.

She felt like the walking dead as she returned to her chambers. How could this possibly go on, day after day?

Oh God—she realized she was praying—*show me what to do.*

A knock on the door. Rosalind stepped in. "May I see you a moment?"

"Of course," Millie said, relieved to have the company. For the last week Rosalind had been a quiet support, doing the work of two clerks. It was, Millie knew, Rosalind's way of saying she would stick it out.

"I have something on my mind I have to talk about," Rosalind said. "It's driving me crazy."

Rosalind looked at her hands, rubbing the palms together. "I . . ." She stopped suddenly, turning her head back toward the door as if she might leave.

"Please," Millie said. She went to Rosalind and gently guided her to one of the two leather chairs that faced her desk. It was obvious that whatever Rosalind was trying to say troubled her greatly. "It's all right," Millie said. "Whatever it is."

Rosalind took a deep breath. "I did something and I feel bad about it. I went out with Russell, Riley's clerk."

That wasn't a big deal. Clerks sometimes went out on dates, even crossing ideological lines. Still, the fact that it was Riley's clerk made her wonder what was coming next.

"He wanted to buy me a drink to start, and I said okay. Only I got up and went to the bathroom, and I told the waiter instead of a Seven and Seven, bring me just 7-Up with a dash of Coke in it. And keep them coming."

"But why?"

Rosalind looked at her boss, eyes smoldering. "Because I can't stand what they're doing to you."

"Who is they?"

"Everybody. The whole machine. And I had to find out what Russell knew."

"About what?" Millie's whole body was starting to tense up.

"That day Riley walked out of conference, and you went to see him in his chambers?"

"Yes."

"Well, Russell was on the other side of the door, listening to the whole thing."

"He was eavesdropping?"

"He called it spying. Riley's other clerk wasn't even in at the time. So he did that thing with the glass on the wall. And he listened."

Millie recalled that conversation with absolute clarity. She had told Riley she was a Christian. He had said he would have to fight her.

"He admitted this to you?" Millie asked.

"We kept getting drinks. I'd finish ahead of him, he'd be amazed, we'd order another round. It finally got to the point where he actually bragged about it. He wrote a memo about your conversation with Riley. He told me he knew a guy that knew Biff Burrow, you know, of the *Burrow Bulletin*?"

"I know it," Millie said, "only too well. So Russell leaked the story?"

"Well . . ."

"There's more?"

Rosalind looked distressed, as if this were the most painful part. "Just before Russell left with it, he printed a hard copy. He had it on his desk. He went to the bathroom. And when he got back he said Riley was standing there, reading it."

Millie felt an emptiness starting to swell inside her. It was getting upsettingly familiar.

"And Russell thought he was going to get in trouble," Rosalind said. "But then Riley threw it back on the desk and walked away."

Now the emptiness engulfed her.

"I'm so sorry," Rosalind said, and then her eyes filled with tears. "I wish I hadn't done that. I feel dirty. And I feel dirty telling you. But I couldn't keep it to myself."

Millie came to Rosalind and put her arm around her. "No, don't. You wanted to help me. That means more to me than anything."

Rosalind wiped at her eyes. "What's going to happen to us?"

Us. That this young woman had used that word was more important to Millie than Rosalind would probably ever know. Millie squeezed Rosalind's shoulder.

"I don't know," Millie whispered.

| 5

Anne could not shake the feeling that the walls were closing in. Was it just a panic attack?

She hadn't heard from Levering, hadn't been able to track him down. Where was he? Off in an alcoholic stupor? It wasn't like him to be so far removed from communication. That had to be part of it.

Then there was Ambrosi. He was going to do something, and she didn't know what. That wasn't like him, either. It meant something big. She'd get caught up in it, maybe that was the thing. He was going to bring her down with him.

But there was something else, worse than mere professional anxiety. It was a deep disquiet of some kind, a big black hole inside her, swirling, sucking up galaxies.

Self-analysis was not something she was into. No money in it. No time for it. She usually dealt with uneasiness through action. Planning things, twisting arms. Even shopping. But this was something worse. She knew it wasn't going to shake loose with a few purchases from Saks.

So what was this?

It felt like something calling to her. Searching for her.

The knock on her apartment door jarred her back into the present. She was startled to see that detective, Markey, through her peephole.

"What is it?" she said through the door.

"Ms. Deveraux, open the door, please."

It was official-speak. She had no choice. Not to open would be like an admission of guilt.

She let him in.

"I'm sorry, Ms. Deveraux, but you'll have to come with me now," Don Markey said.

"Whoa, whoa," she said. "Not now. I've got a meeting in ten—"

"You don't understand. You are under arrest."

Her skin started to climb upward. "Arrest?"

"For complicity in the murder of Tad Levering."

"Look," she said, "I don't know what you're talking about, but you're way off base."

"You have the right to remain silent," he said.

"Wait a second, hold it. Can't you explain all this?"

"You have the right to an attorney—"

"This is ridiculous."

"Are you waiving your right to an attorney?"

"I'm not waiving anything."

"Then come with me and we'll talk about things at the station."

"Things?"

"Unless you want to talk right now, tell me the whole thing. Corroborate what the senator said."

Anne tried to keep her face from twitching. "Senator?"

"Levering. He's told us quite a tale."

Anne's face did not cooperate. She felt her cheeks go into weird gyrations. He knew. The guy knew it all. She could see it in his eyes. And he knew she knew. It was all over, baby. She could almost hear Ambrosi's voice telling her that.

With a swift precision honed over many years, Anne's mind clicked and calculated in her moment of deepest crisis. Survival mode she sometimes called it. When the chips were down, you had to find the best way out.

The detective just waited, as if he knew what she was going to say.

"What kind of deal can we work out here?" she said.

CHAPTER SEVENTEEN

| 1

Now, at last, her moment had come.

Millie walked out of her chambers, Rosalind by her side, and proceeded through the Great Hall. Bill Bonassi was waiting for them just outside the doors.

"You ready?" he asked.

"As I'll ever be," Millie said. She clutched a card that had notes for her statement. It would be respectful, but forceful. Every politician, every citizen, would know that she would stand against the onslaught. The question was whether she could hide the whirlwind inside her. She had thought peace would come with her moment. It had not.

"Then let's go." Bonassi took her arm and started down the great stone steps toward the snarl of reporters below. A clump of microphones was set up on the first level, with half a dozen television cameras placed at strategic locations and angles. Behind the reporters a large crowd of the curious thrust forward, kept at bay by four uniformed D.C. police officers.

Just before her final descent, Millie paused to look back at the Court building. The same marble figures flanked the portico, and the same immortal words, *Equal Justice Under Law,* moved her with their majesty. When she had first seen them she thought they had come from the mind of man. Now she knew they could only have come from the God who gave mankind the very capacity to be just.

At the knot of microphones, Bill Bonassi put his hand up to silence the few shouted questions.

"We have a statement to make," he said. Cameras flashed and snapped, like hungry piranhas.

"It's been a long time since I've stood here," Bonassi said. "It was back in 1953 I first climbed these steps to make an argument before the Court. It was a free speech case. I argued on behalf of a school teacher from Nebraska. I argued that the Constitution gives every citizen the right to think and express ideas that might offend some folks, without the fear that such expression will result in being fired. And we won."

Millie marveled at him. His voice and carriage were magnificent, as if he had been preparing all his life for just this moment.

"Today, after so many years," Bonassi said, "I stand upon desecrated ground. I will say no more than that. As counsel for the chief justice, whom I was proud to serve with, I will step aside and allow her to speak for herself. But I want two things made clear. The first is, the charges leveled against Chief Justice Hollander that are the basis for this indictment are false. Second, I want the word to go out loud and clear that what is happening in our legislative halls is an atrocity. It is the antithesis of the ideals this country was founded on. It has to stop. Fairness and justice, which know no party, must once again be pursued, or we can just wrap up this experiment in democracy right now."

Bill Bonassi, standing tall and proud, took a step away from the microphones.

That was Millie's cue. Silently, she prayed.

She looked down at her notes. She could hear the relentless clicking of the cameras.

When she looked up again she saw a girl. She was around eight years old, and was toward the back of the large crowd. How was she so visible?

And then Millie knew. She was on a man's shoulders, looking perhaps for the first time at the great temple of justice. Feelings rushed back to Millie, fresh and alive, of the first time she was here. Feelings of sacredness, of *spotlessness*. The majesty of this place.

The reporters were looking at her expectantly. She was not speaking. Bill Bonassi put his hand on her arm, as if to ask if she was all right.

Millie looked into the eyes of the Old Lion. "All things for good," she whispered to him.

Then she handed him her notes.

"Ladies and gentlemen," she said into the microphones. "The proudest moment of my life was when I was named to serve as a justice of the United States Supreme Court. To come and join men like William T. Bonassi, Thomas Riley, and all the rest, was more than a dream come true. It was as if I had gone to heaven."

She cleared her throat; it was like moving sand. "But I know now that this institution is not heaven. It is a very human institution. That is its reality but also its glory. What we have is indeed an experiment in democracy. But it is more. It is a glorious testimony to the finest instincts in man. There have been those who have disparaged this Court, found it wanting, cast it in political terms. And yes, because we are human beings we make human decisions. No one is going to agree with every opinion that is rendered, even when the vote is 9–0. But I know in my heart that every justice whom I have been privileged to serve with—everyone who puts on those robes—has tried to do the very best that he or she can."

The whir and click of cameras reminded Millie that what she was about to say would be memorialized for all time, and become fodder for endless analysis by pundits, students, and the politically curious. Yes, her moment had truly come. And far from feeling hesitant, she felt a boldness rush in.

"I have made a human decision," she said. "It is one that I am entitled to make under the greatest document for human freedom ever penned. The Constitution gives every one of us the right to worship as we so choose. This past summer I decided that I would worship the God of the Bible. I have come to believe in the truth and the principles of Christianity. I will not take back that decision for any reason."

She paused, and looked again at the little girl on top of the man's shoulders. She was smiling.

"It has become clear, however, that my personal decision has resulted in something I never wished to see happen. I won't pretend that the lies spread about me don't hurt. They do. But in the end what is said about the Supreme Court itself matters more. The Court is the guardian of freedom and dignity for all citizens, and must remain above distraction."

Millie paused for a deep breath.

"That is why I am stepping down, effective immediately, as a justice of the United States Supreme Court. And as I leave this institution, which I love, I have only these final words to say. Each time we begin a session of the Court, the marshal calls all to draw nigh and give their attention. And then he says these words, that I now adopt with all my heart: 'God save the United States and this honorable Court.'"

2

For the first time in as many years as he could remember, Sam Levering did not crave a drink.

Watching what he once would have termed his ultimate political triumph, he only barely noticed his lack of craving.

Millicent Mannings Hollander was gone. Resigned. The strings had been pulled, by himself and others. Everything was just as it was supposed to be.

He watched it all happen on the TV in the hotel room. He barely remembered checking in, and the hangover was still gripping his temples. Normally he would have hunted a little hair of the dog. And the Oramor Hotel had a great bar.

But the bar was not the reason he was here. He wanted to be where no one could contact him.

The voices were louder in his head. He was passing over the edge, certainly. Drink used to be the way out. That hadn't worked last night. The voices remained.

Tad. Is that you?

One voice sounded distantly familiar. When he was eight his parents had taken him to a tent meeting in Tulsa. Revival fire, they called it. Sam was excited to go, it was the talk of the town in those days.

What he heard scared him to death. An old fire-and-brimstone preacher spoke, he couldn't remember the man's name, but he had a voice like an avenging angel and held his Bible like a club, high over his head, when he wanted to make a point.

Sam was scared of the man and what he said. But there was one moment when the man spoke softly, when he offered up the invitation. That odd rustic ritual was something Sam knew about from his parents and church. It always seemed a little awkward, walking up there in front of people to be "saved."

But the very contrast of the voices this evangelist used—the harshness of fire and the cool balm of invitation—was striking.

Funny, Sam mused now in the opulent hotel room. He hadn't thought about that softer voice in maybe fifty years. But that was the voice he seemed to be hearing in the clamor of his own head.

He brought himself back to the TV, to the talking heads on the news channel discussing the Hollander situation. Where would the Court go? Was she guilty of the charges leveled against her? Will we ever really know?

Idiots. Complete, clueless idiots. They knew absolutely nothing.

Soon, they would know everything, because telling all, Sam decided, was the only way to make the voices stop.

3

Ambrosi Gallo stepped out of the Carnegie Deli on Seventh Avenue and wiped a spot of mustard from his cheek.

It was his last act as a free man.

He knew they were feds the moment he saw them. And when he did, it was too late to make a move.

They had a gun in his back before he could say John Gotti.

Play it cool, Ambrosi thought as they cuffed his hands behind him. Call the lawyer as soon as possible. Say nothing. And . . .

Anne. Oh yeah, Anne had given him up. He should have known. He should have stuck with Italian women.

She'd get hers, though. Even if he was put away. Anne would get hers, all right. He'd see to it.

4

"What made you do it?" Bill Bonassi asked.

"I'll probably ask myself that for years," Millie said. They were in Bonassi's library, the room that had become an island of comfort in a sea of chaos. This was where they had discussed strategy and tactics. Everything had gone according to plan, until the press conference.

"When one justice becomes the center of debate," Millie said, "it diminishes the Court as a whole. I hope I did the right thing."

Bonassi did not seem upset with her, as she thought he might be. In fact, he looked rather rested.

"It would have been a good scrap," he said. "I feel ten years younger because of you."

"That makes it even. I feel ten years older."

After a short silence, Bonassi said, "Ever heard of a man named Telemachus?"

"I don't think so."

"He was a Christian hermit who had come to Rome, toward the end of the Empire, when it was falling into decadence. He felt called to do something about the scandal of the gladiators. To celebrate a military victory, they were fighting to the death in the Coliseum for the amusement of the citizens."

Bonassi paused, his face becoming radiant with the telling. "So Telemachus went to the Coliseum, walked right into the arena where two gladiators were fighting. He put his hand on one of them and told him to stop shedding innocent blood. The crowd roared at him. They shouted in outrage. Telemachus put up his hand for silence.

"Then he said, 'Do not repay God's mercy, in turning away the swords of your enemies, by murdering each other.' The crowd shouted him down, shouted for more blood. The gladiators pushed Telemachus into the dust and resumed their fighting.

"Telemachus got up and placed himself between the combatants. The gladiators seemed to react as one. They killed Telemachus with their swords. And suddenly, realizing that a holy man had been killed, the crowd fell silent. There was no more combat that day. Nor ever again in Rome. His death brought an end to mortal combat."

Bonassi fell silent himself, for a long moment. "Maybe you're a Telemachus. Maybe because of what you did the country will look at what politics has done to the Court."

If only she could believe that. Perhaps, in time, she would.

The door opened. Dorothy, out of breath, said, "You need to come."

"What is it?" Bill said, rising.

"The news. They said Sam Levering shot himself."

EIGHTEEN

1

New York Times
Friday, November 21

In a stunning recorded interview with the D.C. police, the late Senator Sam Levering gave full details of abuses of power and conspiracies of corruption. According to sources, Levering names names and does not spare himself.

Sources say many of the admissions relate to the impeachment of Chief Justice Millicent Mannings Hollander, who resigned from the Court two weeks ago. Levering and his chief aide, Anne Deveraux, orchestrated a pattern of lies designed to drive Hollander from her position. Others were involved as well, including the recently named president of the National Parental Planning Group, Helen Forbes Kensington.

The major accusations against Hollander were false, according to the statement. One charge, that Hollander was under the influence of alcohol when she stumbled into the street and nearly died last June, was false according to Levering. It was he who was drunk, he states in the document, and made unwanted advances on Hollander, who attempted to get away from him.

Also named as co-conspirator was a reporter for the *National Exposure*. Daniel Ricks, the statement claims, was hired to collect dirt on Hollander during her recuperation from the accident in Santa Lucia, California.

Calls to the *National Exposure* went unreturned.

But perhaps the most stunning admission from Levering was that the Hollander campaign was tacitly approved by President John W. Francis.

Arnold Rutledge, chief legal counsel to the president, issued a statement late last night denying the allegation.

2

"You probably hate me, don't you?" Helen said.

Millie shook her head. "I couldn't hate you, Helen. Not after all these years."

"That's funny."

"What is?"

"I hated you."

They were standing at the perimeter of the Jefferson Memorial. It was where Helen had wanted to meet. For Millie it was like a scene out of a political thriller. She made sure she wasn't followed by reporters. She had even told the taxi driver to make sure they were free and clear.

"Why?" Millie asked, as surprised by Helen's admission as anything else in the last five months.

"I thought you were a traitor," Helen said. "I thought you had gone off the deep end and that you would start rolling back everything I believed in."

"I gathered that much."

"And I hated your—I don't know—integrity."

"Why didn't you talk to me about this?"

"I didn't know how."

"But you talked to that reporter for the *Exposure?*"

Helen nodded. "Levering convinced me I had to do it. He and that Gestapo agent of his, Anne Deveraux. We ruined you."

"I don't feel ruined."

"How can you not?"

Thinking of Bill Bonassi, Millie had to smile. "I'm a reverse paranoid."

"A *what?*"

"Let's just say I'm ready to start a new chapter. I'm moving back to Santa Lucia."

"No."

"My clerk, Rosalind Wilkes, and I are going to open an office."

"A lawyer? You're going to be a lawyer?"

"Why not? Maybe even be a TV star. Fox has been calling. They want me to be a commentator on national legal news. I don't know what God has in store."

They were near the portico now, the majestic figure of Thomas Jefferson deep in thought inside. Millie watched a group of children being led toward Jefferson by a woman who was obviously a teacher. Hope for the future, went the cliché. But she couldn't think of a better place to start than with the author of the Declaration of Independence. Millie thought of the stirring final words of that document. "With a firm reliance on Divine Providence, we mutually pledge to each other our lives, our fortunes, and our sacred honor."

When she looked back she saw Helen with her face in her hands.

"What is it?" Millie said.

"Can you forgive me?"

Millie put her arms around Helen. It was not a natural gesture for Millie. Or maybe it was. Now.

3

Rosalind was waiting for Millie back at Millie's house in Fairfax County. Who was it Rosalind had wanted her to meet?

It was a young, rather slight, but confident-looking African American woman who shook Millie's hand with gusto.

"Meet Charlene Moore," Rosalind said.

Over tea, Charlene Moore told Millie her story, up to the filing of the *certiorari* petition by Larry Graebner.

"He's formidable," Millie said. "And your case sounds like one the Court may grant cert on."

"Which is why I came here," Charlene said. "I've been asking God who would be the right person to help me with this. I kept flashing on you."

"I've never been flashed before," Millie said.

Charlene Moore laughed. "But will you do it?"

"You don't waste time, do you, Miss Moore?"

"So I've been told."

"I'll really have to think about this," Millie said.

"You know," said Charlene Moore, "sometimes God kicks thinkin' in the pants."

Millie laughed. "The strange thing is, I think I understand exactly what you mean. Why don't we pray, right now, and whatever God wants, we'll do."

"Right on," Charlene said.

"Roz," Millie said. "Do you mind?"

The young woman shook her head. "I'd like to join you, if I may."

"This is very cool," Charlene said.

Three women joined hands. And sought God.

PART
THREE

Upon these two foundations,
the law of nature and the law of revelation,
depend all human laws.

SIR WILLIAM BLACKSTONE

CHAPTER NINETEEN

1

"Oyez, oyez, oyez."

The Supreme Court marshal solemnly intoned the medieval French words handed down from more than a thousand years of English common law. Though Millie had heard them countless times before, she now felt them entering into her like trumpet blasts.

"The honorable, the chief justice and associate justices of the Supreme Court of the United States," the marshal continued. "All persons having business before this honorable Court are admonished to draw nigh and give their attention, for the Court is now sitting. God save the United States and this honorable Court."

And there they stood, her former colleagues—Byrne, Facconi, Johnson, Parsons, Weiss, Velarde, and Chief Justice Atkins, along with the judge who had replaced her, Walter Saxon. And, finally, Thomas J. Riley. His face, as far as Millie could tell, was a mask of impassivity.

The justices sat in their high-backed leather swivel chairs as Millie's knees trembled. That she was here at all was still unbelievable to her.

It was June again, the time when she would have been wrapping up her Court matters before the summer break. Instead, she was about to argue for the first time as an advocate in front of the Supreme Court.

She had spent the last six months going over and over the case, researching precedent, scanning the transcripts from the lower court for every nuance of legal reasoning. In that time, through e-mails and phone calls, Charlene Moore had come to be something of a little sister to her, more than just in a spiritual way. She was a support, a sharp legal mind, and full of energy.

But as Millie sat at the Respondent's table, she realized that after all that work, she still did not know how her argument would do. It was, she and Charlene had decided, to be directed at the newest justice, Saxon. Millie knew she would have the four conservatives with her. Riley, of course, would oppose her, as would the three other liberal-moderates. Saxon, even though he was a Francis appointee, was at least new enough not to have set himself permanently in any coalition.

If she had any hope of winning, it would be in convincing Saxon. From her research on his opinions from the Ninth Circuit, she got the impression that he was a logical technician. He liked his arguments tight, to the point, and without fluff. So, for the last month, Millie had practiced her presentation with Saxon in mind.

Millie silently prayed, thanking God for trusting her, asking one more time for her mind to be primed and ready.

Then she saw Lawrence Graebner approach the podium. "May it please the Court," he said.

The justices allowed him to argue for nearly five minutes without a question. Millie felt herself wanting to engage Graebner herself. Old habits.

"The use of the term *unborn child* in the statute is clearly unconstitutional," Graebner was saying. "It is a loaded term with only one view in mind, to stop an approved medical procedure from taking place."

Ray Byrne spoke. "Don't you think it's time we looked at this whole question again? In *Roe* Justice Blackmun tied up this issue with medical knowledge. Haven't we had progress in medicine in thirty years? Aren't we behind the times?"

Graebner did not hesitate. "On the contrary, *Roe* has proven its worth over the last thirty years, and this Court should resoundingly reaffirm it. A world of expectations has been built upon it. It has allowed a national controversy to be resolved, however contentious that effort may have been. To overrule or eviscerate *Roe* now would open up the floodgates of disaster."

Byrne did not follow up. Millie saw Thomas J. Riley nodding slowly.

2

Anne Deveraux, inmate number 03–99873, could not stop crying.

She'd done fairly well for two months. She had managed to get a good night's sleep for a change, even with a new cell mate who snored like a Georgia chainsaw. But when she woke up and realized she was still in prison, she broke out in a torrent of hot tears.

Her cooperation with the feds in the case against Ambrosi Gallo was enough to garner her a ten-year sentence, and with the right breaks she could be out in seven. But seven seemed like forever, and what would she do when she got out? The Calibresi family would have her on their short list for early retirement.

She'd probably have to stay away from New York City for the rest of her life. Some life. She felt all of the toughness she had built up so carefully over the years turning to warm putty in her stomach. She was no longer the power monger, the mover and shaker, the politico with an unlimited future. She was just another number in a cage.

She had not cried like this since she was a little girl. And no one was going to help her. She had no family, and those with whom she had so carefully networked over the years were dropping her faster than a politician's promise. Even Cosmo had not contacted her since the arrest.

Damaged goods was a generous description of what she was now.

Her crying drew a response from Sheela, her cell mate. She had been a prostitute who sold crack to an undercover agent and got twenty-five years. She seemed strangely serene about it. "Won't do you no good to keep on like that, honey," Sheela said.

Anne couldn't help it. Maybe part of it was the irony of this day. She'd seen the *Post,* which she got days late in the prison library. Arguments were scheduled today in that abortion clinic case, and one of the lawyers was Millicent Mannings Hollander! Unbelievable, after all she and Levering had gone through over her.

Yet there Hollander would be, standing in front of the Supreme Court, while Anne was locked away in a cell, losing the best years of her life.

She kept her face in her pillow, wondering if Levering's way out was perhaps the best solution after all.

The whole thing with his son had been so weird. It was like he knew something, knew *her.* Those times she had seen him had been creepy. But creepy in a way that was almost too real. *It's not too late,* he had said.

How did he know she was going to end up in here? Now it really *was* too late.

The tears kept coming.

3

And then it was Millie's turn.

As she stood she gave a quick glance into the gallery. Charlene Moore sat with Sarah Mae and Aggie, all three looking nervous. Jack was in the back, having flown out with Rosalind from Santa Lucia for this slice of American history. The rest of the place was packed with reporters, politicians, and a handful of the public, the ones who had lined up at 3 A.M. in order to get a seat for the show.

And what a show Larry Graebner had just put on. He was brilliant. Millie had heard him argue half a dozen cases when she was a justice. Never had he been more eloquent, more on top of the issues. Every question he was asked gave him another opportunity to demonstrate his legal virtuosity.

Millie placed her notes on the podium and looked up at her former colleagues. For a second their faces seemed to melt into one another. The chamber seemed suddenly as silent as a tomb. But she was ready. "May it please the Court," she said. "The informed consent law at the heart of this case has one purpose, as clear from its language as its statutory history. That purpose is to protect the health of women who are considering the most important moral choice of their lives, the decision to end a life."

Justice Arlene Prager Weiss immediately interrupted. "Counsel," she said, "aren't you assuming the very question you ask us to decide? Part of your argument, it seems to me, assumes that a fetus constitutes a life in the sense of personhood. The statute says *unborn child*. But we have rejected that argument in the past. You yourself penned an eloquent defense of *Roe* in the *Messier* case to that effect, did you not?"

Millie had anticipated this query, either from Weiss or Riley.

"My rationale in *Messier*," she said, "was expediency. The question now is whether that rationale was sound. Yes, the case itself is precedent, but this Court has not hesitated to overturn precedent when convinced the rationale should no longer hold. It happened when *Brown* overturned *Plessey v. Ferguson* and brought equal justice to people of color. I am suggesting that this case is another of those times."

"But Justice Hollander," Preston Atkins said, "to do that we would have to find that the fetus is a person within the meaning of the Fourteenth Amendment, would we not?"

The question cut right to the heart of things. Of course Atkins—and Weiss and Riley—were right to put that challenge to her.

But as she opened her mouth to answer, the words stopped in her throat. She looked back at Atkins, then, to his left, caught the eye of Thomas J. Riley. He was staring, almost as if looking through her.

She found herself answering Atkins's question while looking at Riley. "That inquiry must be secondary, Your Honor, it seems to me. There is a preliminary question that must be answered. This Court must decide, once and for all, what first principles will be used to decide these issues."

Riley's eyes ignited with fire. "Just what first principles are you talking about, Counsel?" he asked.

4

Anne Deveraux got that feeling again, the one she'd experienced right before she'd been arrested.

That called-to feeling, from somewhere beyond her understanding.

What was that all about?

She was alone for a moment now, her cell mate out for yard time. It was eerie, and she thought for a moment she was going to go certifiably crazy.

Wouldn't that be cute? Get out on a mental, and spend the rest of your life on drugs, shuffling around in slippers down white-walled corridors?

The image reminded her, for the first time in years, of her room as a little girl. The one time she could remember being happy in her childhood. Her stepfather was gone, her mother was there, and she wasn't drinking.

She came into Anne's room, where the walls were painted white, and Anne was almost asleep. And her mother rocked her in her arms and sang a song. It was a silly song, Anne couldn't even remember the words. But the words were not important. Her mother's arms were.

No more arms. Not here. Not ever.

5

"We must start with the founding documents," Millie said. "All men are created equal, and endowed by their Creator with certain inalienable rights."

"The Declaration of Independence is not the Constitution," Riley snapped.

"That is not the view of the Court in the past," Millie said, marveling at her own words. A year ago such a sentiment would have been unthinkable coming from her. "Our decisions throughout the 1800s consistently called the Declaration 'part of the fundamental law of our nation.' Only in the last forty years have we drifted from that view. Are we going to say now that our predecessors on the Court were wrong or naive?"

Millie glanced left and saw Larry Graebner watching her, a look of complete bafflement on his face. He seemed to be thinking, *Are you absolutely crazy?* That only emboldened her. "I am calling upon this Court," she said, "to reaffirm the basic tenets of our founding. Without those principles, we will continue to be a nation on a collision course with itself. This case makes that clear. That a young woman can be denied—"

"We've guided our ship of state pretty well under the law of the past thirty years," Weiss interrupted. "Shouldn't we consider the drastic political consequences of changing course?"

"The decisions of this Court do have political consequences," Millie said. "We all know that. But the Court was never meant to have political *intentions*. In a Constitutional democracy, this Court was not conceived as the institution that creates law. Or that overturns laws duly passed, so long as such laws do not violate any Constitutional provision."

For the next few minutes several of the justices asked questions about that very thing—the constitutionality of the informed consent law and its various sections. The larger issue Millie had begun to argue was lost. But she knew she had to answer the questions asked. In the back of her mind, she was hoping for—praying for—one more chance to return to the issue.

Oddly, Justice Riley was silent now, though Millie sensed he was deep in thought.

Finally, just before her time was up, Riley leaned forward in his chair. "Aren't you asking this Court to decide in such a way that will tear at the very fabric of our nation?"

Millie saw in him a real anguish. How well she understood it. "Your Honor," she said, "like one of my judicial heroes, I believe truth conquers all things. It may be a long struggle before the conquest, but ultimately it is the only struggle that counts. It counts for Sarah Mae Sherman, and for all the future Sarah Maes. But it also counts for the soul of the law, and for this great edifice we call justice—"

The red light on the lectern illumined. "Thank you," Chief Justice Atkins said. "Your time has expired. This Court is now adjourned."

The nine justices stood and filed slowly out of the room. Millie watched them, her former colleagues, as they disappeared behind the velvet curtain.

She had never felt so spent. She turned and looked into the gallery. Her supporters were all there, nodding in affirmation.

And then she looked up. Her gaze fell on the marble frieze depicting the eternal struggle for justice, the one she had come to know so well when she was sitting on the dais. She smiled, and silently thanked God that she had had the chance to be part of the struggle.

6

Sheela came in from her yard time, holding something. "Hey," she said to Anne, "you were a lawyer, right?"

Why the sudden questioning, Anne wondered. "I never finished law school," Anne said. "Started working in D.C."

"Honey, you sure did take a wrong turn."

Anne heard herself admit, for the first time in her life, "Yeah, I messed up pretty bad."

Then Sheela tossed her some papers. "Got that at the chapel," she said. "Thought you might be interested."

Anne looked at it. It looked official, like a legal brief.

"Maybe you want to come hear the Word sometime with me," Sheela said. "Keep you from cryin' so much."

Sheela was into Jesus. Talked about him constantly. Anne didn't want to hear it. Now, she thought, maybe sometime she'd go to chapel with Sheela, if for no other reason than to break the monotony.

Anne lay down and took a look at the brief. The first page had a section called "Statement of Facts."

> I have been in jail. I have nearly died. I have lost the people I loved more than anything in the world. I wonder sometimes why I didn't take my own life. I think I know why now. God isn't finished with me yet.

What was this? Anne looked for a name on the brief and found it on the last page. Some guy named Jack Holden. Now who was . . .

Then it hit her like a rifle shot. Wasn't that the guy's name, the minister, the one who had been tied up with Hollander when Dan Ricks was on the job?

Same guy! Had to be. She looked back at the page. It was blurred and Anne realized, once more, she was crying. Only this time the tears were not out of deep despair. She had no idea what they were from, but it was like her heart knew—*beyond the edge, better than the edge*—there was something *other*, out *there*, as if on the other side of a door.

Anne wiped at her eyes, amazed, and started once more to read.

CHAPTER TWENTY

1

Friday, December 3

The Supreme Court's 4–4 deadlock in an abortion rights case earlier this week raises serious issues of national policy, experts say. What is baffling, leading court watchers note, is that the Court announced its decision in *Sherman v. National Parental Planning Group* by way of a short, *per curiam* opinion, meaning it came from the Court as a whole with no individual justice signing an opinion.

"It's obvious one of the justices refused to rule," said Yale Law Professor Lawrence I. Graebner, who argued on behalf the NPPG before the high court. "Frankly, I can't imagine which justice would do that. What's worse is that this leaves the door open to a possible rollback of *Roe v. Wade* sometime in the future. I'm very troubled."

The court's decision has no national effect. It leaves in place the decision of the Eleventh Circuit Court of Appeals which had remanded the case for trial.

"This is a victory for the one who counts most, Sarah Mae Sherman," said Millicent Mannings Hollander, the former chief justice who argued Sherman's case before her one-time colleagues. "She will have her day in court, and the NPPG will be held accountable for its actions."

Speaking by phone from her office in Santa Lucia, California, Hollander added, "The larger debate must also continue. We now have an opportunity to engage in a new national discussion about what's best for us as a nation of laws."

Helen Forbes Kensington, president of the National Parental Planning Group, could not be reached for comment.

2

"Who do you think it was?" Jack Holden said.

"I have a feeling," Millie answered.

They were outside on the basketball court behind the church. The warm winter had preserved the wildflowers of the Santa Lucia valley, and today they seemed to have dropped directly from the palette of God.

Across the valley the sleeping giant was still flat on his back. Sometimes, as a girl, Millie had wondered what would happen if the giant suddenly woke up, stood, and made his way toward the town. How would the people react? Would they run, or would they welcome him as an old friend?

Then she wondered—if enough people awoke from their moral slumbers and began to return to the true source of all law, what would the rest of the country do? Scream? Or recognize a forgotten friend? She knew much of her future work was going to be tied up with those questions.

The partnership of Hollander & Wilkes had made national news with the Sherman case. The *Washington Post* ran a piece entitled "From Big Time to Small Town." But the partnership did not feel small to Millie. It felt perfectly woven into the tapestry of her life.

"So who?" Jack said, bouncing the ball in front of him with staccato impatience.

"Thomas J. Riley," she said.

"Riley? No way. Why would he do that?"

"I don't know. To give the debate back to the people, maybe. I do know Tom loves the Court as much as I do, and has a deep well of integrity. I know he believes that sign on his desk. *Vincit omnia veritas.* Truth conquers all things."

Jack thought a moment. "So he was the judicial hero you quoted in your argument?"

Millie nodded.

Jack bounced the ball a few more times. "Do *you* believe truth conquers all?"

"I believe a lot of things I didn't used to. For instance, I believe God weaves patterns."

"I do too," Jack said. He held the ball. Then he smiled. "Maybe," he added, "part of the reason this all happened was so you could come back to Santa Lucia and marry me."

He bounced the ball once, as if to create an exclamation point. Then he waited for a response.

Millie felt a gust of desert air, pure and clean. She was back home, but Santa Lucia was not the place it once was. The past, with all its hurts and confusions, had somehow faded, like an old sepia-toned photograph left out in the sun. The place where she was living now was new; it gave her the feeling of starting over.

But with a minister? As a wife? What sort of pattern was *this?*

"Tell you what," Millie said, her heart beginning to dance. "You make a ten-foot hook shot, and I'll consider it."

The preacher's smile widened as he turned toward the basket.

"Right-handed," Millie said.

Jack pointed at her. "No problem."

He bounced the ball a couple of times, looked at the basket, then launched his shot into the air. It arced beautifully, then hit the front of the rim and clanked out.

Jack stood there, frozen, as if couldn't believe he'd missed.

"Good thing we've got all day," Millie said.

ACKNOWLEDGMENTS

This novel would not have been possible without the help of many special people.

Professor John Eastman of Chapman University School of Law, former clerk to Justice Clarence Thomas, walked me through much of the Supreme Court's day-to-day operations as well as many of the legal aspects of the novel. One of the "smart guys," he is a credit to his students, his school, and the enterprise of American law. Any mistakes that appear in the book are mine alone.

On the issue of the role of the Declaration of Independence in modern Constitutional jurisprudence, I am indebted to one of my old law professors, Ronald Garet, of the law school at the University of Southern California. His insights were invaluable, and he continues to challenge his students to think about the law from a moral and religious angle, and not merely as a high-paying profession.

Profound thanks for their time and knowledge go to my colleagues and friends Randy Alcorn, Terri Blackstock, Mel and Cheryl Hodde, and Angela Elwell Hunt.

I owe a huge debt to my editor, Dave Lambert. Dave knows whereof he speaks when it comes to fiction, so when he spoke (or, rather, issued one of his famous "Dave letters") I listened. His insights made this a better book. Thanks, Dave.

Sue Brower, and indeed the entire team at Zondervan, are likewise a pleasure to work with. I'm honored to be part of their list.

As always, my first editor was my wife, Cindy, who is everything a husband—especially the pesky writing kind—could hope for. My children, Nathaniel and Allegra, have also come to accept that their father is a writer with certain odd quirks, and love me anyway. I couldn't ask for better support than that.

I consulted dozens of resources in the research phase of the book. The Ohio case mentioned in the novel is based upon an actual decision of the Sixth Circuit Court of Appeals, and a superb opinion by the Honorable David A. Nelson, Circuit Judge. The main issue of this book is also as stated by Judge Nelson: "We might wish that the framers of the Constitution had chosen to give us the powers of a council of revision," he wrote, "but they did not do so." Which means we must continue to grapple with the proper role of judges in our Constitutional system.

That issue is fully and fairly explored in *A Matter of Interpretation: Federal Courts and the Law* by Justice Antonin Scalia (Princeton University Press, 1997). This is an exchange between Justice Scalia and four distinguished critics, including Harvard's Lawrence H. Tribe. For further discussion, the interested party should not neglect *The Tempting of America: The Political Seduction of the Law* by Robert H. Bork (Free Press, 1990).

For those who desire a picture of the Supreme Court from the ultimate insider, I cannot recommend highly enough *The Supreme Court* by William H. Rehnquist (Knopf, 2001). It is a warm tribute to the Court, detailed and well written. For those who want to analyze a view of the Court from the other side of the political spectrum, see *Closed Chambers: The Rise, Fall, and Future of the Modern Supreme Court* by Edward Lazarus (Penguin, 1998).

Bill Bonassi's quotations from Jefferson, Madison, and John Adams, and his discussion of biblical metaphysics as part of the American Constitutional fabric, are taken from Michael Novak's *On Two Wings: Humble Faith and Common Sense at the American Founding* (Encounter Books, 2002). This is a brilliant and scholarly review of the founders' system of political belief. Not many books can be considered so authoritative that they should be required reading for every American citizen. Novak's is one of them.

"Once the heart hears the music it is never really happy unless it is dancing." That insight comes from Robert Benson's book *Living Prayer,* which I highly recommend to all seekers of the open door.

The issues surrounding abortion continue, of course, to divide our nation. David Pollock, Executive Director of the Pregnancy Resource Center of the San Fernando Valley, was an incredible help on this topic. Others who offered insights on the legal, moral, and medical aspects of abortion procedures were Dr. David C. Reardon of the Elliott Institute; Kurt Entsminger, Esq., Executive Vice President and General Counsel for Care Net; and Dr. Kari Scott, M.D. I regret that my attempts to secure interviews with leading abortion rights spokespersons did not meet with more success. William Lutz, media relations contact for the National Abortion Rights Action League, did give me an overview of NARAL's position on informed consent laws. I also turned to a good deal of the abortion rights groups' publicly disseminated material, much of it online. Please note that the National Parental Planning Group is a fictional entity, and any resemblance to an actual organization or clinic is purely coincidental.

On the political side of the abortion debate, I am grateful for time and information from the following: Rep. Bob Shaffer of Colorado, his press secretary William Mutch, and his chief legislative assistant Erika Lestelle; Rep. Joe Pitts of Pennsylvania and his press secretary Gabe Neville.

Finally, heartfelt thanks to my church family, who continue to support me with their prayers, encouragement, and good fellowship.

7/04   9   7/03   11/15 85 7/14
11/08   10   8/08
3/14   24   8/13

ABOUT THE AUTHOR

James Scott Bell is the best-selling author of eight previous novels. A winner of the Christy Award for Excellence in Christian Fiction, he resides with his family in Los Angeles, where he is at work on his next book. His Web site is www.jamesscottbell.com.

We want to hear from you. Please send your comments about this book to us in care of the address below. Thank you.

ZONDERVAN™

GRAND RAPIDS, MICHIGAN 49530 USA

WWW.ZONDERVAN.COM